I0598748

The Last Hemlock

The Last Hemlock

The Shenandoah Series

Larry M. Arrowood

WOODSONG
P U B L I S H I N G

Seymour, IN

The Last Hemlock

Copyright © Pending 2017 by Larry Monroe Arrowood

This is the second book of *The Shenandoah Series*. The first book in the series is *Bloodroot*.

All rights reserved. No part of this book may be used or reproduced by any means, graphic, electronic, or mechanical, including photocopying, recording, taping or by any information storage retrieval system without the written permission of the publisher except in the case of brief quotations embodied in critical articles and reviews.

This is a work of fiction. All of the characters, names, incidents, organizations, and dialogue in this novel are either the products of the author's imagination or are used fictitiously.

Woodsong Publishing
5989 Spring Meadow Lane
Seymour, IN 47274

www.woodsongpublishing.com

You may purchase additional books written by Larry Arrowood from Woodsong Publishing's website or through your preferred booksellers.

Cover design by Vision Graphics, Seymour, IN

Printed in the United States of America

ISBN: 978-0-9979146-6-5

Library Of Congress control number: 2017912820

Dedicated to the memory of
Harry Thomas (Bud) Weatherholtz
February 26, 1893
March 7, 1970

He is the beloved grandfather of my wife.

Chapter One

The distinctive smell of coal oil permeated the air. A flickering lamp projected shadows larger than life on the adjacent wall, reminiscent of the big drive-in movie screen south of Woodstock. With the tip of his finger, he traced the outline of her nose and lips, until she gently pushed his hand away. It cut to the quick, but he tried to hide his feelings. Lately, he didn't want her out of his sight. That caused frustration, and she raked him over the coals more than once. He tried to understand her grown-up talk, but he grew clingier still. His need for her affection consumed him, and he couldn't comprehend his fear of losing her.

She adjusted his blanket and tucked it around his neck. He smiled, and she gave him a quick kiss on his forehead. He grimaced when she snuffed the wick. The darkness terrified him. She softly stroked his hair. The pounding in his chest subsided, and he relaxed to her calming touch. This routine worked wonders.

She startled him awake as she slipped out of bed. Dawn peered through the pale-blue veneer curtain that covered the single window. He observed her shadowy movements as she quietly dressed. The door squeaked as she eased it open, slipped out and pulled it shut behind her.

Why does she leave without me? I don't like her sneaking away. Someday she may never come back. He tried to push such nagging thoughts aside and fought the impulse to call out to her. She had scolded him before for his negativism—a word he couldn't quite say—explaining that she had to work for them to survive. Her having to work so hard troubled him, and he wanted to do something about that, but who would hire a five-year-old?

A dog barked as she left the house through the back door. He quickly retrieved his overalls from the bedpost and found his shoes he had kicked underneath the bed. He crammed his bare feet into the cold leather, and leaving the strings untied, he hurried into the kitchen. Grabbing a threadbare, denim jacket from a wall peg, he slipped out the back door and stepped onto the worn path that led past a woodpile, around the chicken house and to a gate at the fenced barnyard. His untied shoes shuffled on some river stone, and she turned toward him, paused briefly and reached out to him. He caught up with her and clasped her hand. She looked down at him and smiled. He was glad she didn't mind him tagging along.

Fog hung low, obscuring the distant mountains. A misty rain fell lightly, and he shivered. She gently snapped his unbuttoned coat, then knelt and tied his shoestrings.

Movement in the partially opened door of the hayloft startled him. Someone crouched in the opening. Was it him? Again? His heart raced, and he wanted to run away, but he could not leave her alone, especially not alone with him. He had seen what that had done before.

He strained to make out the face. He wanted to warn her as she rose from her crouched position and advanced toward the barn, holding his hand, softly singing.

"Oh Beulah land, sweet Beulah land—"

He pulled back on her hand, wanting to sprint her to safety, but she pulled him along as she proceeded toward the double-wide barn door leading to a dozen hungry cows dripping milk and lowing to be relieved of the pressure.

The flash and the instantaneous puff of smoke were unmistakable. The tranquil morning exploded into chaos. Her hand went limp in his. Sounds amplified, and the scene around him became a cinematic slow motion. Her milk pail crashed to the ground and rolled away. Warmth splattered his face, and he wiped it with the back of his hand. She toppled beside him.

The man leaped from the loft, falling hard. He limped across the barnyard, then started running. He was always running away.

He glanced at her crumpled body and tugged at her hand, trying with all his strength to drag her to safety, but he could not. Instinctively, he bolted toward the house, but his steps slowed, a force held him back.

"Bud!"

She called to him. She needed him. Was she okay? He must return to her and help her.

"Bud!"

"Momma. Oh, momma. ... His words seemed slurred. He began to cry. "Somebody, please, somebody help my—"

Harry Weatherholtz tumbled onto the floor, pulling the quilt with him. He lay for a moment, adrenalized and embarrassed, before pulling himself onto the bedside.

"Another dream?" Evelyn sat up in bed. His wife was not startled, for she was used to his nightmares.

"Yes." He sat quietly, offering no explanation.

"I tried to wake you."

"Thanks."

"Your mother?"

"Yes."

"You okay?"

"I think so," he said, rubbing the right side of his forehead. It felt moist near the right temple.

"What time is it?"

He retrieved his pocket watch from the nightstand and held it toward the moonlight streaming through the window. "Five."

"I'll make coffee." Evelyn eased out of bed, snatched her robe from the bedpost and headed to the kitchen.

Chapter Two

Harry Weatherholtz was a dreamer. Literally. It seemed every incident stashed away in memory eventually surfaced in a dream. His dreams, like a scrapbook, kept alive the events of his past. After such a dream, he'd lay awake and rehash the event he hadn't considered in years, and he'd compare the dream with what he actually remembered. His dreams kept a blessed past alive, and the ugly as well. The latter, he'd prefer to forget, but the dreams wouldn't allow it.

Lately, he'd dreamed of a childhood experience, the only pleasant memory he had of his father. He wasn't sure the details of the dream were accurate, for he was only about four years old at the time. In this singular event, he and his older brother Lawrence sat under a towering pine and listened as his father described the various trees of the Shenandoah. His father had composed a poem about the Hemlock and expressed, "Someday you'll understand its meaning." In the dream, his father recited the poem again and again as they sat under the tree. The memory of the poem was accurate, for his father had scribbled it on a scrap of paper which Harry kept tucked away in his army-green footlocker, but he hadn't looked at it for years. It was his only possession from his father. After the murder, Lawrence had thrown the poem away, but he had retrieved it from the trash. Through the years he had many times contemplated destroying it but could never bring himself to do so.

The destruction done to forests, and the lack of reforestation offered Harry much concern. The Skyland Resort, started by George and Addie Pollert up on the Blue Ridge, and now a part of the Shenandoah National Park, offered protection for nearly two hundred thousand acres. Early on, Mrs. Pollert purchased a hundred hemlocks and named the protected forest "Limberlost," after the naturalist author Gene Stratton-Porter's famed novel, *A Girl of the Limberlost*. Some of the trees in the park were four hundred years old. It seemed unfathomable, but a hemlock left undisturbed could live a thousand years. A sapling could have sprouted the same century Crusaders answered the call to reclaim the Holy Land for Christians. Though a logger himself, he was glad for the national park protecting the aged hemlocks. He felt both a biblical and civic obligation to replenish trees destroyed by ax and saw, even though legally logged.

Other than the oft-occurring nightmares, from which he awakened in a cold sweat, life was good to Harry. The past year's pinball effect ranged from despair to intrigue to joy. He was riding that wave of joy. His plans to build Annie a cottage by the lake energized him. His health seemed okay. He'd celebrated his sixty-fifth birthday logging. Throughout the winter he'd taken advantage of the ice-crusted ground to haul logs chained behind ole Sam—his white, dappled Belgian—from the foothills bordering the Shenandoah Park. After the felling and hauling away of fifty trees, his chilled bones welcomed the spring of '58.

The unsolved fire that destroyed his mill set him back financially, but he knew how to live within his means. He'd tasted poverty and survived, so the only direction from poverty was up, and his balance sheet was moving slightly. Evelyn didn't seem to mind the tight budget, or at least she didn't complain. One issue did concern him. She hadn't forgiven whoever set fire to their sawmill, and she insisted the Bufford brothers did it. She struggled with letting go, but he'd learned a long time ago that she tended to work through her emotions by talking, so he'd learned to listen without overreacting. He was wired differently. His response to problems was the opposite of Evelyn's. Solitude seemed to help solve his perplexing situations.

The morning sun glistened off the last pockets of snow that spotted the distant peaks of the Blue Ridge. Skyland Resort had recently opened from its winter break. The first wave of weekend guests created activity in the valley. Politicians arrived from Washington, and teachers and students and naturalists and hikers and entire families from all over the Commonwealth jammed the roads, all seeking a reprieve from winter's rigors.

Harry breathed deeply and exhaled slowly. Sights and smells of the temperate spring morning invigorated him. He braked as a whitetail darted across the road and leaped a split rail fence, stopping a few yards from the road to graze. A patch of white, flowering bloodroot lined the edge of the field. He immediately thought of Annie. Her depiction of Hurley Cutshaw did the flower no favor: "As deceptive as the poisonous flower." For one never having any formal education, she expressed herself well. Nature and toil had been her teacher, and she had been an observant student. Just the thought of Hurley Cutshaw chafed him. He tried to think like a Christian toward Hurley, but doing so was difficult. "Whatsoever things are good … think on these things," he repeated to himself.

The bloodroot flower was native to Virginia. Though beautiful in bloom, Harry would forever associate the poisonous roots of the plant with venom that flowed in Hurley Cutshaw's veins. Harry was shed of him, and he was glad, for himself, but more so for Annie. She'd delivered the death toll to his racketeering of Negro children in the valley by defiantly proclaiming her freedom when she realized she was eighteen years old, therefore, free from the need of the foster care Cutshaw was responsible for.

Harry mentally replayed the scene of last year. Ann had stood up against the man that had beaten her with a strap more times than she could begin to remember. Her body shook as she faced Cutshaw, staring defiantly. Harry could still hear her trembling voice and Cutshaw's threats. "Mistuh Cutshaw, I ain't going home with you now or never, because I don't have to no more." She stood up to him for the first time. Cutshaw challenged, "You'll do as I say, girl, as long as I'm your legal guardian." Ann would not relent. "No, I won't, Mistuh Cutshaw, cause I'm of age." Cutshaw realized he was beaten but wouldn't acquiesce. "What you talking about, girl? You done gone loco. You just get in the truck like I told you." Ann delivered the knockout punch. "No, Mistuh Cutshaw. I's not going with you. You said just today in the courthouse you'd been caring for me for more'n eight years, and you said you took me in when I was ten. That makes me at least eighteen. I can count, 'cause that's the only thing you ever done good for me ... taught me to count your dirty dollars."

Harry couldn't help but smile. That single act by a scared orphan girl had set in motion the compromise arrangement that ended Cutshaw's amoral involvement in the foster care system. Further, it removed Judge Jenkins—for years the controller of the foster care system in the valley—from the bench. Neither Cutshaw nor Jenkins received the justice they deserved. Annie's anguish wasn't nearly avenged, but it ended. The compromise avoided the trauma of the legal battle that would have had to be fought in a system that may have exonerated both Cutshaw and Jenkins. This all would have been at her emotional expense. Harry vacillated in whether his decision to push for a quick resolution outside the courtroom was right. His gut legal instincts troubled him, but Annie's cheerful disposition consoled him.

A layer of wintry grime dulled the green color of his wood-paneled Hudson. The blinding sun accentuated the film on the windshield, making visibility difficult. He adjusted the visor to block the glare. His trip was business, but he wanted to visit the new car wash that had recently opened. Evelyn viewed such as vanity, but he stood his ground. The Hudson deserved a little pampering to ease the aging process.

The narrow, unmarked blacktop road meandered alongside the winding Shenandoah River. Harry adjusted the rearview mirror.

A line of closely packed vehicles jostled for a chance to overtake him. An occasional horn blared what he assumed was disapproval of his pokey driving skills. He glanced at his speedometer and simultaneously engaged the clutch, turned on his blinker and coasted onto a pull-off along the Shenandoah. Vehicles sped past; some drivers offered a conciliatory wave, while others yelled their displeasure. In no hurry, other's schedules need not dictate his.

Evelyn had opted to stay home. For the past few days, she and Annie worked on a Nine-Patch, the last of the winter quilting projects. They planned to donate it to the Daughters of the Confederacy raffle, though neither qualified as members. All Evelyn's relatives hailed north of the Mason-Dixon line; Annie's relatives were unknown, but her skin color told the tale of whose side they favored. The quilt project had been excuse enough for them to have Annie spend nights with them during the coldest part of the winter. Shy and unassuming, she enjoyed her independence, but the old goat shed on the back of Harry's farm was inadequate for habitation in the coldest weather, even for animals. Annie never complained, even though Harry's weatherproofing of the shed still proved insufficient for human occupancy. With the help of some community volunteers, he'd build her a suitable house before next winter. The winter logging had been good, and he could spare enough lumber for the small cottage he planned for her by the lake. That was the least the community could do for reparation for her, but they could never compensate for little Eddie's death.

Harry had purchased Will Compton's old mill at an estate auction. No one seemed to want it, not even collectors, so he bought it for a reasonable price. He'd reassembled the mill on the same site of his burned out mill. A fifty-two-inch replacement blade should arrive any day. That's all he needed to be up and running. The new blade almost cost as much as he paid for Will's entire equipment.

Miss Ann, as he generally addressed her, could barely survive on her scanty income from domestic jobs. His plan was to find her a better paying job. That was another reason for this trip. She had dreams of seeking custody of the lad Cutshaw had been keeping. With the ending of Cutshaw's guardianship, the boy was probably in temporary care and needing a home. Ann's dream might be somewhat premature, but when the timing seemed right, he'd speak to the newly appointed judge, Jack Brady—now the judicial overseer of foster care placement—about the possibility of her being a foster parent. The state might object, Annie being so young and lacking resources, so her new house would surely help with her application. Right now, a steady job would certainly enhance her resources and chances of approval.

Harry wasn't a stranger to the concerns regarding childcare. While sheriff up in Ohio, he had to investigate way too many complaints of neglect and abuse. He'd like to forget some of the sights, but he could not. They were etched in memory. His emotions ran even deeper. He'd lost both his parents in a single year. His grandmother had stolen him away to Ohio, where she tried to protect him from further harm. With all her good intentions, she could not erase the memories. The sights and sounds and pain and longing were embedded deep in his psyche. After more than half a century, nightmares still plagued him. He could not remove the images of his mother's brutal murder. They were etched in detail somewhere in his brain. After more than sixty years, he still missed her, especially during the long and frigid hours of winter's nights—she left in the winter. After retiring from the office of sheriff, he moved back to Virginia, but his extended family lived up north. Their absence accentuated his loneliness. Having Annie around somewhat dulled the edge of his melancholy moods over missing his grandkids. Their visits were too few, so letters had to suffice. He hoped for a letter soon, and he eagerly looked forward to their summer visit.

Last year's tragedy remained an open wound. A child had drowned in his farm pond. Harry felt it was a preventable drowning, but the foster parent, Hurley Cutshaw, was negligent and may have contributed to the drowning. He grieved over little Eddie's drowning, and he sometimes second-guessed pushing Jack Brady to let Hurley Cutshaw walk, instead of prosecuting him. He remained convinced Hurley forced the child into the lake to retrieve a snared fishing lure. He kept that small piece of evidence tucked away in his army foot locker, though it was evidence he'd never be able to present. His decision boiled down to one thing: the jury would have to decide between the word of Hurley Cutshaw and that of Miss Ann. And convicting a white male on the word of a female Negro was a difficult sell for an all white, male jury in Virginia. Considering all the circumstances, it seemed the prudent thing to do: bargain with the guilty for some semblance of justice for the innocent.

Harry scratched at the annoying spot on his forehead. Blood on his fingertips surprised him. Evelyn had expressed concern for the umpteenth time. She was at the point of nagging, something she seldom did, reason enough for him to take it seriously. Perhaps she was right. He planned to have Doc Stout take a look, but it never seemed convenient. He retrieved his handkerchief and dabbed the blood. His continuous scratching had created a scar, as permanent as the deep wounds that scarred his soul. But his long-ago tragedy now seemed trivial compared to Annie's emotional scars caused by years of trauma at the hands of Cutshaw. He found it difficult to conceive of such cruelty from those responsible for the care of children. He wondered what kind of nightmares she must endure.

Judge Jenkins barely escaped the judgment he deserved when his plane crashed along the eastern seaboard. Newspapers up and down the coast heralded his survival a miracle. Harry couldn't envision God in the equation of a miracle for Jenkins; rather, death seemed more judicious. Luck, not divine intervention, was the determiner. And luck and the miraculous were as distant as night and day. Twilight forever divides the two. His evil deeds were the twilight that prevented this fortuitous event from being a miracle. "By their fruits," Jesus condemned the Pharisees. Still, Pilate sent Jesus to the crossbeam, no miracle saved Him. The Pharisees hurled their barbed accusations, shielded by their pious positions within the community. Their sins remained cloaked by their priestly robes.

The community didn't know the truth, nor would they ever know. They joined in the revelry made over the celebrity status of a local figure. The plane crash made national headlines, but Jenkins' diabolical actions against children in the valley never made local news—not even local gossip. Only a few knew the truth, and that truth was locked in their hearts for various reasons. Evil existed in camouflaged garments of good: Judge Jeremiah Jenkins seated on a bench, dispensing judgments; Hurley Cutshaw seated on a stump, pretending to care for orphans but disallowing the life of a child. By the position of the thumb, a Caesar decided the fate of a gladiator. By the signing of a document, Jenkins enslaved Negro children into the custody of Hurley Cutshaw. By the crack of a belt, Cutshaw enforced child labor.

Harry slammed his fist against the steering wheel. How could this have happened? How could men be so evil? He fended off the blasphemous questions. Where was God in the mix? Why does God let such men coexist with decent folks? He didn't question God's providence, he simply didn't understand it.

The theme of yesterday's sermon from the Psalms perplexed him: *A righteous man will be remembered forever; the wicked will be forgotten.* He didn't challenge the Divine inspiration of Scripture, but he did sometimes challenge man's interpretation. In his days as sheriff, he met a lot of wicked men who made quite a name for themselves. Judge Jeremiah Jenkins fit that category: honored by the governor, retired with a government pension and remembered in the history books for his good deeds to society. Seems like the wicked do prosper. Did anyone even notice his efforts in rescuing Miss Ann from Cutshaw's evil clutch? "Sorry, Lord," he whispered. That thought seemed prideful, and it wasn't about him. Annie's freedom was the only thing that mattered, and God knew he had a hand in that. Any decent man would have acted accordingly.

He turned the Hudson onto a long, tree-lined drive. The sudden strobe effect of the sun penetrating the oak foliage and streaming through the windshield, created a dizzying effect. He decelerated.

A colonial-style brick mansion stood at the end of the verdant canopy of aged hardwoods. It had somehow survived the devastation of the civil war; its occupants had not, and without heirs, it became a home for the aged.

The fading letters identifying Twelve Oaks Nursing Home cleverly exemplified the waning of life, something Harry tended to give more consideration these days. Had the plantation home of the Wilkes family in Margaret Mitchell's novel *Gone With The Wind* inspired the name? Six towering oak trees had originally lined each side of the drive. Three stumps scattered between the budding oaks hinted of the inevitability of death. Twelve Oaks was down to nine, and some dead branches in the remaining trees warned of future casualties. Death was a natural process he accepted, but, even after all these years, he had not come to closure with the death of his mother. She could well have been alive if she had not met such an untimely and violent death, murdered at the hands of her husband—his father. He found it difficult to consider the man his father, though he bore his name. He pushed aside the angst that momentarily surged. Anger had long ago subsided; still, there was a part of him glad his dad hadn't survived prison. That prevented a host of issues with which he didn't have to contend.

Instinct from years as a law enforcer immediately kicked in, and he quickly assessed the scene before him. Half a dozen pensive residents in wheelchairs, attended by two women in matching white uniforms, lined the expansive veranda of the old mansion. The residents wore the same blank expression, like matching masks. What is it like waiting on death?

The Hudson coasted to a stop in front of a fading sign with a missing last letter. "Guest? Or guess?" He chuckled.

To his right, four men sat around a table underneath a red and white striped umbrella. The tallest and stout looking one sat in a wheelchair, typical of the irony of life: time and chance happen to all. The man tugged at a white bandage that wrapped his head and completely covered his eyes, evidently a victim of an accident, or he'd had recent surgery. Frames of memories flashed—some friends, others complete strangers, but all bonded in a common cause—of young men carried from the field of battle in Europe. Pity welled, and he swallowed hard, for he disdained life without sight. Too much of life's gratifications hinged upon visual, from the Easter lilies soaking the morning sun, to the Blue Jay splashing in a brook. Helen Keller's story should be told to every child in grammar school if the teacher would just leave out her political affiliation. Any party whose philosophy delineated the gallantry of war veterans of the first great war, or opposed the halting of Hitler's Nazi advance in Europe, rated low in Harry's view. That was the one thing to which Miss Keller remained blind. How did such a brave soul become a socialist? Harry spent enough time in the trenches of WWI to speak his mind. His Purple Heart endorsed that right. But this wasn't about him; it was about all who fought. It was about the four hundred and eleven crosses aligned symmetrically around a white stone chapel, and for them, the torch of freedom must ever be held high. *In Flanders fields the poppies blow, between the crosses, row on row.* … Lieutenant Colonel John McCrae's poem moved him to tears. He had been there, not the cemetery, but the field of battle, wave after wave of men scrambling from the trenches into the face of a barrage of enemy fire. Many left the trenches, but some never returned. Over and over, like the waves of the ocean, this scene still played out in his mind, as if it happened yesterday. For a veteran living in the valley, nothing was more beautiful, yet melancholic, than the springtime fields of poppies with the Blue Ridge Mountain backdrop. He had hoped to someday visit Flanders Field Cemetery.

Harry snapped open his pocket watch as if time now mattered but quickly slipped it back into his pocket, for he had no appointment but hoped to speak with a friend regarding employment for Miss Ann. Still, time did matter, and where had all the time gone? Forty years had zipped by since the war, but not a day passed that he did not remember the fighting that cost the lives of over nine million soldiers and almost as many civilians. Was the gentleman in bandages a veteran? How had he received his wounds?

The conflict had shifted from Europe to Asia. Fighting in Korea had ended, but the area remained a powder keg. The French had withdrawn from Vietnam, and the temporary boundary between the north and south—the seventeenth parallel—was definitely drawn with chalk. Would America be drawn into another war? He hoped not, but when decent governments become passive toward aggressively evil regimes, democracy will eventually crumble like a dried up fruitcake.

He adjusted his fedora in the mirror before stepping onto the cobblestone sidewalk leading to the veranda. Blades of grass poked through the cracks of the aged walkway. The mansion had originally been the showcase of a thriving plantation, but that was long ago. Time was definitely taking its toll. Money received from the patients certainly wasn't going into the upkeep of the grounds.

One of the men under the umbrella hastily stood and strode toward him. Harry hesitated, readjusting his hat. Why would Jack Brady be here, and why would he be here with Hurley Cutshaw? Who was the classy dressed man with a cane? And the man in bandages? He seemed familiar.

Chapter Three

"Good morning, Harry." Jack extended a hand and flashed his customary, political smile.

"Mornin', Jack." Harry glanced at the others and clinched Jack's hand harder than necessary. "What's going on?" He hesitantly released his grip.

"It's not what you might suspect." Jack held up both hands, palms open in a passive defense.

"Suspect? What else would I think? The only time Hurley Cutshaw socializes is when he's plotting with the devil."

Jack glanced at the others as if to see if they could hear the conversation. "Hurley was already here when I arrived." He spoke in a hushed tone. "Just a coincidental meeting. I came to see Judge Jenkins on official business. He's convalescing here, from the plane crash. You've met him?"

"No. Seen him but never met him."

"I'll introduce you if you like."

Harry offered a tight-lipped smile.

"Harry Weatherholtz, surprised to see you here," Cutshaw called out. He waved like they were old friends.

Harry hooked his thumbs on his pants' pockets. For Cutshaw to act so friendly, something had to be amiss. He nodded to Cutshaw.

"Let me introduce you to the judge." Jack took Harry's arm and nudged him forward. "I'm sure you've heard how he miraculously survived the accident, along with his aid, Winston Pratt. That's the gentleman with the cane."

"I heard they had survived." Hesitantly he walked with Jack across the patchy but otherwise green lawn—that already needed to be mowed in places—toward Cutshaw, Pratt and Jenkins.

The judge sat with folded arms, his face in the direction of the sun, cocked upward.

"Judge Jenkins, this is Harry Weatherholtz. I think you've heard of him."

Jenkins turned toward them, but he didn't respond.

"The plane crash left him blind," Brady said. "A miracle he survived."

"Sorry, your honor." Harry knew his condolences were insincere, and he wanted to recall them, but it was right to be civil. His heart screamed that Jenkins got what he deserved but still not enough to call it justice.

The judge's face remained fixed in Harry's direction, as if looking at him through some invisible slits in the bandages, still without responding. From behind the bandages, he seemed to study Harry's features. Cutshaw fidgeted but remained silent. Harry refused to engage him.

"The judge has been here a few weeks. They're not sure about the diagnosis for his sight, but doctors are cautiously optimistic. We're all praying." Brady's political savvy kicked in, perhaps to relieve the awkwardness, though Harry perceived it as hypocritical. Brady was noted for characteristics other than those of a praying man.

Jenkins' head snapped aloof, his hands slammed against the wheelchair's armrests, clinched, still the judge, ever wielding the gavel of authority. He repositioned himself before speaking, as if weighing his words. "So I finally get to meet the man who stopped social progress in Shenandoah County. Can't say that I'm pleased to meet you, sir."

"I don't consider child labor progress." Harry crossed his arms and stared at the judge.

Brady placed a hand on Harry's shoulder. "I'm sorry, Harry, the judge isn't feeling well—"

"I hear you're a baby-sittin' that wench of mine." The words grated from Cutshaw's high-pitched voice. Ever since the day Harry found him sitting on that stump, having not twitched a muscle to attempt to rescue a drowning little boy, his animosity toward Harry remained obvious. Guilt has a strange way of surfacing in other emotions.

"If you're speaking of Miss Ann, she doesn't need babysitting. She's making do on her own, working odd jobs and paying her way." Harry determined to remain calm. He'd already won this battle, and he wasn't allowing it to be fought again.

"So you should thank me for beatin' the laziness from her." Cutshaw's eyes emanated a sinister hatred as he made a jack-in-the-box leap from the lawn chair. "I taught her everything she knows. She should be grateful—"

"This isn't the time or the place for such confrontation, Hurley." Brady clutched Cutshaw's forearms and forced him back into the chair, his wiry body squirming like a worm being hooked.

"Our program was the best thing that's ever happened to the black children in this community. It cut welfare costs and created self-esteem." The judges' wheezy voice and gasping between words hinted of the effects of the fiery plane crash.

Momentary pity silenced Harry.

"It's behind us gentlemen." Brady postured for calm.

"We were training them to be industrious and independent of the dole," Jenkins jabbed his finger into the air toward Harry, "until this outsider stuck his nose where it didn't belong." He tried to rise from his wheelchair but gave up the idea. His face flushed and he breathed in heavy gasps. "It's not over, Weatherholtz."

"What's going on?" A nurse rushed their way.

"Everything's fine, ma'am." Brady gave the nurse a reassuring wave.

Jenkins' candor didn't surprise Harry, and for a blind man in a wheelchair, the judge spoke with unusual confidence. Any sympathy he felt for the judge vanished. He sought to suppress his disdain for Cutshaw, but everything within him screamed for retribution. In his years in the law-enforcement community, he'd seen their equal in scorn for human life, but he'd never seen such contemptuous criminals go unpunished. A jury of citizens had always seen to that, and on a couple occasions, a victim's kinsman or advocate did the job, not that he condoned such.

"So what brings you to Twelve Oaks, Harry?" Brady redirected the conversation.

Harry hesitated. "Wanted to visit a friend that works here."

"How's Evelyn?"

"She's fine."

"Good to see you again."

"Good to see you, Jack."

Harry tipped his hat and headed toward Twelve Oaks' main entrance.

The confrontation opened wounds. Flashes of the lad lying lifeless by his lake still haunted Harry. He tried desperately to save the child's life. Cutshaw observed from a sitting position on a tree stump, heartless. Against the pleas of Miss Ann, Cutshaw had sent her brother, who couldn't swim, into the lake to retrieve a snared fishing lure. Even after the incident, Cutshaw maintained custody of Miss Ann, treating her like chattel and hiring her out as a domestic worker, but keeping the income. The horrible ordeal finally ended when Miss Ann realized she was old enough to be on her own and defiantly declared independence from Cutshaw's guardianship.

Judge Jenkins was complicit in the scheme. He signed the legal placement of orphaned children in the valley. Jack Brady, as county prosecutor, had investigated the case. Motivated by a lingering hatred modeled by his ancestors, Jenkins discriminated against the black children and purposefully placed them in dangerous and cruel environments like that of Hurley Cutshaw. Further, he purposefully removed children of unwed black mothers and, likewise, placed them in homes from which Harry believed the judge received a kickback from the money paid by the government to the guardians of the children. Most of these children were branded as retarded and therefore not eligible for schooling. This saved the county money and made the children available to do demanding errands for their guardians or to be farmed out as workers within the community. The guardians received compensation directly from the employers of the children, and the employers got a good deal. Jenkins and Cutshaw, both complicit in these acts, had escaped prosecution by Brady at the strong urging of Harry, both agreeing they could not get a prosecution, and a trial would cause great mental anguish to Miss Ann, who would be a primary witness for the prosecution. The motive to drop the investigation was pure, and Miss Ann had escaped the predictable challenging ordeal that would have ensued with a trial of such a high-profile political figure. The unofficial deal that Brady brokered ended Jenkins' seat on the bench and also stopped the exploitation of black orphans in the valley, but it offered no reparations to the victims.

Their criminal mentality seemed the only commonality between Jenkins and Cutshaw. Otherwise, they were worlds apart socially, economically and intellectually, but here they were together again. What did Jack mean by "the scene was not as it appeared?" Harry's mind raced and his pulse quickened. Mental frames from the past months flashed in split second timing: the beaded water glistening on the face of little Eddie's listless body; a frail and fearful Miss Ann running for help; Cutshaw sitting on a stump without attempting to rescue the boy; a grand jury dismissed without a verdict;

front porch conversations with Sheriff Flin; the initials JJJ—Judge Jeremiah Jenkins—brazenly embossed on a license plate of Jenkins' car parked in Cutshaw's store lot; the suspicious and unsolved fire that destroyed Harry's sawmill; his dog Shep lying amidst multiple tire marks that had crushed out life.

Harry breathed deep and slow, trying to calm his palpitating heart. Why was Jack Brady with them? These three together—Jenkins, Pratt and Cutshaw—reeked of wickedness. Had he been wrong about Jack? Why would he visit with Jenkins and Cutshaw knowing their criminal activities? Their meeting smacked of treachery? What conspiracy were they plotting? Were they reneging on the deal that removed Jenkins from the bench and stopped Cutshaw's mistreatment of black children? Would such exploitation of black children start up again? Who now had custody of the black child Cutshaw had temporarily gotten to replace little Eddie? Was he back under Cutshaw's care? There could be nothing good from a meeting of these three. Maybe Sheriff Flin was right after all. It's not enough to corner the skunk; you've got to bag him. Flin had pushed for the investigation to continue, but Harry had convinced him otherwise.

This chance meeting made him wonder about last year's decision. Had he underestimated the depravity of the powers that controlled this valley? Would his blunder endanger children again? In all his years in law enforcement, he had done his best to protect the innocent. This time, could he have miserably failed. Jenkins was right; it wasn't over.

Chapter Four

In spite of the ruckus with Jenkins and Cutshaw, Harry's meeting with Celia Tucker went well. Celia was a former neighbor who had moved away, gotten her degree in nursing and had returned back to Woodstock. Though short on help, still, Miss Tucker expressed her concern in hiring Ann, and she reluctantly agreed to interview her. Ann would be the only colored worker at Twelve Oaks. Finding out that Jenkins was a resident, He now had misgivings of his own regarding her working there.

Twelve Oaks had long ago lost its elitist status; it catered to welfare clients. A few were mental patients the government had relocated in its effort to reduce the population of asylums—assimilation, they called it, more humane. He wasn't sure about that, the mentally ill residing in nursing homes with under-trained staffing. His greatest concern wasn't that Ann couldn't cope with the residents; rather, he feared for her safety because Judge Jenkins was a racist with a personal vendetta against her and her kind. Then again, Jenkins was blind. Would his blindness make him colorblind? Harry hoped so. Perhaps he could coach Ann to not let Jenkins know her identity, but to do so he might have to reveal information regarding his involvement in dropping the investigation. She had no idea of Jenkins' role in placing her and little Eddie in Cutshaw's care, nor that he might have been prosecuted had he not pushed for dismissal.

Harry puzzled over another question. Why would a man of Jenkins status choose for rehab an out-of-date institution like Twelve Oaks? Jenkins could afford the finest and most up-to-date rehab center in all of Virginia, but he settled for a nursing home that catered to the poor and insane. What was he up to? Was he feigning blindness? He was definitely conniving with Cutshaw.

Harry slowed for the flashing lights of a utility truck. Two workers in painters' whites wielded brushes on the wooden *Welcome to Woodstock* sign. The freshly-painted, bright green background accentuated the white letters. He thought he recognized one of the workers. From the VFW? They returned his wave.

A row of cherry trees lined the road, their pale pink blossoms signaling the arrival of spring. He inhaled deeply. Their blooms released a pleasant aroma. Springtime in the Shenandoah brought life to more than plants; it invigorated the human soul.

Woodstock was the center of Shenandoah County activity. He and Evelyn visited at least monthly, especially when his retirement check arrived. He loved the historical significance of this colorful community. Woodstock was one of several county seats that punctuated the valley landscape, others being Harrisonburg, Luray, and Staunton. Woodstock and her neighbors boasted a background story predating the Civil War.

A column of young Massanutten Academy cadets—under the watchful eye of the looming mountains for which the military prep school was named—practiced a marching routine on the front lawn. He pulled alongside the curb and killed the engine. Their matching blue and white uniforms, with gold insignias, moved as one unit under the midday sun. He didn't know any of the students who attended the school, for many came from around the country, some even from other countries. These saw their families sparingly. Perhaps the lengthy separation from families prepared them for a lifetime of military service. The sight of boys away from home sparked memories of his childhood in Larue, Ohio, a quiet little community south of Lake Erie and in the middle of nowhere. He, too, was away from parents and family, but the difference, he could never see his parents.

He pulled a handkerchief from his pocket and blew his nose. Had his allergies already kicked in? A bugler caught his attention, signaling orders to the trainees.

The academy opened when Harry was six years old, about a year after he had left the valley. He'd lived his first five years in the valley, but after the killing of his mother by his father, his grandmother sought refuge for him and his brother and moved with them to Ohio. Originally, it was protection from his alcoholic father's vengeance, but after his father's incarceration—where he died the first year—it became revenge toward his father's family. They never again associated with his dad's parents, something he regretted but was too late to change. The death of his father in prison removed any threat on his life, but he never returned to the valley until years later. Without formal education, he'd made a decent life for himself: numerous military honors, sheriff of Wyandot County, Ohio, for six years, and he had earned respect from his fellow man. His honorable reputation followed him to the valley, a reputation he worked hard to maintain. His was a reputation that contrasted his father's, and it was a reputation he prayed compensated for the lingering memories of his father's dastardly deeds.

The color guard paraded in front of the unit: the Virginia state and Academy flags flanked the stars and stripes to the left. He restarted the Hudson. An upperclassman shouted orders; the cadets obeyed in unison.

Harry had served under the command of a Massanutten graduate in the first Great War. The officer reflected the code of honor drilled into the students: honesty always and intolerance for any soldier who is dishonest.

The impressive campus, with its three-story brick buildings lining Main Street, slowly disappeared in his rear view mirror. That's how he tried to live life: seeing the past from a smaller view in the rear view mirror and viewing the present through the wide front windshield. On some days that was a challenge. Circumstances robbed him of growing up in this historic community, but he now claimed it as his home and savored its history. George Washington had sponsored the town charter in the Virginia House of Burgess in seventeen sixty-one, almost two hundred years earlier. He slowed the Hudson as he approached the courthouse, designed by Thomas Jefferson and built of native limestone. The legend of Peter Muhlenberg lingered in this center of Shenandoah County legal activity. Reverend Muhlenberg, an Anglican pastor, preached his final sermon in Woodstock in seventeen seventy-six by removing his clerical robe to reveal a uniform of the Continental Army. Three hundred volunteers followed him out of the valley to fight in George Washington's army against the imposing Red Coats. Harry knew locals sometimes embellished their history, but he also knew truth and courage and honor flowed through this valley as constant as the winding Shenandoah River.

He eased the Hudson into a parking spot in front of the county jail alongside Sheriff Flin's black cruiser. A layer of rusty red Virginia clay camouflaged the sheriff emblem. A couple *Dogs n Suds* hot dog wrappers littered the front floorboard. The new fast-food craze was sweeping the country. Flin looked to have eaten his share. He wasn't into appearance, as his weight attested. Such persona often disarmed criminals, for they equated overweight with laziness and incompetence. He certainly was overweight, but lazy he was not, and all in all, he was a good cop.

"If it ain't my good friend Harry Weatherholtz." Flin bounded from his swivel chair and greeted Harry with a firm handshake. A wadded wax paper beside an empty coffee cup, along with a wet spot on the front of his shirt, revealed a recent lunch. Evelyn's biscuits and molasses wouldn't tempt him today, at least not for a while.

"Afternoon, Sheriff. Brought you a little something." Harry placed a brown paper bag on Flin's desk.

"What's this?" Flin studied the bag. "Where you been hidin' all winter, Harry?"

"Been busy … mostly logging. Rebuilding the sawmill."

"Thanks, Harry, or should I be thankin' the wife?" He glanced inside the bag.

"Biscuits straight from Evelyn's oven. I had a hand in the molasses."

"Appreciate it … already had lunch but them biscuits will keep. You remember Irene?" Flin pointed toward his dispatcher.

"Certainly. How are you, Miss Irene?" He removed his fedora and gave a slight nod.

"Fine. Nice to see you again—" The telephone interrupted the conversation.

The legs of an oak chair grated Harry's eardrums as Flin scooted it across the wooden floor toward him. "Here, have a seat and take a load off that mind of yours." He dropped back into his desk chair and studied Harry's face, while he tapped the top of his oak desk with the eraser of a tooth-pocked pencil. "What brings you to town?"

"Couple errands. Thought I'd stop by and say hello. How are you?"

"Never been better. You?"

"Good." Harry toyed with the brim of his hat.

"Coffee?" Flin pointed toward the coffee pot. "Irene, could you pour—"

"No, thanks." Harry waved away the offer.

"Never mind, Irene. How's Evelyn? Sure appreciate her sending them biscuits." He peeked into the bag again, like maybe he wanted to try one, but closed the bag.

"She's good."

"I need to get out there and see you folks."

"We'd like that. We still have plenty of that molasses left over from last year. You'll have to help me get rid of it before fall."

"You sure do a fine job preparin' it. Got a knack for it, Harry. And I've been craving it like you can't imagine." Flin laughed as he patted his bulging belly.

Harry crossed his legs at the ankles and placed his hat on his knees.

"Something on your mind, Harry?" Flin resumed tapping the eraser against his desk.

Harry glanced at Irene and back to Flin. "You got a minute?"

"Sure. Something troubling you?"

Irene ended the phone call and fumbled with some papers at the filing cabinet, too nonchalant to not be eavesdropping.

Harry glanced at her and hesitated.

"Let's take a walk." Flin stood. "Be back in a jiffy, Irene."

"Sure thing," she said, her scowl obvious. Harry didn't mean to offend her, but he wanted the conversation confidential. After all, he could be wrong with his assumptions, and he didn't want rumors feeding more paranoia within the valley. A dispatcher was the third best source of gossip in the community, next to the local telephone operator and the barber. Charlie Campbell could cut your hair in twenty minutes, but he'd stretch it to thirty for a salacious story. Some folks say Zelma Gilpin, manning the local telephone switchboard, could listen in on five conversations at a time, but she sometimes got the customers crossed, causing much consternation.

"Nice to see you again, ma'am." Harry smiled.

"You too." Irene blew a bubble that popped onto her bright red lips. She closed the filing drawer and returned to her desk.

Flin grabbed his Colt .38 from the desk drawer and slipped it into his side holster. "Grandma's Kitchen is empty this time of day. I sure miss her, but Cindy's carryin' on her momma's tradition quite well. You had lunch?"

"No. Not really hungry, and Evelyn is expecting me. Just had something I wanted to run by you. It'll only take a minute."

They stopped at the bust of the Reverend Peter Muhlenberg. Harry rested a hand on the shoulder of the bust, tracing the furrows of the bronze statue. "You recall the story?"

"Sure do. His last sermon in Woodstock … from Ecclesiastes … a time of war and a time of peace … a time to pray and a time to fight."

"Maybe embellished a little by the Daughters of the Revolution?" Harry smiled.

Flin chuckled. "You got that right."

Harry hesitated. "I'm afraid we may have made the wrong choice regarding our handling the situation with Miss Ann and Cutshaw."

"By letting Cutshaw walk?" Flin retrieved a handkerchief from his hip pocket and wiped his brow. "I was afraid of that. Never was comfortable—"

"Not just Cutshaw." Harry stooped and pulled a blade of grass from a crack around the base of the bust.

"Whatcha mean?" Flin continued to wipe his brow.

"Cutshaw was just a pawn. Judge Jenkins was the real kingpin."

"Mighty big accusation. Any proof?"

"Yes. I suspected it, and Brady confirmed it."

Flin replaced the handkerchief in his hip pocket. "You knew this and didn't tell me?"

"I wasn't positive. It would've been a task proving it to a Shenandoah County jury. You know that."

Flin nodded his agreement. "True, but I'd still liked to have known."

"You're right. I should have told you, but I thought mostly about Miss Ann, how to protect her. Brady had reservations about prosecuting an old family friend, and we got what we wanted, Miss Ann's freedom. We all … Brady, you, me … we all agreed it was too tough a fight … and at the expense of Miss Ann."

"But you should've at least told me about Jenkins." Flin tugged at the collar of his shirt as if to loosen its pressure on his jugular.

Harry didn't respond.

29

"Why didn't you tell me? We could've tightened the noose had I known that." He jabbed his fist into his open palm.

"With Jenkins' resignation and Brady's appointment to be the one to make placement of orphans, the problem seemed fixed."

"At least it worked for a while. Now we're in a fix." Flin retrieved his handkerchief again and wiped his brow.

"What do you mean?" Harry removed his fedora and rubbed his fingers through his thinning hair.

"You ain't heard?"

"Heard what?" He aligned his fedora to his brow.

"Brady got a special appointment at the statehouse, by the governor. Jenkins' party will appoint a new judge and prosecutor. We're stuck with whoever Jenkins and his cronies come up with for prosecutor, and believe you me, that person won't have our interest in mind."

"So that's why Brady was meeting with Jenkins?" Harry traced the brim of the Revolutionary War hero's bronze hat.

"At Twelve Oaks?" Flin asked.

"You knew Jenkins was at Twelve Oaks and didn't tell me? I assumed he was out of our life, him leaving the county after he was removed from the bench."

The tables had turned. Both had withheld information from the other, and both were disappointed in the other.

Flin's shoulders slumped. "Didn't see any need. Now we're even. Anyhow, I kind of figured out Jenkins was involved with the placement of those black kids under Cutshaw's care. I didn't mention him at Twelve Oaks 'cause I knew we couldn't touch him. And I didn't want you doing something stupid."

"Well, aren't you the actor, Sheriff. You knew about Jenkins association with Cutshaw but never let on." Harry scratched the back of his hand. "Got into some poison ivy in Evelyn's flowerbed. Should have known better." He had grown to respect Flin but had certainly underestimated his prowess as the county sheriff. He suppressed a grin.

"I've kept this job a long time by learning when to keep my mouth shut, Harry. A long-term sheriff keeps some eggs in a different basket. I knew Brady had to cut a deal with Jenkins, but I wasn't sure about Brady's motives ... of course, I trusted you. You didn't push for prosecution. Anyways, now that things are going the way they are, you best keep a protective eye on Miss Ann ... and watch out for poison ivy."

"You think so?"

"I know so." Flin studied a '57 Fairlane, bearing a West Virginia plate, as it eased alongside the curb across the street. "Hate boils the blood. Makes a man's rage rise to the surface and turns his thoughts devilish. That girl's in danger of their revenge. Those two, Jenkins and Cutshaw, make a dangerous duo." Flin's right hand rested on the handle of his Colt. He stroked the nape of his neck with the other. "You be careful too, Harry. Watch your back."

"Thanks. What about Brady? You think he's clean?"

"Not sure. Money and power make an intoxicating mix. Time'll tell. I think I'll check out that car. Is that a 500 Skyliner, retracting-roof hardtop?"

"I'm not up on cars, Sheriff. I'm still driving a Hudson." Harry chuckled. "It may be."

"I think it is. Haven't seen it's like before around here. And its driver, evidently, didn't notice he's in a no parking zone."

"You have to admit that's a mighty beautiful vehicle parked along our street. Maybe he thought the yellow curb was reserved parking just for him."

A young man in white spats, with his sunglasses pushed back on his head, exited the vehicle.

"I'd say his daddy bought it for him for Christmas, so I'd say he can afford a parking ticket? See you 'round, Harry."

Flin ambled across the street and struck up a conversation with the young man. He could make a crook feel at ease. He had the typical small-town cop appearance, but underneath his graying hair was a brilliant mind with a knack for judging character.

"Glad we're on the same team," Harry mused.

Flin was too far away to hear the compliment, or see the grin on Harry's face.

Chapter Five

The Hudson bounced along the rutted driveway and scattered a flock of bantams as Harry decelerated in front of his house. Evelyn pushed open the screen door and stepped onto the porch, wiping her hands on her blue and white gingham apron. She descended the steps as he exited the car. Something was wrong. She seldom left the kitchen to greet him. Their relationship had long ago lost any melodramatic moments. Dinner should be the issue at hand; something was amiss.

"How's Celia?"

"Good. Agreed to see Annie. She still here?"

"No. Left to clean the Carnahans' house."

He fiddled with his hat, restructuring the indentation of the front crown.

"Is everything alright, Bud?" She seldom called him Harry. She always called him Bud, a nickname his older brother gave him as a child. Harry preferred her to call him Bud. The ring of it kept alive the special bond he and his brother had shared.

"I think so." He rubbed at the corner of his eye. "Why do you ask?"

"Jack Brady stopped by to see you." She swiped a strand of hair from her forehead and repinned it to the side.

"Really? Did he say why?"

"No."

"That's strange. I just spoke with him at the nursing home a couple hours ago."

"Brady was at the nursing home? I wonder why?"

"Never really said."

"I appreciate what he did for Annie. I really like that boy, but he seemed nervous, like something troubled him. Did he indicate anything to you?" Evelyn tugged on the shoulder straps of her apron.

Harry shrugged, but he didn't answer.

"What's going on, Bud?"

Harry tossed his hat onto the hood. "Brady is leaving for Richmond. Accepted an appointment on Shockoe Hill."

"The Capitol?"

"Yes."

"He told you that?"

"No."

"How'd you find out?"

"News like that travels fast. Flin told me."

"That's a dangerous place to work." She smirked.

"Jack will do alright. He's a politician, more so than I realized."

"I was referring to the building itself, not the job. You remember its history?"

"Oh, that. Quite a tragedy."

Shortly after the Civil War, a balcony on the second floor collapsed, crashing through the floor and sending people and debris to the House of Delegates chamber forty feet below. The mishap wounded more than two hundred people and killed sixty-two, including the grandson of Virginia's famed "Give-me-liberty-or-give-me-death" statesman, Patrick Henry.

"I'm happy for Jack. I imagine he'll do just fine at the statehouse. But why does that trouble you?" Evelyn asked.

"Oh, I liked having him here to keep the valley peaceful." Harry scratched a bug off the windshield.

"Is that poison ivy on your hand?"

"I got into a spring patch the other day."

"You should put something on that right away before you have it all over your body."

"I will. Did Jack say why he wanted to see me?"

"No, just said he had some unfinished business to discuss. How come it took so long to get home?"

"Took longer at Sheriff Flin's than I expected. Lots to talk about."

"Anything in particular?"

"Just … you know … stuff. I gave him the molasses and biscuits."

"I'm sure he liked that."

"He did." Harry scratched at the sore on his forehead.

"Didn't happen to stop in and see Doctor Stout about that sore?"

"No. Maybe next week."

"What'd you and Jack talk about that needed more discussion to the point that he'd make a trip out here?"

"Nothing really. I'm surprised he stopped. He was visiting Judge Jenkins, who's recuperating at Twelve Oaks."

"That can't be good … Jack visiting with varmint."

"Cutshaw was there, too."

Evelyn cinched and retied her apron strings. "Lord, have mercy. I'm afraid this thing isn't over. What's that boy getting himself into talking with those two?" She turned toward the house.

"Let's not jump to conclusions." Harry retrieved his hat from the hood of the car. "Did Jack say where he was headed?"

"No." She stopped at the top of the steps and kicked a clump of chicken droppings onto the ground. "Them chickens need to be fenced in. Making a mess everywhere."

"Was Miss Ann here when Jack stopped by?"

"Left right after he arrived."

"Which direction did Brady go?"

"Drove in the direction of the Carnahans' place?"

Harry stared in that direction. "The same direction of Miss Ann?"

"Yes, why?"

Harry did not respond.

"Surely you don't suspect Jack Brady—"

Harry brushed by her toward the door.

"There's something else. ..." Evelyn hesitated.

Harry turned abruptly. "What?" He reached for her hand, something he seldom did, for life had stifled any outward display of affection. Evelyn had long ago adjusted to his lack of affection. "What else, Evelyn?" He awkwardly released her hand.

"I didn't give it much thought at the time, but the Buffords' car passed the house, real slow, right after Annie left. I was talking to Jack and never gave it much mind, but once he left, I got to thinking about it and got worried. I know they apologized for what they did to Annie, but I still have a difficult time trusting those boys."

Harry didn't answer.

"Bud? What are you thinking?"

"Let's drive over to the Carnahans' and check on Miss Ann."

"If them no account boys did anything to her—"

"Just precautionary, Evelyn. We have no concrete reason to believe anything bad has happened. I certainly have no reason to suspect Jack would harm her in any way. Then again, I never thought he'd renege on his arbitration with Jenkins, but that wasn't necessarily on purpose. If he accepted a job at the State House, he can't run things locally. That's just a matter of fact. Can't blame him for a promotion. Anyway, Miss Ann can use a ride home."

Chapter Six

Harry vividly recalled two heinous crimes in the valley that went unpunished: the murder of his young mother, Minnie, and the death of little Eddie. His mother's death was due to alcohol and jealousy. He was convinced Eddie's death was due to Cutshaw—aware the lad couldn't swim—forcing him into the lake. Though helpless to prevent either, Harry still bore a sense of responsibility for both. What if he could have warned his mother in time? If he had been more alert, perhaps by a few seconds, he could have recognized his father hiding in the hayloft and somehow warned her. And what if he had gotten to the lad a minute earlier.

His mother's murder should never have happened. His father had been in jail but somehow escaped before trial. He'd made threats before, so she wasn't safe with him afoot. What if the system had done its job better? If they'd prevented the escape before the trial, he wouldn't have had the opportunity to kill his mother. He would have been sent to prison for his pending crime. If his family had moved to Ohio earlier, he would not have found them, and his mother could still be alive. But Harry was only a child himself. Why did he hold himself to such high standards of responsibility? For little Eddie's death, he felt a greater sense of remorse. What if he hadn't dug the lake on his farm? If he had been a minute earlier at the lake, perhaps he could have revived the lad. He still grieved for the child.

And after their deaths, the court system failed both his mother and little Eddie. Hers was a first-degree murder trial for which a jury brought back a manslaughter verdict. The ill decided verdict prompted the judge to dismiss the case on a technicality of the law regarding first-degree and second-degree murder cases. Little Eddie's was a manslaughter case brought before a grand jury, which Harry encouraged Brady to dismiss due to the emotional threat to Miss Ann. Harry now had regrets about his action.

Though an upholder of the law much of his life, Harry fought cynicism all his life regarding the legal system. How could his father escape a prison sentence on such a ridiculous technicality? The judge threw out the second-degree murder verdict because the act was definitely premeditated, thus a first-degree murder. The judge's ruling didn't make sense, but it followed the letter of the law: due to the circumstances, if the murderous act was not first-degree, it could not be second-degree. Although a murderer, his father avoided prison because of the wording in a law-book. Students of law still study the case and argue its concept. Harry pondered the stupidity of the ruling, a loophole shrewd lawyers abuse.

His father eventually went to prison, for a previous crime of threatening to murder Harry's grandma on his mother's side of the family. He walked for murder, but he was convicted for a threat of murder. That didn't make sense any way Harry considered it. The only consolation was that his father went to prison. And that was where he died a year later, though Harry had no concrete evidence of the death: no death certificate, no proof of a funeral, not even a grave plot. Nor did he seek such.

Likewise, Jenkins and Cutshaw used the absurdity of the law to break moral principles the law was written to provide. Their system to provide food and shelter for children created an enslavement of the children. That had been Eddie and Annie's situation: two orphaned and illiterate black children were given a place to live and food to eat, but they were mistreated and forced to work for their keep. Jenkins and Cutshaw profited financially. Their conniving plan fed both their greed and their hatred. Harry thought this had come to an end but now realized it could well start back up. Though blind and residing in a nursing home, Jenkins was still conspiring. What technicality would he and Cutshaw use to victimize another child? Ann was too old to be placed back into the system, but she was unprotected from their hatred. "It's not over," was Jenkins statement. No, that was more than a statement; it was a threat.

The squealing tires attested that Harry pressed the Hudson harder than usual. Evelyn, generally pleading for caution, didn't protest. He gripped the steering wheel with both hands and sat forward in the seat, squinting against the blazing sunset. Silence permeated the atmosphere as they sped along, escalating the sound of the occasional gravel, trapped in the tire treads, which gave loose and clanged against the undercarriage. Evelyn braced her hands against the dash as Harry braked abruptly.

The Carnahans' house was a showplace. Recently strewn gravel formed a perfectly circular driveway to the front door. Early blooming Virginia bluebells lined a perfectly edged flower bed uniquely designed to soak up the warmth of the springtime sun. Mrs. Carnahan's green thumb gave the parsonage a beautiful street appeal. It was an older house, with a gingerbread cornice adorning the wraparound porch, and the intricately designed wooden décor was meticulously painted with complimentary contrasting shades of brown.

Harry had never intruded on the parsonage's privacy. He understood well the importance of solitude, for he had spent six years as sheriff in Ohio, raising a family of six in the upstairs apartment of the castle-like county jail. Too many felt the liberty to drop by and have a word with the sheriff. After all, as a law-abiding taxpayer, they paid his salary. He'd regretted allowing drifters to hang around the jail, sometimes feeding them, for, on one occasion, his own daughter's innocence had been threatened, or at the least she was forever scarred with the trauma of the event. Ironically, his reasoning for going easy on drifters had to do with his father. Rumors abounded that his father had escaped prison—or else bribed authorities—and did not die in prison. Harry speculated that if the rumors were true, he would have wanted someone to make sure his father didn't go hungry. Though his reasoning was admirable, it was flawed. He realized his consideration of the rumors was a pipe dream created out of uncontrolled emotional rationalization, and he vacillated from disdain to regret regarding his father.

Too many interruptions destroyed the sanctity of home for his family while he was sheriff. He regretted those years for his family's sake. For that reason, this was the first time he had dropped in on the parsonage. He hoped it to be the last.

Harry waived the usual small talk and uncharacteristically blurted the reason for their visit. Pastor Carnahan acted delighted to see them, but the reason for the visit set him aback. He stood in the doorway, without an invitation to come in, to the point it became awkward to Harry for invading his space.

"We haven't seen her, Mr. Weatherholtz." Pastor Carnahan responded apologetically.

Harry rubbed his fingers through his hair and stared at the floor before questioning, "She hasn't been by to clean?"

"No, we haven't seen her … though she generally comes on Mondays to clean. You think something has happened to her?"

"We're not sure." Harry toyed with his hat.

"I'm sorry Harry, Evelyn, how impolite of me to leave you standing in the doorway. Come in." Pastor Carnahan stepped aside and motioned them in.

"Is anything wrong?" Mrs. Carnahan began straightening magazines on the coffee table. "I'm sorry the house is a bit messy."

"Can't say for sure." Harry continued to study his hat as he turned it clockwise by the brim.

"She left our place a couple hours ago … said she was cleaning for you today." Evelyn's voice cracked and she snapped open her purse and retrieved a handkerchief.

"Yes, she generally never misses a Monday, and she was supposed to clean this afternoon. I just said to George, 'I wonder where Miss Ann is.' That's why the place is a mite messy. Can I get you some coffee?" Mrs. Carnahan rearranged the pillows on the sofa a couple times.

They declined the offer for coffee.

"I said to George just before you showed up, 'Miss Ann must be sick or something, because she never misses work.' Didn't I just say that, dear?"

"You did."

"I worry about that child, after what happened to her last year." Evelyn dabbed her brow with a lace-edged handkerchief. Her complexion had gone from red to clammy in a matter of seconds. "I'm sorry, we shouldn't have troubled you folks." She fanned her face with the handkerchief. "Don't think I'll ever get over these hot flashes."

Mrs. Carnahan clasped Evelyn's arm. "You're shaking dear. You think something has happened to Miss Ann?"

"Can't be sure, but I'm concerned." Evelyn stuffed her handkerchief into the pocket of her gingham dress. "Sorry, my hair's a mess. You know I don't usually travel away from home looking like this, but we are worried about Annie."

Harry stood. "She's probably fine, but we can't dismiss the fact that she isn't where she should be, and no one seems to have seen her since she left our house. We'll let you know otherwise."

"There's something else, isn't there, Mr. Weatherholtz?" Pastor Carnahan unfolded an arm and extended an open palm, as if beckoning a troubled heart to open his soul to the caring Savior.

Harry hesitated. "Could I use your telephone?"

"Sure." Mrs. Carnahan hastily stood, led him to her husband's study and straightened up books cluttering the desk. She pulled the door partially shut as she backed out of the study. "Take your time."

"Thank you, ma'am."

Harry picked up the receiver and dialed. He balanced the receiver between his head and shoulder, while cracking the joints of his intertwined fingers. Hints of arthritic symptoms gave him some concern. He'd always prided himself in his physical prowess. Lumbering hardened muscles but intensified the aging process, especially the joints.

"Sheriff's office." The voice was familiar.

Harry grabbed at the receiver as it slipped from his ear. "Miss Compton, Harry Weatherholtz. Is Sheriff Flin in, please?"

"Out on a call. Can I take a message?"

"Well … yes. Tell him I'm concerned something may have happened to Miss Ann … the colored girl that lives over by us. She left home some time ago, but she hasn't shown up at her domestic job."

Irene didn't respond.

"Miss Compton?"

"Something you may need to know, which may or may not have any bearing … what did you say her name was?"

"Miss Ann. She's the sister of the little fellow who drowned last year in my lake."

"Oh, yes, I remember her. Like I was saying, this may, or may not, have any bearing on her missing, but the Sheriff's looking into the report of a beating of a colored girl."

"When? Where?"

"Just happened today, not sure 'bout the time. Over New Market way. Isn't that near your place?"

Harry rubbed at the nape of his neck.

"Mr. Weatherholtz? You there?"

"Yes. Any description of the victim?"

"No, other than a young Negro female. They'll probably take her to Dr. Stout's office there in New Market, and if she's bad enough probably bring her here to Woodstock Memorial."

"Thank you, Miss Compton."

"You're welcome. I'll radio and tell Sheriff Flin you called."

Harry stepped into the living room, walked past Mrs. Carnahan and grabbed his hat from the coffee table before speaking. "We've got to go. I think I may have located her."

"She okay?" Mrs. Carnahan asked as she helped Evelyn from the low setting sofa.

"No. If it's her, she's not okay." Harry headed toward the door.

"Thank you," Evelyn placed a hand on Mrs. Carnahan's shoulder. "Thank you for everything."

"If we can do anything. ..." Pastor Carnahan again assumed his pastoral invitational stance.

"Just pray," Evelyn pleaded, as she rushed after Harry toward the car.

Chapter Seven

They sped past two workers who stripped paper from a billboard that for the past three months had promoted the Lee-Jackson holiday. The fallen clutter formed an unsightly mess around the base of the sign. One of the workers waved and Harry reciprocated.

Every February, Virginians, as far back as eighteen eighty-nine, celebrated the birthday of their own General Robert E. Lee. They added Thomas Jackson to the celebration around the turn of the century. Stonewall, as he was affectionately nicknamed by his troops, was a familiar name in the valley. Virginians were indebted to his military genius, courage and loyalty to the cause. They forever speculated the outcome of the war if General Jackson hadn't met his untimely death by friendly fire at the Battle of Chancellorsville. Harry didn't attend the local celebration this year, but he had deep respect for both generals.

He jerked the steering wheel hard and the Hudson swerved to miss a rabbit.

"Be careful, Bud." Evelyn gripped the dashboard.

He slowed at the sight of a state highway truck, yellow lights flashing. A flagman waved him into the opposite lane to avoid the fresh steaming blacktop the workers tamped into potholes created by the winter's freeze. One of the main accesses through the valley, much attention was given to the upkeep of the Valley Turnpike. The road was part of US Route 11, which stretched over sixteen hundred miles from the Canadian border down to New Orleans. It flowed through the valley in a northeast by southwest route, with the Appalachian Mountains enclosing the valley to the west, and the Blue Ridge creating a natural fortress to the east. This main road followed the natural geography of the valley. This was the same path General Jackson marched his "foot cavalry" during four trips through New Market in their efforts to protect the valley from the northern invaders. "If this valley is lost, Virginia is lost," Stonewall wrote to a staff member. With only seventeen thousand men, he successfully protected the valley by outmaneuvering a combined Union force of sixty thousand. The valley descendants never forgot; the annual holiday made sure of that.

They approached the grounds of the Hall of Valor Civil War Museum. Preparations were already underway for the mid-May reenactment of the memorable Battle of New Market. Was a century old war still being fought in the hearts and minds of the valley inhabitants? Or was the reenactment to honor the memory of the fallen? Perhaps both: honor mingled with animosity. Harry had lived on both sides: he loved the Union; he loved the Shenandoah Valley.

The Battle of New Market was unique among Civil War battles. Union troops outnumbered the Confederates by two thousand men. The Federal force had pushed deep into the valley, approaching the city of New Market. General John Breckenridge commanded the Confederate troops, and knowing he had to stop the advance of the Federals through the valley, he called on a group of cadets from the Virginia Military Institute in Lexington. The cadets, who were no more than eighteen years old, with some as young as fourteen, marched into battle under their commander, Lieutenant Colonel Scott Shipp, who was only twenty-four years old. In the heat of the fight, with fixed bayonets, the boys charged into a deadly barrage of musket shots and cannonballs. Eight boys died, and over forty youngsters were wounded, but they captured the Union battery and turned the tide of defeat into a victory at New Market. The townsfolk never forgot, and each year they showed their pride with the reenactment.

Harry knew war; he bore the scars of the first Great War. He touched the brim of his hat as he observed the headstones of the fallen.

They spied Flin's black and white cruiser, lights flashing, double-parked in front of Doctor Stout's office. Flin descended the stone steps of the office as they pulled alongside his cruiser. Harry rolled down the window as Flin approached.

"Hello, Sheriff." Harry loosened his grip on the steering wheel.

"Harry." Flin stuck his head inside the opened window. "Mrs. Weatherholtz. You folks in town to do some shopping?"

"Afternoon, Sheriff," Evelyn said.

"Are things okay in there?" Harry gripped the steering wheel again.

"A domestic quarrel turned bad. I swear this generation's going to the dogs. Man beat his young wife half to death."

Harry released his grip on the steering wheel. "You know them?"

"Somewhat, but never had any trouble out of the husband before this. Gonna have to find him. Colored boy who had too much liquor, and now he's run off and's hidin' somewhere in those hills." He nodded toward the mountains.

"Miss Ann's missing again. We're not sure—"

"How long?"

"A couple hours."

"Too early to tell if she's truly missing. Check down by your lake?" Flin removed his hat and wiped his forehead. "Seems that's where she likes to go sometimes … to think and all … maybe depressed or something."

"I think she's accepted little Eddie's death ... going on with her life ... still grieves sometimes, but all in all, she's doing okay. Stopped by our place just today, but afterward, she didn't show up for a domestic job. I don't know how to say this without sounding like a conspiracy nut, but Evelyn thinks she saw the Buffords' car pass our house right after Ann left."

"Them boys are headed for the big house as sure as shootin'." Flin rapped his knuckles against the roof of the car.

"Jack Brady showed up at my house also," Harry said. "It was before I got home from seeing you, but Evelyn was home. He said he needed to see me. He left in the same direction Miss Ann had gone, and she never showed up at the Carnahans' where she was to do some cleaning. Maybe he's seen her, if we can find him."

"You spoke to the Carnahans?" Flin asked.

"Half hour ago."

"You think the Buffords might have taken her?"

"Can't say anything for sure at this point." Harry tapped his fingers against the steering wheel.

"Surely you don't suspect Brady of anything." Flin repositioned his body to lean against the car door.

"No, but I can't help wonder why he was with Cutshaw and Jenkins at Twelve Oaks. I don't know why or what, but I'm concerned something's going down. And now Miss Ann turns up missing right after that meeting. Sheriff, I'd never forgive myself if anything happened. ..." Harry slammed his hands against the steering wheel.

Flin leaned into the open window. "What do you think, Mrs. Weatherholtz?"

"We're probably overreacting, but you know how I feel about those Bufford boys."

"Probably need to check it out." Flin tugged at his collar squeezing against his jowl. "I'll drive over your way, take a look and ask around. If she shows up or not, either way, you be sure and stay in touch. I'll let you know if I come up with anything."

"Thanks, Sheriff. Sorry to bother you without more information." Harry cranked the ignition to the Hudson. "Maybe we're overprotective, but she's been through a lot."

"I suppose it was the other girls that got you worried?"

"Not sure what you're talking about." Harry turned off the engine.

"There have been a couple other beatings of colored women lately we haven't solved. One of them was a spittin' image of Miss Ann, just an older version."

"I wasn't aware."

"Got me concerned. You and I both know it's best to err on the side of caution, especially when someone has no one in the world that cares about 'em. Ann girl's lucky to have you folks."

"We'll get back home. Maybe she'll show up there. Stop by anytime." Harry restarted the engine.

"I'd like that. Oh, almost forgot something." Fin pulled an envelope from his shirt pocket. "Hurley Cutshaw dropped this off at the office … just after you left … and asked if I'd deliver it to you. He said he'd deliver it to you personally, but seein' as you two have your differences, he thought it best to have me drop it off. I assumed he thinks you owe some back grocery money."

"Nope. Paid him in full. Got a signed receipt to prove it," Harry said.

"Hang on to that receipt." Flin chuckled.

Harry opened the envelope and slowly unfolded the paper. His body stiffened as he read the scribbled note.

> Weatherholtz,
> I know a secret you need to hear. Your daddy ain't dead. We need to talk soon.
> H. C. Cutshaw

"You okay, Harry?" Flin scratched at the stubble on his jowl.

"Sure. Just the typical Hurley Cutshaw. Always stirring the pot."

"Anything I need to know about?"

"Don't concern yourself with him, Sheriff. You know how he works."

"Wasn't necessarily concerned about Hurley. It's you that concerns me, Harry."

"I've got to go, Sheriff," Harry said.

"You be careful," Flin called after him as Harry pulled away.

Chapter Eight

"What's going on, Bud?"

Harry tossed the note to Evelyn. She scanned its contents but did not comment.

Evelyn seemed to know when a situation played out best in silence. Still, Harry was somewhat surprised she didn't ask what it meant, debunked its content or asked where they were headed. Then again, she knew him well.

He pulled slowly into the parking lot of Cutshaw's store and braked. Two cats scampered underneath the front steps of the store. Cutshaw's truck, its fender wells caked with red mud, sat alongside the building.

"Not sure I should do this." Harry gripped the steering wheel with both hands.

"You don't have to." Evelyn placed a consoling hand on his shoulder.

"I will sooner or later."

"Well then, I don't remember who said it, but if you have to swallow a frog, don't look at it too long. Just keep a cool head, Bud."

"I will. This should only take a couple minutes."

"Be careful, Bud." Evelyn's voice was more a plea than a command.

"I will." He paused as she rolled her window down and wiped the side-mirror with a Dogs n Suds napkin. "Probably best you stay in the car."

Harry hadn't frequented Cutshaw's store all winter, and he assumed that was the way Cutshaw wanted things. At least it was the way he wanted things. The less he saw of Cutshaw, the better. He'd taken his business to the new store George and Louise Zirkle had opened the first of the year.

Little had changed with Cutshaw's building. The same loose handrail and rickety steps signaled for caution. The steps still sagged in the middle. The torn screen on the door remained in need of repair, but someone had painted the front of the building as far up as they could reach. It was either a short adult or a child. That thought—a child—concerned Harry. The damage to the window frame by the pellets from a shotgun remained, but the broken glass had been replaced. The new windowpanes contrasted with the old, which had not been washed, and the fresh glaze remained unpainted.

Harry stepped inside the store and paused, adjusting to the dim lighting. Cutshaw jumped up, knocking a rickety cane chair backward. He defiantly hooked his thumbs around his suspenders and smirked. "Didn't think you would come."

A cat scampered from the counter. Cutshaw kicked at it, then adjusted a grungy white apron underneath his potbelly.

"I'll state my business and be gone." Harry pulled the note from his pocket. "You write this?"

"Sure did."

"What does it mean?"

"Just what it says. Your daddy never died in jail. Got released and lives in the mountains." He nodded toward the Blue Ridge.

"And how did you come by this information, since no one else knows?"

"Cause I have connections."

"With who?"

"Not telling."

"Then why should I believe you?"

"'Cause I'm telling the truth. No need to lie, 'specially 'bout somethin' so far-fetched. Course I've known fer years, jist never bothered to tell you."

"Why, after all these years, would you tell me now?"

"Cause I never needed to tell you afore."

"Why do you need to tell me now?"

"'Cause I think you'd want to know. …"

"And?"

"Cause I want you off my back, Harry Weatherholtz."

"What do you mean? I'm not on your back. All I did was stop injustice among children, though Miss Ann pretty much got free of you on her own."

"Judge said it right. You stopped social progress. Now, I want you to back off, and I'll tell you where your daddy is, laying on his death bed right now, wantin' to see you and—"

"If my father is alive, which I don't think he is, why do you think I'd care to know, much less see him?"

"You care alright. Human instinct. It eats at you night and day. And you need to see your daddy, 'cause he ain't got long to live, and he's beggin' to see you. Bein' a Christian man and all, it'd be a sin not to go to his side when he's breathing his last breath. Broke my heart just hearin' him asking about you, beggin' me to fetch you. It's the Christian thing to do."

"And what do you get for giving me this information?"

"You stop harassin' me and my business. That's all."

"I've never harassed—"

"You turn your head and let me have my foster child, and I'll tell you where your daddy is. I'd never mistreat a child, but I'll teach 'em how to work and be respectable and know his place in society. I won't lay a hand on him 'less he sasses me and needs it. What's so hard about that?"

"And if I don't turn my head and let you go on mistreating children, then what?"

"I'll tell your daddy his highfalutin son refused to come to his dying bedside. And then I'll tell the law where your daddy's been hidin' all these years, and they'll go up the mountain and bring him down in cuffs. And the newsmen will be there, and word will spread like wildfire in dry pine needles. Everything you've tried to forget all these years will be plastered as headlines all up and down the valley. And it'll all be raw again in your head, and you'll be to blame."

Harry tossed the note onto the counter. "I don't believe a word you're saying, and if I did, it wouldn't change my response. You've got me figured all wrong, Hurley Cutshaw. Nothing will allow me to conscientiously turn my head while you mistreat another child."

"Then maybe you should think again. I didn't come to the card table without a full hand."

"What do you mean?"

"Nothin' particular. How's my no good for nothin' Ann girl doin'?"

Adrenaline exploded throughout Harry's body. He pounded clinched fists against the counter. Cutshaw leaped backward, knocking over a chair. Harry swiped a metal ashtray from the counter and it clanked against the wall.

His entire body shook uncontrollably. He clasped his hands behind his head and stared at the ceiling. Revenge surged, clouding reason. He could end this here and now. He could stop this evil game once and for all. He closed his eyes and tried to reason. Scriptures wrestled within his head. *Blessed be the Lord my strength which teacheth my hands to war, and my fingers to fight ... smite Amalek, and utterly destroy all that they have, and spare them not ... vengeance is mine, I will repay saith the Lord ... love your enemies, bless them that curse you, do good to them that hate you, and pray for them which despitefully use you, and persecute you ... he maketh his sun to rise on the evil and on the good, and sendeth rain on the just and on the unjust.*

All his adult life Harry had consistently read the Holy Script, impressed by its instruction, encouraged by its wise counsel. He now tried to balance the myriad of Scriptures that bounced around in his head. He weighed the judgment of the God of the Old Testament against the grace of God offered in the New Testament. However, the thundering of Mt. Sinai drowned out the Sermon on the Mount. But there was another voice. Whose was it? At first, distant, then it came nearer, calling him.

"Bud."

His mother? No, she never called him by that name. Whose?

"Bud!"

Harry hesitated, his body quivering as if chilled to the bone. In the Great War, he had waded through chilly water waste deep until his body shook with hypothermia. He survived on pure adrenaline. He survived an entire war, with friends falling around him. This singular conniving man would not defeat him now. Still, he instinctively grabbed the neck of a bottle from the counter.

"Bud, no."

He hesitated.

"Please, Bud. Listen to me. He's not worth it. Let's get out of here."

"Help me, God...please, God, help me..." He struggled to gain composure. Evelyn's hand on his shoulder and her pleas slowly filtered his scrambled thoughts.

Cutshaw stood smugly behind the counter. Harry placed the bottle on the counter and with one quick motion reached across the counter and grabbed Cutshaw by the elbows, yanking him forward. "You're a conniving, lying scalawag, and I will not be manipulated by your deception." His words came slowly, deliberately, almost monotone. He hesitated and then released his grip. His fists thumped onto the counter.

"Bud."

He turned toward Evelyn.

She clasped both his arms and pulled him close. "Don't do something you'll regret the rest of your life. He's not worth it. Let's get Sheriff Flin and let him deal with this."

Cutshaw breathed heavily, in short, wheezy gasps. He reached under the counter.

The movement startled Harry. He grabbed Cutshaw's arm and twisted hard. "Don't do something stupid, Cutshaw."

"Not doing nothin' stupid. Let go of my arm, Weatherholtz. Got something to give you."

Harry hesitantly released his grip.

Cutshaw pulled a small, rusty tin from underneath the counter, pried open the lid and retrieved an envelope.

"If you don't believe me, then read for yourself." He held the envelope so Harry could read the fading cursive writing addressing the recipients of its contents.

To my sons Lawrence and Harry
To be opened after my death

The edges of the envelope hinted that it had been opened and resealed. Harry vacillated from wanting to slap the insidious grin from Cutshaw's face to wanting to snatch the envelope from his hand. Cutshaw taunted him with the envelope, flicking it as if it was a switchblade, probably wishing that it was, and more so, desiring to slice Harry's throat.

Harry exhaled slowly. Is it humanly possible to be this wicked, or must one be possessed? He hesitantly reached for the envelope with an open palm, expecting Cutshaw to withdraw it. Cutshaw placed the envelope into Harry's open hand and lifted his hands in a gesture of peace. Or did the smirk betray victory? He was not to be trusted, and he should never be underestimated.

Harry slipped the envelope into his hip pocket and walked toward the door where he paused until he heard Evelyn's footsteps on the hardwood floor as she followed. He pushed the screen door open, stepped into the afternoon sunshine, inhaled deeply and slowly exhaled.

Evelyn patted his shoulder gently and quickly descended the steps ahead of him. "Let's call for backup, Sheriff Weatherholtz."

It had been a long time since she had called him that.

Chapter Nine

Gravel scattered as a black, Ford Coupe slid sideways into the space facing Harry's Hudson. The exterior sun visor, mounted low over the windshield, partially concealed the faces of two occupants. Harry surmised who they were, for he knew only one such car in the county whose drivers were so reckless. His body involuntarily stiffened for the impending altercation as the occupants exited.

Evelyn grabbed Harry's forearm and held tight. "Be careful, Bud."

He hadn't spoken to Bill or Bradley since visiting with them last year at the old homestead on Holman Creek. They'd halfway accepted his apology for his behavior—a mixture of condescension and disdain and vengeance—toward their shenanigans. He hoped they'd changed their ways, but evidently, they hadn't.

"Howdy, Mr. Weatherholtz, Mrs. Weatherholtz." Bradley partially removed and replaced his '57 Milwaukee Braves World Series cap. "Been lookin' for you."

Bill walked around the back of the car and opened the trunk.

"Evelyn thought you fellas drove by our house today. What can I do for you?" As Evelyn withdrew her grasp from his arm, he opened the door, forcing Bradley to step backward, and he quickly exited the Hudson.

"That was us but saw your Hudson was missin', so we drove on by. We got something for you. Show 'em, Bill." Bradley motioned to Bill, who retrieved a corrugated box from the trunk.

"Sorry I missed you." Harry studied the box, but the closed flaps concealed the contents. He detected movement, a slight rattle and a strong odor. A rattlesnake could easily be concealed in the box. Surely they wouldn't.

"We've been needin' to talk to you." Bradley nodded towards Bill. "Both of us owes you an apology."

"For what?" Harry studied Bradley's eyes, seemingly as kind as a kitten. He detected no mischief, but psychopaths conceal emotion.

Bradley dropped his gaze and rearranged some loose gravel with the toe of his boot. "About what we done."

"Just what did you fellas do?"

"You know ... all the stuff we done ... to that Annie girl ... and your dog. We ain't proud of none of it." Bradley's voice depicted sincerity.

Harry pondered the seemingly sincere expression on Bradley's face and considered many a criminal sobered up right after his crime. Shame does that. Had they done something else and just wanted to soften the consequences? "You fellas have done a number of things that have displeased me, but I'm most interested in what you've done today."

"Like what?" Bradley asked, seemingly surprised.

"Have you seen Miss Ann today?"

"No, sir." They both answered almost in unison.

"You sure?"

"We're sure," Bradley said. "Has something happened to her?"

Was that a sincere question or mockery? Harry had read them wrong before. He didn't want to be too specific, but he needed to know what they knew about her disappearance, if anything. "She left our place shortly before Evelyn saw you pass by our house. Did you happen to see her?"

"We passed by your house, but we didn't see no girl," Bradley said.

"Then why are you here, now, a couple hours after Miss Ann has gone missing again? That's quite a coincidence since I haven't seen you around for months. Has Hurley Cutshaw hired you to aggravate that girl again?"

"No, sir." Bradley's voice and animated expression seemed more honest than defensive. "Swear on my momma's grave."

Something in the box moved, and Bill slightly shook the box. It rattled. Was that a smirk or a smile? Why? Harry stepped closer, crowding them. "You're sure you didn't see her?"

Bradley hesitated and looked toward Cutshaw's store, but then like a geyser he erupted, pleadingly. "Cutshaw tried to hire us some, but we said no, cause we done learned our lesson before. You gotta believe us, Mr. Weatherholtz. We done nothing wrong this time. We don't know what Cutshaw may've done but not us. We ain't—"

"Really?" Anger surged through Harry's body. He breathed deeply and slowly exhaled. "He tried to hire you for what?"

Bradley studied his the knuckles on his right hand, rubbing his fingers across scabs. "To mess with that girl—"

"You're talking about Ann?" Harry asked.

"Yes."

"What do you mean by mess?" Harry asked.

"Scare her, stuff like that, but we didn't do it." Bradley tossed Bill a commanding glance. "Ain't that the truth, Bill?"

"It is, sir. God's our witness."

"If you turned Cutshaw down, then why were you at my place just after she turns up missing?"

"We ain't got nothin' to do with her missin', and I sware it." Bradly lifted his right hand. "We knew for a fact something was going down, and we decided not to get involved, but we figured you'd think it was us. We wanted to prove we didn't have nothin' to do with whatever it is." He stuffed his hands into his pocket. "You've got to believe us, or you can ask Sheriff Flin. We already talked to him a little while ago, and he gave us a number one shakedown. We ain't done nothin' wrong, and we'd already planned before this happened to give you somethin' to say we got nothin' against you. Show 'em, Bill."

Bill opened the flaps to the box and stepped toward Harry.

Harry instinctively braced himself to face Bill and whatever was in the box.

Bill reached into the box and retrieved a small tan and black puppy. The puppy twisted to get free and nipped at Bill's hand as he handed it to Harry.

"Well, I'll be." Harry could not believe these boys could be so thoughtful, after being so cruel. The look on their face showed no malice, only pleasure for their good deed. He cradled the pup in the crook of his arm and scratched its head. The puppy moved its head as if to direct the massage.

Evelyn exited the car, retrieved the puppy and cuddled it to her cheek.

"We think it's from a litter your Shep sired. We'd given him to you sooner but had to wean 'em first. That's why we come out to your place, to give 'em to you, but we saw your car wasn't there, so we drove on by. And that's a fact, Mr. Weatherholtz," Bradley said.

Harry shook his head. "Well, boys, I … I … I don't know what to say."

"A thank you would be appropriate." Evelyn smiled. She rubbed the pup's perked ears. "Looks just like Shep when he was this size. Don't you think so, Bud?" She handed the pup back to Harry.

Harry smiled and nodded. "I appreciate this, fellas. You and me had our difficulties … I thank you for the dog … and sorry I accused you so hastily, but with Miss Ann missing and all … you understand."

"You had your rights. We ain't been no saints." Bradley extended a hand. "We'd gladly help you look for her."

Harry reached for Bradley's hand and the pup leaped from his arms. He caught him in mid-air. The envelope fell from his pocket. Bradley snatched it from the ground and handed it back to Harry.

"I heard your Daddy died a long time ago, in prison." Bradley had seen the writing. He cocked his head sideways, his curiosity piqued. "I didn't mean to snoop … just happened to notice."

"Yes, he died in prison when I was just a child." Harry stuffed the letter into his pocket. "Can we have the cardboard box?"

"Sure. And the baby rattle, too. The pup really likes it." Bill handed the box to Harry.

"For a moment there, I thought you fellas were giving me a rattlesnake." Harry chuckled. He placed the puppy in the box and started toward the car but stopped and turned toward the Buffords. "It's like ole Shep's raised from the dead. You've made my day."

"Thank you, Mr. Weatherholtz, and our offer's still good," Bradley said. "We'll help you locate the girl."

Bradley's eyes seemed to reveal sincerity. Harry had seen it before in interrogations. "Any idea where she might be?"

Harry's question seemed to catch them off-guard. Bradley studied the ground but didn't answer. The sincerity quickly turned to suspiciousness.

"She might be in danger, Bradley. Anything you know may help us find her."

Harry glanced at Bill, who looked away. "Do you know something you should tell me, Bill?"

Bill remained silent.

"It'll be between you and me. I won't tell anyone you told me. You have my word." Harry tried not to push, but desperation drove him.

"Go ahead and tell 'em, Bradley," Bill blurted out.

"We did see a colored girl in Jack Brady's car. Didn't get a good look at her, but she was black for sure. Wondered at the time, but who are we to question the county prosecutor. He's the one who asks the questions. Nobody'd believe us accusin' him."

"When? Where?" Harry asked.

Bradley kicked at the gravel. "Aw, shucks. Jack Brady will destroy us for sure if he hears we told."

"He'll do nothing of the sort." Harry placed an assuring hand on Bradley's shoulder. "Surely there's a good explanation."

"When we drove by your place, right down the road from your house, we passed him."

"Any idea where they were headed?" Harry asked.

"Not a clue." Bradley glanced toward the porch. "We'd best get out of here, Bill. We're as good as dead if Brady gets word of us snitchin' on 'em."

Harry turned toward Bradley's gaze. Cutshaw stood on the porch, rubbing his chin with the back of his hand. How long he had been there, and how much he had heard, was difficult to know. The look on his face offered Harry concern.

Chapter Ten

Jack Brady eased his Studebaker onto the driveway of the colonial mansion that clung to the side of Great North Mountain. He paused to observe the expansive valley. An afternoon shower left a lingering mist, a common sight to the valley dwellers, but inspiring awe from this elevation. A half-dozen ravens soared within eyeshot, waltzing upon the spring air.

He exited the car, retrieved his briefcase from the back seat and walked to the passenger side. She sat pensively, staring at the massive house. He opened the door, and she exited the car but stood transfixed, staring at the house.

"Ever see anything like this, Miss Ann?"

She shook her head no. He nudged her toward the house with the corner of his briefcase, and she walked slowly toward the front door.

He fumbled with a key ring, trying a couple keys before he found a fit. "It's almost frightening, isn't it?" He chuckled, nodding at the grotesque gargoyle that served as a door clapper.

She shook her head in agreement.

Brady stepped into the house and tried a couple switches before he flicked the right one, and a dozen lights of an ornate chandelier blinked on in the center of the massive entryway. She slowly followed him into the house, holding her purse tightly underneath her arm. White sheets covered chairs that lined the wall in the long foyer. He hung his hat on the coat rack and reached for her purse. She reluctantly handed it to him, and he hung it by the strap onto the rack. She slowly untied her scarf and placed it with her purse. The house seemed chilly, so he didn't ask if she wanted to remove her threadbare sweater.

Their footsteps echoed off the polished oak floor as Brady led her across the foyer and into the massive, mahogany-paneled library.

"Sit there." He pointed toward a high-back, leather sofa that sat in front of an enormous desk.

He walked to the desk and clicked on a lamp. The desk was just as he remembered it. A bronze eagle, its wings spread in flight and clutching a salmon with its talons, adorned the burl-inlaid top. The last time he stood in this room he felt more kinship to the fish than the eagle. He smiled, removed his tweed sports coat and tossed it onto the oversized swivel chair. Things were different now than they were last year. He no longer cowered before Jenkins, concerned for his future. He was now in charge. The master.

She stared at him, clasping one hand with the other and holding them close to her stomach. He sat on the corner of the desk, his legs crossed at the ankles.

"You ever seen a library this big before, except the public library?"

"No." She spoke in a whisper.

"Of course New Market's library doesn't compare to this. Woodstock's library might equal it in volume but not content."

"I never been inside no library afore this."

"Really? Not even the public library at New Market?"

"Never had a need to go to the library."

Brady didn't respond. He reached inside his briefcase, retrieved a piece of paper and handed it to her. "Take a look, Miss Ann."

She stared at the paper. The dimly lit room accentuated the whites of her eyes. His ambivalence toward the colored community made him aloof. He didn't share Weatherholtz's affection toward Miss Ann, but he did not necessarily dislike her. That made this task easier.

"I'll be back in a couple minutes. Go ahead and read it … then sign it."

"Why sign it?"

He masked his impatience. "So there'll be no questions later."

Chapter Eleven

Were the Buffords lying? Harry wanted to believe their story, though they were the likely culprits. Were they leading him away from their crime? He glanced at the box in the back seat of the Hudson. Was the puppy merely a diversion? He certainly didn't want to believe Jack Brady was involved with something as insidious as harming Miss Ann, but if the Buffords were telling the truth, she may well have been the person in Jack's car. Still, if it was Ann in Brady's car, that didn't mean she was in any danger. Perhaps he gave her a ride. But why didn't he drop her off at the Carnahans' place? Where is she now? Was his paranoia unwarranted?

"Bud, are we going to sit here all day?" Her words were beyond teasing.

"Sorry, dear." He was obsessing again. A weakness and a strength. He lost a lot of sleep in his lifetime obsessed with details. He just couldn't turn off his brain. He could lay awake for hours looking for a clue under every proverbial rock. But that was how he solved many a crime … viewing all the angles of every possible scenario.

He disengaged the clutch and turned the ignition but again hesitated, his head cocked sideways. "Do you hear that?" He glanced at Evelyn.

"Hear what?"

"She's missing. I'll need to drop her off at Sewell's and get the plugs checked.

"For heaven's sake, Bud, could we get going?"

He did not respond. Evelyn's patience was exhausted. The Bennett in her had boiled to the service. Harry tried to conceal a smile. He appreciated her spunk. It was good she didn't see Cutshaw peeking through the screen door, for she may have had a few choice words for him.

Could this whole ordeal be of Cutshaw's doing? Perhaps a get even ploy against Jack Brady? Cutshaw certainly hated Brady, but was he scheming enough to create such an elaborate plan of retaliation? Then again, Judge Jenkins could well be the kingpin of another dastardly plan.

As Harry pulled away, Evelyn waved goodbye at the Buffords, but on second glance she grabbed Harry's arm, realizing their car wouldn't start. "They might need help, Bud."

Harry braked. He certainly didn't want to leave them stranded on Cutshaw's doorstep, especially after the look on Cutshaw's face. Had he overheard the conversation? Still, Harry questioned why the Buffords showed up just when Ann turned up missing. That was quite a coincidence, and they'd proven the past year to live on the edge of disaster. Evelyn hadn't the time of day for them before, and she was a decent judge of character, but now she had warmed up to them. A puppy changes everything. He'd give them the benefit of doubt, but the jury was still out as to which side of the law they would end up.

Years dealing with the criminal mentality could skew one's thinking against trusting in the good of mankind. Was he being fair to these boys, or should he proceed with caution? As hard as he tried to exhibit trust, he wondered if their story was just a concoction to save their hides. If the Buffords weren't lying, who was the black girl in Jack's car? Ann? And if it was Ann, had Jack simply given her a ride? That seemed a logical explanation, but that didn't explain her whereabouts now. On a more positive note, if Jack Brady had given her a ride, he may well be the last person to see her since her disappearance, and maybe he had an idea where she might be. No matter the scenario, he had to find Jack.

Bill opened the hood to the car and halfway climbed onto the engine, jiggling wires. Bradley continued to crank the starter, which had diminished to a slow growl that was about to go silent.

"You going to give them a hand?" Evelyn asked.

"Let's give it a second."

The scene before him took a backseat position to the thoughts pinballing inside his head. What about the report by Flin regarding two unsolved recent beatings of colored girls? Could Ann be a third victim? Cutshaw now stood on the front porch of his store, leaning against a post. His glare unnerved Harry. Was that a grin on his insidious face? It was highly likely he was behind Ann's disappearance. If the Buffords weren't lying, and Cutshaw tried to hire them to kidnap her, when they refused he had hired someone else. That seemed a likely scenario, but what about Brady. Had the Buffords just made up that story to throw him off the trail? If not, surely Jack just gave her a lift. When he dropped her off, whoever is doing the beatings, may have nabbed her. God knows what they've done by now. He had to find Sheriff Flin and Jack Brady. Jack may be key, for he would know where he dropped Ann off. Flin had to act fast, form a search party and find the girl. Ann was savvy, but she would be no match for hooligans with a hatred for Negroes, or Negroes who had no moral regard for their own female gender.

Could the Klan be involved, especially with the recent beatings? They'd been active in Virginia shortly after the First Great War, fighting against anti-Americanism. You would think that after seeing the brutalities of the war they would have had an aversion to violence. At least that's the effect it had on him. To the contrary, the mid-century saw a resurrection of Klan violence in the Commonwealth. Afterward, Governor Battle pushed through a bill against wearing hoods and cross burnings. That had mostly stomped out their open activity. Now the looming fight for desegregation, and the battle against a lingering Jim Crow mentality, brought a sense of unrest to many, for and against. Some Negroes were calling for equality for all citizens. Had that brought about more retaliation?

The sluggish cranking of the Buffords' starter indicated the battery was dying. Harry killed the Hudson's engine and slowly exited the vehicle, just as their engine roared into action. Bill slammed the hood shut and jumped into the car. He gave out a Rebel yell as Bradley popped the clutch, causing the Ford to launch forward, spraying gravel that dinged off the side of the Hudson.

"Immature boys," Evelyn said, shaking her head. "Will they ever grow up?"

Cutshaw retreated into his store, but Harry glimpsed him peeking out the window. What was he up to? The envelope bulged in Harry's shirt pocket. He snatched it and stared at the inscription. Anyone with knowledge of his past could have addressed the envelope. He didn't care to read its contents. It was probably another of Cutshaw's ploys, always manipulating. He should simply tear it up and stop any further mental aggravation. He grasped the middle of the envelope with both hands.

"No, Bud!" Evelyn grabbed his hands.

"Why not? It's another lie."

"You don't know that for sure."

"True, but I know Cutshaw wouldn't do anything good for us."

"Surely he didn't connive this story; it's too far-fetched for a trick. I think you're giving him too much credit for brainpower. At least read it and make an intelligent decision. You can tear it up later."

"Even if it is from him, I'm not sure I want to read it."

"Why not. Perhaps it could bring some closure."

"It ended long ago."

"Then why are you still having nightmares?"

Harry didn't respond.

"I'm sorry, Bud. Here, your hands are trembling. Let me open it."

Harry released the envelope. Evelyn retrieved a hairpin and sliced open the end. She withdrew the faded paper and slowly unfolded and scanned its contents.

A quarter of a mile ahead Bradley had pulled the Coupe to the side of the road.

"I wonder what they're up to now?" Harry shook his head in uncertainty.

"Is that a siren?" Evelyn lowered the paper.

Harry rolled down the window. "I believe so."

The flashing lights unmistakably identified a sheriff's vehicle. The Buffords sped away when the cruiser passed them. As the car approached Cutshaw's store, the driver braked, and the car skidded onto the store lot, the siren still blaring.

"I'm not sure who's the most childish," Evelyn said, varying her volume to match the waning sound of the siren, "Sheriff Flin or the Buffords."

Flin threw open the door and slowly rocked his frame from the cruiser, readjusted his belt under his belly and donned his hat. He leaned back into the car and retrieved a paper bag from the passenger side.

Cutshaw reappeared on the front porch, his hands tucked into his pants' pockets, taking in the scene.

"Stay in the car, Evelyn," Harry said as he exited.

"Finally found you." Flin breathed heavily as he extended a handshake.

"What's happened?"

"Been looking all over for you, Harry."

"Any news on Miss Ann?"

"Not sure. That's why I needed to see you. Another beating … worse than before—"

"Who?" Harry did not try to contain his emotion.

"A young, female Negro—"

"Oh no, not Annie?" Evelyn crowded beside Harry, taking his arm.

"Can hardly recognize the poor thing. Do you know what shoes Ann wore when she left your place?"

"Yes, her white tennis shoes." Evelyn clasped her hands as if in prayer.

"You sure?"

"Yes," Evelyn answered in a whisper.

Flin pulled a white slipper from the paper bag. "Nothing like this?" Blood covered the shoe.

"No, that's not Ann's shoe," Evelyn said with a sigh.

"Well, you can thank the good Lord up above, cause that's good news for you folks. Sad for someone else." Flin put the shoe back in the bag and wiped his hands with his handkerchief.

"Poor soul, I can't imagine. ..." Evelyn's words trailed as she rubbed the tip of her nose with the back of her hand.

"Yea, she was terribly beat up. About the worse I've ever seen." Flin scratched the nape of his neck and studied the paper sack. "You folk's okay?"

"Have you seen Jack Brady?" Harry asked.

"No. I thought you said he was out to your place."

"He was, but we have eyewitnesses that saw him with a colored girl in his car after he left our place. We suspect it was Miss Ann, and if we can find Jack, I think he can help us locate her."

"What in the world would Jack be doing with Ann in his car?"

"Perhaps giving her a ride, somewhere," Evelyn said.

"Or. ..." Flin stared into the distance.

"Or what?" Harry asked.

"Maybe he hired her."

"To do what?" Harry asked.

"You haven't heard?"

"No." Harry's impatience showed.

"He bought the old Jenkins place. I'd best drive over there and have a talk with Jack."

Chapter Twelve

Ann studied the paper, her hands trembling, before slowly lowering it to her lap, revealing tears that streamed her cheeks.

"What's the matter?" Brady asked. "You don't have to take the job if you don't want it."

She shook her head. "It ain't that. I can't read a lick, Mistuh Brady."

He sighed. "I'm sorry, Miss Ann, I truly am. I completely forgot. Here, let me read it to you." He retrieved a handkerchief from his pocket and exchanged it for the paper. "I haven't used it."

She smiled. "Thank you."

"Okay, here we go. I'll read, and you listen. Work list. Item number one: scrub and wax foyer floor. Item number two: remove, wash and replace all dishes in the kitchen cupboards. Item number three: dust all books in the library."

She gawked at the bookshelves that lined the walls from the floor to the high ceiling.

"That'll keep you busy for a day or two." He laughed.

"And make me a lot of money." She smiled.

"What are you going to do with all your money?"

"I have a plan."

"Like what?"

"You remember that little fella Hurley Cutshaw took in after I left?"

"Yes."

"I reckon he needs a place to stay since Cutshaw got his due and can't take in no more orphans. I'd like to take care of him … maybe start a home for black kids that don't have no momma and papa."

"That's a mighty big dream, Miss Ann, but it's a good dream."

Ann stared at the bookshelves, doing a semi-circle of the room. "Thank you for all the work, Mistuh Brady. I really appreciate it."

"I guess I didn't consider the upkeep when I made the deal to buy this place."

"You bought this big house just for yourself?"

"I have dreams, too, Miss Ann."

"And who you say owned this house?"

"Jenkins. Judge Jeremiah Jenkins."

"Never heard of him. He must be a mighty special person."

He did not answer.

"I guess now you be a mighty special person."

He feigned a smile. If she could look into his heart, she wouldn't think so highly of him. He glanced at the wall clock. "I'd best get you back down the mountain before someone starts wondering where you've disappeared to."

Chapter Thirteen

Harry's silence reflected his troubled soul. He tried to do better, to communicate more with Evelyn, but old habits were hard to change. Answers to her occasional pump-priming questions were coming up dry, and he knew it troubled her, but she gave him space. He wasn't sure how long the charades would go on before an outright confrontation, which she could do when she'd had enough.

Evelyn broke the silence. "That was kind of Jack to offer Ann a job." A steam rose from the Louisiana chicory as Evelyn refilled the transparent cup Harry cradled in his hands.

"Yes, it was." He poured Pet milk, from a yellow Depression glass creamer, into the cup and stirred it to a creamy brown before pouring coffee from the cup into a matching saucer. He held the saucer to his lips and blew gently between sips. He cherished the small cup and saucer, which were his sole possessions from his mother. He sipped the last of the coffee from the saucer and placed the cup back into its center, carefully, as if it might break. "I shouldn't have second-guessed Jack," he said with a sigh.

Evelyn scooped fried potatoes, scrambled eggs and a biscuit onto a plate. She slowly smothered them with brown gravy. "You were just concerned about Annie." She set the plate in front of him and repeated the same for herself. They ate slowly but in silence. Harry downed the last of his coffee and Evelyn refilled his cup and served him another biscuit.

"Jack's a hard one to read. Seems to keep you at a distance. Don't you think?" Evelyn asked as she wiped her fingers on a dishcloth.

"Probably so." Harry buttered the biscuit slowly. "Age difference, I suppose, and he's mighty educated. From good stock. But you're right in your evaluation. He's a bit cool toward me at times."

"We all have our quirks, I suppose. Take for example the way you butter your biscuit. You always tear it apart and butter both sides. Some folks, me included, only butter one side, generally the top."

Harry smiled at her as he smothered both halves of the biscuit with molasses from a pint mason jar. "The more butter the better it tastes."

"And of course you do the same with the molasses ... both slices ... then you stick them back together." She wiped the edge of the molasses' container with a dishrag and slid it beside the envelope that had been laying on the table for two days. They hadn't discussed its contents since the day Cutshaw gave it to Harry.

Harry bit into the biscuit. Molasses squirted from all sides and ran onto his fingers. He licked his fingers, then took a sip from his third cup of coffee. His fingers stuck to the cup.

"I don't think it's safe for Ann working at the nursing home, especially with Jenkins and Cutshaw still conniving," she said as she tossed the dishcloth to him.

"She's got to face her fears." He wiped his fingers with the cloth.

She slowly slid the envelope across the table to him. "Like you're facing yours?"

He stared at it but took another bite of the biscuit and chewed slowly, wishing the subject would change, before taking another sip of coffee. His hand trembled slightly, but he said nothing. He was accustomed to her speaking her mind, and he generally respected her opinion, but this time it bothered him.

She cringed as he sat the cup hard onto the saucer. "I'm sorry, Bud, I shouldn't have said that."

Little Shep whimpered from the box in the corner.

"Hey little guy, you need out?" Evelyn started to get up.

"I'll take him." Harry gulped the last of his coffee and slipped the envelope into his hip pocket as he left the table. He snatched his hat from a wall hook and tipped the cardboard box with the toe of his boot. The pup scampered out of the box and toward the door.

The early morning air contrasted from the heat of the kitchen stove. He rubbed his hands together vigorously, entwined his fingers and stretched them until the knuckles cracked. Logging made him a decent living, but the arduous labor left his hands stiff in the mornings. He was glad spring had chased away ole man winter. He descended the steps ahead of little Shep. The puppy tumbled from step to step until he reached the bottom and then dashed across the yard, chasing a leaf that skipped in the spring breeze.

The morning sun topped the timberline of the Blue Ridge, casting a blood-red sheen across the horizon. Harry adjusted his hat. "Definitely a spring shower in the making little fella." Shep's ears perked.

He pulled the envelope from his pocket and studied the cover. The faded letters were written with steady hands, not the scribbling of the aged. Did his father write it? Probably not. More than likely Cutshaw wrote on the envelope and authored its contents. It is part of some elaborate hoax he's in on. He found it hard to believe the letter was from his father, for he was certain his father had died his first year in prison. And anything the letter might say, Cutshaw could have written in an attempt to purposefully deceive?

Shep carried the leaf in his mouth. Harry stooped and extended an open palm. The pup trotted toward him but a few feet away dropped the leaf and darted after another. His old friend couldn't have sired this little fellow? He had the color and mannerisms, but the time of birth was too questionable. Gestation for dogs is about nine weeks. Allowing another nine weeks for weaning from his mother's milk, and throw in another couple weeks of uncertainty, the little fellow had to be sired in early winter. Shep was killed during the previous summer, months before this little fellow came into being, but it certainly could be from another dog Shep had sired. It was a nice gesture the Bufford brothers had made, but it was not possible that this was Shep's pup. He wouldn't bother to tell them differently.

The sun momentarily pierced the overcast and sent multiple beams earthward. If an artist could capture the radiance and beauty, critics would challenge it as being unrealistic.

He studied the handwriting on the envelope. Faint lines underscored the letters. A meticulous person, or someone with a lot of time on his hands, had addressed the envelope. His mind raced. Could his father have written it? He needed to find something with which to compare the handwriting. Perhaps the court had some legal document his father had signed. But that would have been over fifty years ago. Slowly he withdrew the contents from the envelope, unfolded the yellowed paper and read the first line of the fading ink, perfectly written between faint blue lines. *Dear sons, if you are reading this letter then I am dead, but I wanted to let you know somewhat about me.* Harry refused to believe its authenticity.

He stared at the distant horizon, the red glow slowly fading as the sun rose higher behind the clouds. How quickly nature changes but seldom without some warning: a temperature change, change of atmospheric pressure, wind shifts. But mankind defies the norm. He strikes suddenly. Cain. The Japs at Pearl Harbor. This letter had no warning; it came out of the blue. A plethora of emotions surged. And questions. How could this be? And why, after all these years? He wiped the corners of his eyes with the tips of his fingers.

That life had ended long ago, and he would not allow its resurrection. He had to get a grip on his emotions. Cutshaw was simply plotting another devious scheme. He would not be sucked into the scheme.

The full eastern sky dulled a milky gray.

He read the rest of the letter and quickly inserted it into the envelope. Some things about the message made sense. The timeline of events seemed accurate. He'd heard rumors about his father escaping prison, about sightings, but he assumed them to be just that: rumors. People loved to speculate. And gossip. The letter from the warden stating his father's death seemed the logical thing to believe. At least that's the story he had chosen to believe. As for the accuracy of this letter, Cutshaw could have anticipated all the details and forged the letter accordingly.

The wind picked up, and a few large raindrops splattered onto the steps. The pup scampered to him, bored of chasing leaves and wanting human attention. Harry sat on the lower step and stroked its fur.

"Ready for some warm milk?" He lifted it onto his shoulder. Shep wobbled to maintain balance as Harry stood. "Let's take a walk to the barn and see if the cow's in a generous mood this morning."

Harry folded the envelope and stuffed it in his hip pocket. Could life change so quickly, without warning? In a stretch of imagination perhaps it could, and if so, he knew what he had to do. But it would be on his terms, not Cutshaw's.

Chapter Fourteen

She welcomed the first rays of sun that spotlighted dust particles waltzing on air. She had slept fitfully in a chair beside his cot. A night of coughing bouts left him exhausted, and the coughing continued to interrupt catnaps. The raspy breathing indicated a flare-up of his emphysema, or worse, pneumonia.

He strained to see his image in the smudged mirror hanging on the wall by his cot. It took much effort to run a pocket comb through his tousled white hair. She offered help, but he refused. His taut, red face contrasted the pallid and wrinkled skin that hung loosely on his arms.

He laid the comb aside and spat feebly into a sardine can that balanced on the edge of a crowded nightstand. Spittle clung to his overgrown whiskers, and he wiped at it with a soiled handkerchief, again brushing aside her assistance.

She rearranged the dingy feather pillows that propped him against the rough wooden headboard. The action sent him into another coughing spasm.

She wiped his brow with a damp cloth when the coughing subsided. "Can I do anything?"

"No, thank ya, Vera," he whispered.

She was ten years younger, and she had aged well, despite their harsh lifestyle. Her blond hair camouflaged the gray strands mingled into a single braid and coiled into a bun adorning the back of her head.

"Any word from Hurley?" His words were broken, and his stomach heaved with each word as he forced air through his esophagus.

"No."

"That man's a snake if ever. ..." The coughing started again and he gasped for air.

"I asked him to bring a doctor the next time he comes up the mountain." She continued to wipe his brow.

"How much did he charge ya?" He pushed himself upright, searching for a more comfortable breathing position.

"Didn't charge nothin', least ways, not yet."

"He will."

"Do ya think Harry'll come?" She looked away, dipped the cloth into the pan on the nightstand, wrung out the excess water and gently placed it on his forehead.

"Why should he, after all these years thinking his father is dead?" He closed his eyes and dozed momentarily, but the coughing returned with a vengeance. It drowned out the sound of the wind rustling through the stand of Hemlocks on the north face of their secluded mountain shack. A steady drip of water leaked through the ceiling and landed in a rusty coffee can set on the makeshift kitchen counter, splashing water onto the countertop. It was evidence of the last of the melting ice that had formed on their corrugated metal roof. Vera poured the water from the can into a pot of boiling water on the stove. Until the ice melted from the path to the spring a half-mile up the mountain, the boiled water served for cooking and drinking. She was afraid of the treacherous climb, for what would happen to him if she should fall and break a limb?

Their dog began a low growl that erupted into a yelping fit.

"That may be Hurley." He tried to rise but fell back onto the filthy and disheveled covers.

Vera rushed to the window. Their dog gave chase across the yard, stopping at the edge, where a black bear reared on its hind legs to challenge the aggressor. Two cubs bounded playfully ahead of their mother. "No, Buck, no!" She rapped on the dirty windowpane.

"Who is it?" He struggled to set up on the side of the bed.

"Just a bear and her cubs."

The bear lumbered after the cubs, and Buck returned to his sentinel at the front door. He gave a slow chase of his tail, and after a couple circles settled into a coiled position, his nose snuggled into his ragged fur.

"I need him to come … need him to know about you … to take care of ya. But he ain't coming, is he?" He fell backward onto the bed and turned his face toward the rough-hewn log wall.

Vera stared out the window. Except for the steady drip, the rustling of the hemlocks and the exacerbating wheezing, all remained silent.

Chapter Fifteen

Twelve Oaks housed the elderly but also catered to the mentally ill. The government had released many from its aging mental facilities, some controlled by medications and on the brink of aggressive behavior. Nursing home employees were untrained for such, so they counted on the medicine doing a job they could not. Needless to say, the nursing homes were at capacity and in need of both skilled and unskilled labor. Ann was excited about her job; she loved caring for the residents. Mr. Weatherholtz's promise to build her a cottage by the lake seemed too good to be true. It would be special to live near where she saw her little brother alive for the last time. She was determined to do her part to help with the cottage expenses. With what she received from her domestic jobs, including Mr. Brady's big house, and now this part-time employment as an aid, she planned to save money each week, and she could help make her dream of a place of her own come true. And she longed to take care of Negro foster children, to make a difference in their lives.

Workers had warned her about the peculiarities of some of the residents, especially, "the judge." She wondered if he might be one of the people from the mental institutions. It was her first time to assist him. The door to his room stood slightly ajar, but she knocked before entering.

"Who is it?" He seemed agitated.

"Lunch time." She pushed open the door slowly.

The judge sat by the window, his face turned toward the sunlight, as if it might penetrate the bandages that wrapped his head, covering his eyes. She placed his food tray on the serving table and rolled it toward him.

"What am I having?"

"Boiled potatoes, green beans, ham, coffee and white bread." She embellished the menu with the tone of her voice.

"You have a name?"

"Ann."

"Ann." He studied the name as if it had to meet some approval. "Put my coffee on the left. Butter my bread and place it on the right. I don't remember you serving me before. How long have you worked here?"

"Just started."

"Family?"

His head seemed to follow her movement. "None to speak of." For some reason, his mannerisms frightened her. Could he see through the bandages? She buttered the bread and placed it on the right side of the tray.

"I detect an accent. Are you colored?"

"Yes, suh."

"Are you wearing gloves?"

"No, suh."

"Then take this food back to the kitchen, put on a pair of gloves and get me a fresh plate."

"I didn't touch your food, and I ain't sure they'll let me get more food, suh."

"They will." Jenkins clawed at the lap robe tucked under his legs and across his lap as if it restrained him.

"I'll go see."

"Do it, now!" He swatted the tray from the table, scattering dishes and food across the floor.

Ann bumped into a nurse as she bolted from the room.

"It's okay child," she whispered. "Just do as he says and then clean up the mess before you anger him further."

Chapter Sixteen

"What's troubling you, Annie? Things not go well at the old folks' home?" Evelyn poured iced tea from a sweaty crock.

"It's that judge, Mistuh Jenkins. He's plumb mean."

Evelyn tried to conceal her emotions as she handed her a glass of the tea. "Care to talk about it?"

"He's so rude and demanding. Can't satisfy him with nothin' I do. Have you had any dealings with him?"

"Bud's met him a time or two. I know of him, seen him around, but I've never spoken to him." She weighed her words. "He was a judge here in Shenandoah County for years. Just recently retired, had a plane accident and got burnt really bad."

"That's the reason for the bandages?"

"I think so," Evelyn said. She poured herself a glass of tea.

"He's supposed to not be able to see, but it looks like he's watching my every move." She sipped her tea. "Good tea, ma'am."

"Did he do anything to you, child?"

"Just over-demanding, that's all. The other residents are easy to work with. I don't understand how he gets by with being so mean, but everybody caters to 'em like he owns the place."

"Maybe his authority for years as a judge has left him a might arrogant," Evelyn said.

"Wasn't Mistuh Weatherholtz a sheriff for years? He had authority."

"Yes. He served a couple terms."

"Didn't cause him to get puffed up."

Evelyn smiled. "There's a big difference between a judge and a sheriff. Plus, Bud's a different breed ... and you don't know him as well as I do." Evelyn raised one eyebrow and pursed her lips.

Ann laughed.

It did Evelyn good to see her laughing. She didn't dare tell her how evil Jenkins really was, nor that he was responsible for her and Eddie being placed in the care of Hurley Cutshaw. It didn't seem to serve any purpose to tell her about the judge. Still, she needed to guard her against Jenkins' potential to harm her.

"Do you talk much to the judge?" Evelyn topped Ann's glass. The tea spilled onto Ann's hand. "Sorry, dear. Let me wipe that—"

"It's okay." She studied the tea. "No, I don't talk to 'em much. Asked about my family. Just told 'em my name."

Evelyn's heartbeat quickened. "Did you tell him about Eddie drowning?"

"No. Maybe I should've, him being a judge and all. He'd surely disapprove of what Hurley Cutshaw did all these years, if I told 'em. Maybe he knows someone who could make sure that don't happen no more."

Evelyn readjusted the strings to her apron. "Probably just as well you not ... talk about Eddie to him. No need to relive that ordeal with a total stranger."

"You's probably right."

"We'd best get to work on our quilt. The raffle is coming on quickly." She gathered up the glasses. "How's your work for Jack Brady coming along?" They proceeded to the living room where the quilting frame took up most of the space.

"I clean for Mistuh Brady tomorrow."

"He's lucky to have a hard worker like you, Annie-girl."

She blushed. "I's luckier still to have friends like you and your husband."

"Speaking of my husband, he's a mite late getting home for lunch. Said he needed to visit with Sheriff Flin but should've been home by now. He's missed his lunch, and it's almost time to start supper. Can't imagine what's taking so long."

"They workin' together on another case?" Ann took her seat on the far side of the frame and began tacking the backing of the Nine-Patch.

To tell Annie what was really going on behind the scenes would only disturb her. She had suffered through enough traumas the past year to exempt her from pain for a lifetime, but life doesn't work that way. Jenkins and Cutshaw would harm her in a heartbeat if they had the opportunity. So how do you shield the innocent without leaving them vulnerable by lack of facts? What a fine line to tread!

"It's hard telling what those two, Sheriff Flin and my Bud, are up to. Don't worry yourself about them. You just do your job at the nursing home, keep Brady's house clean and always feel free to talk to us about anything that's on your mind, dearie." Were her words with confidence, or could Annie sense her concern? Bud should have been home long ago. What was keeping him?

A car turned onto the driveway. She raced to the door. Sheriff Flin's cruiser eased to a stop next to the front porch. He exited. Alone.

Chapter Seventeen

Flin tipped the brim of his hat. "Mrs. Weatherholtz."

"Hello, Sheriff. Come in." She pushed the screen door open. "What brings you out our way." She placed a consoling hand on Ann's shoulder but tried not to show alarm.

"Harry home yet?"

"No. I thought he was with you."

"Was. We had coffee this morning. He left right afterward, headed toward the Blue Ridge."

"He never mentioned that to me. You know why he'd be going up there?" Evelyn tried not to alarm Ann, but she found it difficult to contain her emotions.

"Don't rightly know." Flin adjusted his hat. "He had me do a little investigation for him. Figure it had something to do with whatever he's up to."

"What kind of investigation?"

"Well, I wouldn't want it to get out, but he had me stop Hurley Cutshaw yesterday for a traffic violation on his way out of town, then do the same when he returned. Each trip, I logged his mileage and gave that to Harry. Course the whole thing got Cutshaw mighty riled, the traffic stops and all. Don't take much to get that man riled.

Now curiosity's gotten the best of me. Decided to drive over and see what Harry found out."

"I'm not sure, Sheriff. I wish I knew. ..." Her words trailed off.

"You can trust me, ma'am." He placed a hand over his heart. "I wouldn't tell a single soul."

"I know that, Sheriff, but I really don't know. And if I did ... I respect Bud's privacy, so he'll have to tell you whatever he's up to."

"Understood, ma'am. You okay, Miss Ann?" Flin stepped toward Ann and offered her a consoling tap on the shoulder.

"Yes, Mistuh Flin, I's okay."

Evelyn observed the kindness with which Flin treated Ann. It reminded her somewhat of Bud when he was sheriff of Wyandot County in northern Ohio. A sheriff's job wasn't easy, for the law mostly dealt with offenders of the law. It was easy to develop a warped view of society, suspecting all and viewing even the good citizens as potential criminals. Flin served both the white community and the colored's without showing obvious partiality but not without its difficulties. Some white folks accused him of snuggling too close to the blacks, while some in the black community condemned him for ignoring the folks down in the bottoms. Some even chided him for not having a black deputy on the force, but the budget simply wouldn't allow it ... maybe someday, or if one of his deputies quit. Such undue criticism causes some civil servants to develop a cynical attitude. Flin seemed able to keep a good balance in his relationship with the white and black community: not too critical, yet not too gullible. He wasn't color blind, but neither was he color oriented. The more Evelyn knew Flin, the more she admired him. His respect for Ann was obvious. He had witnessed her proclamation of freedom from Cutshaw. Harry had described to Evelyn how Flin laughed until he cried when Ann bested Cutshaw that day down by the lake.

"Heard you got a job at Twelve Oaks, Miss Ann," Flin said in a manner showing he was proud of her.

"Part-time aid." She grinned.

"Good for you. Just keep an eye out for that Judge Jenkins. He'll be gunnin' for you."

Evelyn cringed.

"Gunnin' for me? Why me?" Ann slowly brushed her fingers through her kinky black hair.

Flin looked at Evelyn and realized his error. "Sorry, Miss. I shouldn't have said nothin' like that to you." He glanced at his wristwatch, grabbed his hat and backed out the door. "Be seeing y'all around. Tell Harry I'd like to know what he's up to."

Flin rushed from the scene like he'd gotten an emergency call from Irene, and he never looked back all the way to his cruiser. Evelyn followed him onto the porch and waited until his car spun onto the blacktop before returning to the living room, where Ann stared at the quilt.

"What's going on?" Ann toyed with a needle.

"It's complicated, dear. Best you not know."

"I'm not a child, Miz Evelyn."

"No, you're not, Miss Ann, but neither are you apprised of the ways of man. Let's wait for Bud to get home, and he can explain it to you."

"If ever he gets home." The situation had plunged her into melancholia.

"Don't say it like that, Annie," Evelyn said.

"I don't rightly know what to say." She leaped to her feet, cinched her apron strings and strolled to the kitchen.

Evelyn chose not to respond, partly because Ann's summation was correct, and partly because she was tired of the whole ordeal. For the past year, the problems of others had disrupted what could be the tranquil years of Bud's retirement. Sure, life had its difficulties, but these were brought on by Bud's trying to do good for others. But what did Bud have to show for it? He'd shown kindness but reaped vengeance. Someone torched his mill and killed his dog, and he'd done nothing but try and help a couple orphans. That wasn't the way it should be. She was tired of this battle and was ready to pack up and head north, back to her family, away from Cutshaw and Jenkins, and away from the whole disturbing mess in this lonely valley.

Chapter Eighteen

The unpaved road narrowed, then abruptly ended. Harry was sure this was the general location. The mileage on his speedometer matched what Sheriff Flin had given him as the distance Cutshaw had traveled. Cutshaw was furious when Flin stopped him twice in a single day. That was a ruse to check the speedometer and see just how far he had driven. The plan seemed to have worked. A vehicle had recently turned around in this very place. Harry exited the Hudson, donned his hat and denim jacket and studied the surroundings. Tire tracks were fresh by a day or so, and they matched the studded tires on Cutshaw's pickup, so deduction reasoned this was Cutshaw's destination. Who would visit this isolated area in early spring, and what would bring them to this particular location? Someone with a peculiar interest. He was sure it was Cutshaw.

Booted footprints lead away from the road. Harry followed the tracks on a path that lead into a patch of pinewoods. He walked the path for fifteen minutes before it exited the trees into an opening with a sheer drop, where forty feet below the evergreens snugged against the face of the cliff. The trail circumnavigated the precipice, revealing a mountainside of conifers as far as the eye could see.

Harry paused to observe the breathtaking panorama. He had passed this way before, unaware of its proximity to what could be his past. Now that he knew, he was apprehensive being here. Was he chasing an elusive long-ago wish? Sixty years changes everything, at least somewhat. How had it changed him? For the better? He hoped so. Or was he growing into a worn-out cynic? He shuddered at the thought. Or was it the coolness of the three thousand feet altitude? The wind whistled over the cliff and came in surges that almost sucked his breath. He snapped the top button to his jacket, pulled the collar over his ears and repositioned his hat against the gusts.

A tall grove of eastern hemlock blanketed the north slope of the mountain. The wind whipped the tops of the trees, and they drooped as if avoiding the low hovering clouds that painted a misty glaze across the valley. The creation of the national park, some thirty years ago, spared these hemlocks from the logger's ax. There was rumor an insect had infested some of the trees and brought concern for their future. He saw faint signs of browning among the green. Being a logger himself, he knew how devastating man's greed could be to nature. Still, he could not fathom a tiny insect doing enough damage to endanger the survivor of a thousand winters and the howling and adverse winds of these elevations. Some of these hemlocks could have sprung up from seeds dropped onto the ground five hundred years before Columbus arrived in the Americas. Some towered more than a hundred and fifty feet into the air, with trunk diameters over six feet. With the logger's ax silenced, their worst enemy remained wind and fire: fires caused by both nature and human carelessness, and wind that challenged the root system in the shallow soil in which these giants clung for life.

The path reentered the forest. The high-pitched call of a blackburnian warbler caught his attention. He studied the trees lining the path, hoping to see the black-masked bird. They loved the coniferous forests of the Blue Ridge. Did it object to his intrusion? He caught a glimpse of bright orange flitting from the thick limbs of the flowering hemlocks. A distant female answered the call. Soon they'd be nesting in one of the trees that shrouded the slopes of the Blue Ridge. They'd raise a family high in a nest clinging to the swaying limbs of one of these lush, flat-needled evergreens. It was a ritual of millenniums.

Harry paused, his breathing laborious. A clear stream chuckled across rocks alongside the ascending path, crisscrossing the path at several turns of the rugged topography. Patches of melting snow, white and unspoiled by pollution and the snowplow, formed multiple tributaries. A dense stand of rhododendron followed the primary stream and painted the landscape in hues of pink, violet and purple on a canvass of evergreens. These towering Blue Ridge Mountains acted as a natural fortress that protected the valley for years from the immigrant white man. It must have been awe-inspiring during the latter sixteen hundreds when explorers found gaps through which they could pass over this mountain range. They found a valley that stretched for two hundred miles. Time had not erased the awe.

A dog barked in the distance. Harry paused, focusing both sight and hearing. The distinct snapping of limbs and the crunch of the underbrush advanced slowly toward him. He eased behind a tree and scanned the thicket for movement. A deer? Probably not at this elevation, and the sounds were too careless. He caught movement and focused on the spot. A black bear and her cubs emerged from the thicket and ambled toward him, foraging as they came. The protective mother stopped and sniffed the air. She purposefully changed directions. Harry waited until they passed before he stepped onto the path and continued.

What about the dog? Dogs don't frequent this area, so a dwelling had to be nearby. The mother bear had steered the cubs away from a confrontation with the dog and into the undergrowth. The dog was smart to not give chase. Harry realized the barking had subsided; it was not coincidental that the path led in the direction from where the barking had come from. There was definitely a dwelling to which this path led.

The path emerged again from the forest and followed the edge of a precipice. Off in the distance, he could make out faint sections of the valley turnpike. In the early years, the valley served as a natural warriors' path for the Iroquois and Shawnee. German and Scots-Irish immigrant farmers from Pennsylvania transformed the Indian path into a wagon trail in the early seventeen hundreds. They came by way of the Potomac to stake claim to the valley's rich soil, abundant water supply and mild weather that favored their farming talents. The Indians eventually relinquished the land, for a fraction of its cost—or were cheated out of it altogether—and moved west to seek hunting grounds undisturbed by the plow, and they sought a land where the buffalo still roamed.

The immigrants turned the valley into farmland and orchards that fed a growing nation, and it served as the Confederate breadbasket during the divided years. A strategic pathway to Washington and Richmond, both armies vied for occupancy of the valley. The Blue Ridge Mountains to the east, and the Appalachians to the west, created a natural funnel. An army could march, sometimes without detection, until they were well within striking distance of their opponent. They could break from the valley in a massive surprise assault. The valley saw three major Civil War campaigns. The locals' hero, General Thomas Jackson, combined his knowledge of war and the geography of the valley to create a tactical wall of defense early on in the war. Later, Confederate General Jubal Early forced the Union out of the valley and ultimately marched on Washington. Famed author of *Ben-Hur: A Tale of the Christ*, Lew Wallace, shelved by his superiors for unresolved issues regarding the fateful Battle of Shiloh, ended up a hero in that battle. He stopped the advancement of the boys in gray long enough for reinforcements to save the Capitol city. Ironically, though Wallace suffered defeat, his loss of that battle proved to be one of the greatest victories of the war, by stalling the enemy long enough for blue-uniformed reinforcements to arrive. The Union's General Sherman eventually put the valley to the torch, creating empty stomachs for the boys in gray and thus opened a doorway to Richmond.

In the early nineteen hundreds, the government forced some five hundred families to relocate from the mountains overlooking the valley area in order to create the Shenandoah National Park. The park consisted of rustic resorts and a scenic parkway that snaked the ridges, and much of the land area was protected as a natural wilderness. Authorities removed most of the mountain dwellers from the land, but a few managed to stay. Had his father escaped prison and hid out in this vast wilderness? Rumors abounded that he had been seen in these parts after his supposed death in prison. Were they true? Did a bribe obtain his father's freedom? Did he hide out in these hills and evade capture and eviction all these years? Harry gave little credence to the rumors, until now, and the letter. But he dare not allow gullibility to override reason. Was this whole ordeal just another of Cutshaw's devious schemes?

He paused and studied the sun, its rays piercing the timber at an angle. Evelyn would be wondering about him if he didn't start home soon. The faint odor of burning wood grew stronger: hickory. He deliberated and pushed on. A sharp turn around a boulder as large as an outbuilding opened into a small clearing. A crude log cabin, no more than fifteen feet wide, stood at the backside of the clearing beneath an outcrop that balanced precariously above the roofline. Smoke drifted from a metal flue in the direction he stood. He hesitated by the boulder, to catch his breath and to contemplate.

A collie, its shaggy, winter fur shedding in patches, sat on the single log step to the front door. He stood and sniffed the air. One ear stood alert, while the other drooped at the middle, as if broken. The dog chased its tail a couple times, plopped onto the log step and buried its nose in its front paws. It had not seen him.

He saw movement through the window, a woman. Had she seen him? Was she his stepmother? He really didn't care. His mother had loved him enough in those short years to last a lifetime. The woman disappeared from the window. Harry waited for the door to open, but it did not. He sighed in relief. After all these years, what was he doing here?

The dog stood and walked into the yard. Harry remained hidden behind the boulder. The smoke from the flue drifted toward him. He loved the aroma of burning hickory. With the wind in his face, his scent was not reaching the dog. He studied the situation. His options were few: make himself known, or walk away.

On impulse, he pulled the envelope from his pocket and read again from the lines of faded ink. He had read the letter several times, but for the first time, the date of the note caught his attention: February 26. Was it coincidental the letter was written on his birthday? Did his birthday spark the letter? Probably coincidental. He continued to read:

February 26, 1898

To Lawrence Elmer and Harry Thomas,

Dear sons, if you are reading this letter then I am dead, but I wanted to let you know somewhat about me. I am sure you hate me for killing your mother, and rightly so. I should have been executed for the dastardly crime, but I got off on a technicality and was sent to prison anyway for a lesser crime of which you may be aware. Before my incarceration I hid in the Blue Ridge Mountains on a piece of land I had purchased as a young man. After I was imprisoned, a lawyer purchased the property from me. He was to place the money in a trust for the two of you, and the trust was to be under his oversight. The money is yours by simply identifying yourselves to the lawyer. I do not expect you to understand, and therefore I do not ask you to try, nor do I ask your forgiveness, for even God may not forgive me of the wrong I did.

I wish you well.
Elmer Weatherholtz

P.S. The lawyer has an office in Woodstock, VA. His name is Joshua Mullen.

He felt no emotion toward his father. He hardly saw him, for he was mostly on the run, and the years had dulled any natural father and son attachment. Still, curiosity brought him to this place. The woman in the window, who is she? The wife of his father? That is if the man is his father. And if her husband is his father, how does he treat her? How could he have been so cruel to his mother? Sixty years had not erased the memory of her gentleness, nor the deeds of his violent temper. His mother deserved better, far better than life gave her.

Memories overwhelmed him, and a gush of unexpected emotions erupted. Trying to gain composure, he gasped for air. His chest heaved and ached, but he was not sure the source of the pain. Was he having another heart attack? Not here, not now. His eyes welled with tears but not for whoever lived in this cabin. It was for his mother. He knew now, as he had always known, that he did not want anything to do with Elmer Weatherholtz—or whatever name he went by—even if he was still alive. He did not want to see him, and he did not want his money and he could not forgive him for his crime.

He crumpled the paper and tossed it onto the ground. He hastened back down the path, but stopped abruptly, retraced his steps, retrieved the wadded paper and stuffed it into his pocket. By the time he reached his Hudson, shadows descended upon the eastern slope of the mountainside. The sun transformed into a bright orange sphere that dropped quickly behind the mountains. Evelyn would be worried sick.

Chapter Nineteen

Her footsteps echoed as she walked slowly across the giant foyer and into the massive, mahogany-paneled library. Inspired by the splendor of the study, she paused in the entryway, as if its chambers beckoned reverence. The oval, floral rug—centered beneath the chandelier in the middle of the room—surpassed in beauty any quilt she'd ever seen.

She slipped by the enormous desk, allowing her slender fingers, chapped from the endless hours of domestic labor, to brush across the bronze eagle poised on the corner of the desk. The eagle's wings spread in flight and clutched a fish with its claws. She had seen an eagle in flight crisscrossing the valley, and this statue well reflected its majestic movements.

The leather chair fascinated her, and instinctively she plopped into the cushioned seat and spun around in circles until dizzily she clung to the chair arms. The chair coasted to a stop, and she stroked the leather arms, waiting for her head to clear.

"Pretty impressive, huh, Miss Ann."

She sprang from the chair—staggering momentarily—and subconsciously touched her flushed cheeks. "Yes, suh, Mistuh Brady. Didn't know you was there."

Brady walked to the shelves and ran his index finger slowly across the spine of the books. "There's an order to the books. You must keep them in perfect order. *Comprende*?"

She stared at him.

"That means, do you understand?"

"Yes, suh." She nodded, hoping her expression didn't betray her uncertainty.

"Good."

She glanced at the hundreds of books crowding the polished cherry shelves. They lined the walls from floor to the high ceiling on three sides of the room and between massive windows on the outer wall. How could she keep them in order? The sudden throbbing of her heart startled her. Embarrassed, she wanted to run from the room and never face Jack Brady again. She moistened her parched lips with the tip of her tongue.

"No need for alarm, Miss. I have a simple plan." He pointed to a section of books. "Take these for an example. They are legal works that need to remain together. They are all older books, mostly collector copies entitled *Works on Religious Liberty by Priestley, Blackstone, Philip Furneau and Others.* I once attended some law-school lectures on Priestley and Blackstone. They differed greatly in their views of religious tolerance versus conformity. Blackstone supported conformity and viewed nonconformity to the state-church as a crime. Of course I, and you, disagree with his philosophy."

She shook her head as if she understood. Jack Brady sure was a smart man.

"Of course that is inconsequential to the task at hand. I just want all the books removed, dusted, the shelves dusted and the books replaced in their spot on the right shelf. You simply do it a few books at a time and there'll be no problem. Probably best to go by sections. For example, here's a section of biographies."

Her puzzlement must have been obvious, for his facial expression showed his doubt in her ability.

"They're all books written about people, Miss Ann. A biography differs from an autobiography in that an autobiography is a book written by a person about themselves."

Though embarrassed at her obvious ignorance, she appreciated Brady sharing this information. Having never been in a classroom, she suddenly realized the satisfaction that came from receiving new information; it seemed to work like food to an empty stomach. The difference, food satisfies hunger, but the more information Brady shared with her, the more she desired. It was more like having a licorice stick; you never get enough to satisfy the pleasure of the taste. The receiving of knowledge caused something to come alive within her. She didn't want to infringe upon his time, but she thoroughly enjoyed the information he shared and the way he formed his thoughts. She didn't try to hide her fascination.

"The biographies are organized in alphabetical order by the title ... the name of the book: 'A' includes *Attila the Hun* and *John Adams*." He pointed to another book. "*Jefferson Davis* is in the 'D' section. Last name generally determines the order. You understand what I mean by alphabetical order?"

"No, suh." She dropped her head.

"By the order of the alphabet. The "A's" first, then "B's" and so on." He pointed to specific letters and recited their names.

"Don't know no alphabet, but I guess a biography 'bout me would be first on your shelf, 'cause I know Ann starts with 'A' 'cause you just showed me." She smiled.

"Not necessarily."

Embarrassment wiped away her smile. She had hoped to impress him.

"What's your last name? Remember, the order generally goes by the last name, not your first."

"Shaver." Anticipation overcame the embarrassment. She was more eager to learn than she feared being humiliated.

"Yes, Shaver. I knew that, having done the grand jury investigation on your brother. Let's look at "S" and see who you'll sit beside." He slid his fingers along the edge of the books. "*Sir Arthur Conan Doyle, Hitler, Lincoln, Mussolini, Napoleon,* ah, here we go." He pulled a book from the shelf and opened it. "*Jeb Stuart: The Last Cavalier*, by Burke Davis. Just released last year, published by Random House of New York. You'd be right here, Miss Ann." He pointed at the empty space.

She smiled. "Who's Jeb Stuart?"

"Actually Jeb's not his real name. Those are his initials … the first letter of each of his names. He's James Ewell Brown Stuart but went by the nickname Jeb … J … E … B … ," he pointed at each of the letters, "which is an acronym formed from the first letters of James Ewell Brown."

She methodically repeated the name. "James Ewell Brown. J … for James."

"Ewell … E." Brady coached her.

Something about the sound of the letters and the way Brady spoke the names made sense. "J … E … B. Jeb."

"That's great, Miss Ann. You're a fast learner." He patted her on the shoulder.

"Had to learn fast to avoid Mistuh Cutshaw's razor strap."

"He beat you?"

"Yes, suh. Sometimes just 'cause he was mad at somebody else."

"I'm sorry. Well, you're shed of Hurley Cutshaw now. Let's put Mr. Stuart back on the shelf right here beside Miss Ann Shaver."

"What did Mistuh Stuart do?"

Brady hesitated. "General during the Civil War. Graduated from West Point. Cavalryman. Some say the eyes and ears of General … of his commander."

"For the north or south?"

Brady paused as if studying a title. "The south, mostly because he was from Virginia, you know, loyal to the homeland and all."

"Can't rightly imagine me sittin' on a shelf right beside Mistuh Jeb Stuart."

"Of course, I understand, he being the enemy—"

"Didn't say he was my enemy. I's from Virginia, too, Mistuh Brady."

He stared at her, as if studying her thoughts. "I didn't mean to be presumptuous … assuming … judgmental. I just thought that—"

"I just meant I done nothing to earn a place on no bookshelf, 'specially aside important people."

"You're amazing, Miss Ann. I declare, never met anyone quite like you. Don't think you've ill-will toward anyone."

"Not true."

"Cutshaw?"

"Fraid so."

"By the way, the floor looks great in the foyer."

"Thank you, suh."

"I think you're ready to go to work on these books." He headed toward the door. "I'll check in on you later. Any questions, I'll be around." He closed the door behind him.

Ann pulled the books, a handful at a time, from the shelves and carefully dusted and replaced each to their right spot. Awestruck by the books, some with leather binding and bold lettering, she found it difficult to focus on dusting. She studied the titles, reciting the letters that Brady just taught her. She opened the books and discovered some had pictures she assumed to be the person the book was written about. Recognizing a photo of General Robert E. Lee astride a beautiful horse, she recited the name slowly and tried to say the individual letters in the name. It was difficult, but it all made perfect sense: each letter had its unique sound. "L … E … E." She recited her own name, holding out the letters: "A … N … N." She replaced the biography of Lee, pulled another book and studied the title, repeating the letters she knew. "E … N … E … N." But she couldn't make out all the letters so the word didn't make sense. She opened the book. A wild-haired man with a walrus mustache—she'd seen a billboard of a walrus—stared at her from the inside of the book. She didn't recognize him.

She returned to her work, and in haste to make up for the time she'd spent studying the book titles, a book tumbled to the floor. She examined a photograph that slipped from its pages. It was a picture of a black woman standing inside a large room. The room resembled the Shenandoah County courthouse at Woodstock: high ceilings and fancy woodwork. She remembered from the only time she was ever in the building, the time she was supposed to testify against Hurley Cutshaw, but got so scared she ran away. The woman looked frightened, as did the little boy she held by the hand. She stared at the picture for a long moment, befuddled by what she saw. The child resembled her brother Eddie, and the young woman looked like herself, only an older version. This couldn't be so, for she'd never had her picture taken with Eddie. She would have remembered, but if it wasn't her, who was it that would look so much like her? And could the child actually be her little brother? If so, there was only one explanation: the woman was her mother, and the little boy … he was Eddie. She could not remember her mother—she had been separated from her at a young age—but the picture had to be her mother, for it resembled her too much to not be so.

Her hands shook so violently the picture blurred. She unconsciously picked up the book and stared at the cover. Handwritten across the front was a single word. What did it say? The word had seven letters and she recognized some. The first letter, "R," was the first letter in General Robert E. Lee's first name. Three of the letters were the "E" in his last name. The fifth letter "N" was the letter in her name, and like the "E" in Lee, both letters had obvious sounds. She could not make out the third letter. She formed the letters she knew as best she could. "RE_EN_E." Living in the valley, she was familiar with General Lee. She grabbed his autobiography from the shelf, turned to the page that had his photograph and slowly sounded out, "General Robert E. Lee," focusing on the "G" sound. She returned to the book from which the photograph had fallen, studied the single word on the cover and attempted to recite the letters, including "G" from General Lee's name.

"RE_ENGE."

What was the third letter forming a word she did not know? What did the word mean? She would have to find out. Why would a picture of her mother and brother be in a book in Jack Brady's library?

Footsteps on the stairway interrupted her thoughts. She hurriedly replaced the book onto the shelf and slipped the picture into her pocket. Shame immediately gripped her heart. And fearfulness.

Chapter Twenty

So far, Harry had survived the baited trap. Cutshaw had shown his hand, forcing Harry's move, whose stealth maneuvering sidestepped the snare. Battle lines were drawn. The sides had obvious allies and those not so evident. The uncommitted created the greatest concern. Where did Jack Brady figure into the equation? What was the purpose of his visit with Judge Jenkins at Twelve Oaks? Was it coincidental that Cutshaw's visit coincided with Brady's? Did the purchase of Jenkins' home by Brady incur some type of favor? What new events would unfold at the vacating of the prosecutor's position by Brady? These questions swarmed Harry's mind like yellow jackets on an opened soda bottle, and he mentally swatted at them from multiple angles.

The clandestine trip up the mountain didn't sit well with Evelyn; evidently, he had erred in keeping her in the dark. A furrowed brow and stonewalling at mealtimes revealed her distress. The retrieval of her battered suitcase from the attic hinted of a trip to Ohio, but she showed no enthusiasm toward traveling. Her mother hen hovering over Miss Ann seemed minimized. Ann seemed to feel the aloofness, for her visits waned in frequency and duration. That could be in part due to her cleaning job for Brady, but more than likely she felt Evelyn's coolness. An unfinished quilt in the living room hinted of such.

He was obsessing again. His thoughts kept coming, relentlessly, like the waves of enemy lines that kept coming at them during the Great War. Or like the ocean at Virginia Beach, wave after wave of thoughts kept crashing onto his mental shores. There would not be a let up until he solved the problem.

The nuisance of the community, the bane of their peace, had to be dealt with. But how? Sheriff Flin's dead dog philosophy regarding Cutshaw wasn't working. His poison had somehow seeped into their daily, wellspring of life, and the effects were obvious in Harry's home, his heretofore haven.

Or was all this just his imagination gone wild with his refusal to deal with inner conflicts regarding his past? Within hollering distance of the front door of a man claiming to be his father, he had walked away. Was it pride? Repressed hate? Fear of how he might respond? An unconscious means of punishing his father for his dastardly deed? Then again, chances of his father being alive were minimal to impossible. Surely it was another one of Cutshaw's evil ploys. But why? Twenty steps could have made a difference but not necessarily to the good. Perhaps he should go back to the cabin and bring closure, then again, why should he? The man Cutshaw claimed to be his father had skirted within thirty miles of him for the past fifteen years and hadn't bothered to visit.

He instinctively rubbed at the throbbing in his temple. The sore had scabbed over, so the pain was probably just a headache. The discomfort had intensified the past few days, but so had his stress, a likely duo.

Sounds from the bedroom ceased, perhaps Evelyn was napping. He stepped into the kitchen and poured a cup of coffee. He sipped long and swallowed, repeating the process a few times. The warmth distracted the throbbing in his head.

He stood at the sink and observed through the window a male nuthatch spreading his wings and tail feathers, revealing his black and white markings. The female's head peeked from the same knot-hole the snakes had invaded last summer. She darted across the lawn, landing at the edge of the woods, where she clasped a straw with her beak and flew back to the hole. Harry and Evelyn had observed this courtship the last couple springs. The birds were back, the male attentive to the needs of the female as he cracked pine seeds with his bill and shared his cache, which she downed between breaks in repairing the used nest.

Evelyn stepped into the room carrying her suitcase. She paused to straighten her hat. Harry, totally perplexed, felt speechless.

"I need you to drop me off at the bus stop. I'm going to see the kids."

They'd weathered storms together, battled adversaries in tandem, celebrated victories and survived setbacks. In forty years of marriage, she'd never left his side. She'd had plenty opportunities to leave before but never did. Why now, when he needed her feedback most? Harry started to respond, but she silenced him with an uplifted hand.

"My mind's made up. I need some time away, and you need to get some issues settled."

He'd been kicked by a mule, sucker punched by a convict and hit over the head with a beer bottle while breaking up a barroom brawl, but none of those stung like her words. This pain was different; it solicited no defense, only despair. He had no comeback. He wanted to sweep her up in his arms and beg her to reconsider, but a man of few words, his words seemed fewer still as he looked into her stone-willed face. He had failed to heed the signs. The iceberg had struck, and he could only surmise the damage, hoping all was not lost. He extended his hand for the suitcase, but she sidestepped his assistance and headed out the door.

Chapter Twenty-one

Cutshaw dreaded the meeting. Judge Jenkins' threadbare patience worried him more than he cared to admit. Weatherholtz hadn't taken the bait; the dangling carrot was shriveled and quickly losing enticement. The old man couldn't hold on much longer, and he was their best chance to manipulate Harry Weatherholtz Why not just convince the Buffords to end this whole mess, and he could get on with life? If his plan worked, he'd have enough money to close his store, a business that was all but failing since the Zirkles opened their general store down the road.

He eased the door open and slipped inside. The judge breathed heavily, seemingly unaware he'd entered the room. A pillow over his face would be sweet revenge for all the insults, but it could end a lucrative partnership. If he could make it without the judge's influence, he'd gladly smother the brute.

Jenkins stirred. "Who's there?"

"It's me. Hurley."

"How long have you been here?"

"Couple minutes. Didn't mean to wake you. Tried to be quiet."

"It was the smell, not the noise, that woke me. Don't you ever bathe?"

Cutshaw stared at the pillow, his fists clinched.

"Has Weatherholtz stopped his crusade for the illegitimates in our community?"

"No, sir. He's a stubborn cuss, but I ain't given up yet. He'll break if'n we bend him far enough."

"Then let's bend him."

"I got another plan that might work."

"What?" Jenkins tugged at the bandages over his eyes.

Cutshaw stretched his suspenders with his thumbs. "Kidnap his Miss Ann, since he's so attached to 'er, and threaten to send him a finger ever day he don't agree to cooperate."

"And just how do you expect to do all that without having the law haul us off to jail. Last year we barely survived your antics with that little boy, and now you want to kill his sister?"

"Not kill—"

"Your hatred for Weatherholtz is causing you to lose focus, Hurley. All we want is for Weatherholtz to back off and let us show these tight-skirted wenches they can't keep having illegitimate babies without dire consequences. There's no reason our program for these children shouldn't continue in this valley. It worked well in the past, saved taxpayers money, relieved the burden on local government and taught unwed women that we're not putting up with their shamelessness. Not to mention instilling some measure of discipline in the illegitimate kids."

"And we've gotta be sure no foreigners from up north interfere with orphans like that Ann girl ever again," Hurley said.

"I hear Jack hired her … the colored girl."

"Yep. Can't believe he could be so thoughtless after all you've done fer him."

"That boy's forgotten who's buttered his bread all these years. A disgrace to his daddy."

"Want me to take care of Brady?"

"Later. Right now I want you to take care of Weatherholtz. Every man has his price. He's no exception. You find his price."

The door opened and a nurse entered. "Time for meds, Mr. Jenkins."

Chapter Twenty-two

"How's Evelyn doing?" Flin asked.

Harry had stopped by the sheriff's office on his way from the bus stop. Of all the questions Flin could have asked, why did that have to be the first? Harry hoped his countenance hadn't belied his secret. "She's still the best biscuit maker in these parts." He evaded the question.

"You got that right, but I 'bout shot myself in the foot last time I was over't y'all's place. Had to leave before she got a chance to offer any biscuits. She tell you?"

"No. What happened?"

"Miss Ann was there, and I spoke out of turn about her being careful around the judge. Didn't really think through before I spoke, kind of forgot Ann wasn't aware of Jenkins' involvement with her plight. Evelyn gave me the dirtiest look. Thinking maybe I should come over and apologize."

"I don't think that's necessary. I can smooth it over for you."

"Appreciate that. By the way, whatever come of that information I got for you from Cutshaw? I asked Evelyn, but she wouldn't tell me what you are up to, but she acted like it is some big deal."

"You know women, Sheriff, they can exaggerate something fierce in their mind."

"But neither did you offer me any kind of explanation. What's going on, Harry, to cause you to spy on Cutshaw so?"

"Well, since you asked, he's been spending a lot of time with Judge Jenkins at the nursing home. You know that's not good."

"Right." Flin studied his pudgy knuckles, like a palmist looking for a sign. "What do you think they're up to?"

"Not sure. Trying to figure that out. Thought it good to keep track of Cutshaw, where he's going, and who he's seeing." Harry pulled a matchstick from his shirt pocket, stuck it in his mouth and twirled it with his tongue.

"Did you find anything out?" Cutshaw insisted.

"Not sure what all he's up to, but I think if we keep a short leash on him, all's the better. We can control him with a short noose. So I just like to know where he's spending his time," Harry said.

"Keep me in the loop and—"

The phone interrupted the conversation.

"Sheriff's department, Irene Compton." Her face revealed concern.

Harry eased toward her desk.

"Where?" The tone depicted concern. "How bad?"

Flin pushed himself up from his swivel chair and walked toward Irene's desk. Harry saw an opportunity to end the sheriff's interrogation. He'd like to keep quiet about the possibility of his dad being alive. It could get complicated, a man who was supposed to have died in jail fifty years ago living unnoticed in Flin's jurisdiction. And Flin was a stickler for the rule of the law. Neither did he want to tell him Evelyn had skipped town. That would raise a lot of questions he didn't rightly have the answer for.

"We'll send help right over." Irene scribbled on a notepad. "Yes, I'll notify the hospital."

"What's up, Irene?" Flin hooked his thumbs on the front of his sagging belt.

"Multi-car pileup on Valley Pike, five miles out, plus a passenger bus. Some people injured, not sure the extent."

"North or south?" Harry already had his hat in his hand.

"North."

"I'll go with you, Sheriff, if it's okay?"

"Sure. Get all available deputies out there, Irene."

"Will do, sir."

Harry beat Flin to the cruiser. He wanted to pray, but words eluded him. A Bible verse screamed at him, one he didn't want to consider right now. "Forgive us our debts as we forgive our debtors." He feared for Evelyn. That could well be the bus she was on. He feared his wrath had rained back on him, but in the worst of ways, harm to his wife. Under his breath, he begged God for mercy.

Flin, lights flashing, weaved the cruiser around the crawling traffic. The CB squawked incessantly. Harry strained to make out scrambled conversations. There were casualties, but no deaths mentioned, but you never know the extent of injuries until a medical team arrives to assess the situation. Through the side mirror, he glimpsed the flashing lights of a wrecker that followed close behind them. The flashing lights chased drivers onto the brim of the road. Harry didn't understand why Flin wasn't using his siren, and he fought the impulse to switch it on himself.

"Any idea which bus line?" Harry asked.

"No. Let me call Irene and see what she's heard." Flin grabbed the mic and keyed in.

Harry stiffened at Irene's report. It was the evening Grey Line that had departed from the Woodstock station, the one from which Evelyn waved to him from the third window behind the driver.

"You seem a bit nervous, Harry. Anything I should know?"

"Evelyn … worried about Evelyn."

"What's wrong with her?"

"She was on the evening bus that left Woodstock, and I assume it's the one in the accident."

"Why didn't you say so sooner?"

Harry braced against the dash as Flin braked suddenly when a car zipped from a side road in front of them.

"Crazy drivers." Flin flipped the switch to his siren. The driver jerked onto the brim and Flin accelerated past him, glaring at the driver who tightly gripped the steering wheel and avoided eye contact.

Flin rode the bumpers of cars until they edged to the side of the road. He slowed as he approached the accident. A state trooper directed traffic around the pileup. The bus had pulled to the side of the road, the left front tire flat and showing damage to the left front fender. Passengers crowded alongside the road, but no one seemed injured. Harry's fear eased. He scrambled from the cruiser and walked swiftly to where the passengers congregated, but Evelyn wasn't among the crowd. He spotted the driver by the name-tag attached to his shirt pocket, his hat tilted back on his head, puffing nervously on a cigarette.

"Mr. Johnston, Harry Weatherholtz. My wife was on your bus. Mind if I step inside and check on her?"

"Not at all, but I don't think anyone is on the bus."

Harry followed the driver up the steps. It seemed empty.

The driver pointed toward the "Occupied" sign above the restroom door. "Let me check." He walked to the back and tapped on the door. "Mrs. Weatherholtz?"

No one answered. He looked quizzically at Harry and knocked harder.

"You in there, Mrs. Weatherholtz?"

"No, I'm Sarah Jamison."

"Sorry, ma'am." He turned to Harry and sighed. "We did have an older lady get into a car with a couple of people and drive away. Thought it a mite strange at the time, but with all the commotion around here, I didn't give it any more thought. Just figured she knew them and needed to get somewhere in a hurry. Looking back, that might have been the same car that had followed us all the way from Woodstock. Tried to pass me a couple times. Don't quite know what

126

to make of that now. Probably them that caused the accident, weaving in and out trying to pass me."

"Did you get their license number?"

"Didn't think about it at the time."

The door to the bathroom opened and the heavy-set Sarah Jamison exited, straightening her dress.

"Excuse me, gentlemen."

They squeezed between the seats and allowed her to pass.

"What did the men look like … in the car that drove away?" Harry leaned forward, pressing for an answer, but not wanting to create undue concern. "Old? Young? What kind of car? Did they go north?"

"Yep. Spun gravel on the bus heading outta here awfully fast, like a getaway car just robbed a bank. Can't rightly recall what they looked like, just noticed there were two of 'em, maybe three." He paused and stared into the distance. "It all happened so fast. Kind of hard to keep everything straight, which car was which. Then there was the lady the ambulance took." He abruptly descended the steps.

"From the bus?" Harry followed closely, ducking as he exited the bus.

"Yeah, with a huge gash on her forehead. Hit the back of the seat when the accident happened." He drew a line across his forehead with his index finger.

"How old?"

He took a deep drag and blew smoke that drifted into Harry's face. "'Bout your age, maybe a little younger. Wearing a hat."

Harry swatted at the smoke. "What color dress?"

"Don't recall, but she got blood all over the front." He dropped the cigarette onto the gravel and crushed it with the toe of his shoe.

"You recall what row of seats she sat in?"

"Not sure. Second, maybe third. Can't rightly recall. Everything happened so sudden like."

Harry processed the information. Two possibilities: one a kidnapping, the other an injury. Time was critical for the former;

a trip to the hospital could determine the latter. Neither choice was desirable, and not knowing who was in the car and not knowing the extent of the injury intensified his angst.

"Find 'er Harry?" Flin hastened toward him.

"No, but I got a lead." He quickly relayed to Flin his conversation with the bus driver.

"I'll put an APB on the car as a precaution, headed north you say?"

"Yes. Can you give me a lift back to Woodstock to check at the hospital?"

"Better still, I'll radio and check. That'll be much quicker." He placed a hand on Harry's shoulder. "We'll find her, Harry." He headed for the cruiser.

Harry paced while Flin radioed Irene and explained the dilemma. Flin finished with Irene, then radioed all available officers to be on the lookout for the car, giving the few details they had.

Irene's voice interrupted the squawking of the CB. "Sheriff Flin, Irene here. Tell Mr. Weatherholtz to relax. It ain't his wife at the hospital."

Flin engaged the mic. "Too premature, Irene. If it's not her at the hospital, then she may be the victim of a kidnapping. Get as much information on the wire as you possibly can for a car with two men and a woman. Call me on any leads you might hear."

"Roger that, Sheriff. Oh, one more thing. The Buffords are at it again. Got stoned at Sam Tompkins' place and hit a car on their way out of the parking lot. We're looking for them as we speak."

Some disciplines are a science, and you can gauge the outcome from the beginning. Math is a science: two plus two always equals four. Gauging character isn't as simple, but there are some basics that are obvious. The profile of the criminal mind is an example, for you can predict the outcome of a life early on. Harry sensed some basic flaws in the Buffords, but he didn't want his inclinations to be true. "Never judge a son until he's thirty" was an adage he clung to regarding his own boys. All things considered, they had turned out pretty good. He maintained such hope for the Buffords. Surely deep down there was good that would surface with maturity. He had pushed for tolerance in hopes that kindness would facilitate rehabilitation. Had he lapsed into gullibility in his senior years? Evelyn tried to warn him about those two, but he wouldn't have any of it. His poor judgment may have brought harm to the dearest person in his life. His failures in judgment were adding up to a fiasco. How could he ever forgive himself for such naiveté?

Chapter Twenty-three

Harry chose a corner chair in the sheriff's office, leaned the chair onto its back legs and balanced it with his head against the wall. He closed his eyelids in an attempt to relieve the prickly barbs jabbing his eyes. The cracking of his knuckles eased his tetchy emotions. A snort from Flin startled him, and he tumbled forward in the chair, slamming the legs against the hardwood floor. Flin's sumo-sized head bobbled incessantly, a telltale sign of a night without sleep, but he didn't rouse. Harry was glad. He checked his pocket watch: twelve hours with no news regarding Evelyn.

A Rockingham County deputy had arrested the foul smelling and stupefied Buffords around midnight. Their Coupe had run out of gas near Coots Store. They were headed in the opposite direction the mystery car—the one suspected of taking Evelyn—had traveled. Then again, the Buffords could have doubled back, which could explain why they ran out of gas. The Rockingham sheriff and his deputy had hauled the cuffed and babbling brothers into Flin's jail, glad to be shed of them. After a few head dunks in a bucket of cold water, they still held to their story. Yes, they faintly remembered hitting a car leaving Sam's bar. No, they didn't know anything about a bus wreck. And no, they never gave Mrs. Weatherholtz a ride, and they certainly didn't kidnap her.

Harry couldn't turn off his brain as it calculated the time-line of events. In a short time span, the Buffords would have had to stop by Sam's place, commit a hit and run, abduct and hide Evelyn and end up at Coots Store drunk and out of gasoline. The time scenario worked close enough for suspicion. Sam had called in the report of the hit-and-run around five-thirty. A call to him verified the Buffords had gotten to the tavern around four o'clock and had left with plenty of booze under their belt and a carton to go. The bus wreck was called in around six in the evening, enough time for them to arrive and abduct Evelyn. Where were they from six until nine? They'd had plenty of time to do something to Evelyn, double back to Rockingham County and drown their guilt in beer. Still, unanswered questions left room for doubt. How did they know Evelyn was on the bus? Had they been following when he took her to the bus station? Why didn't he notice? It wasn't like him to miss the obvious: like a car tailing him.

He rubbed his itching forehead with the back of his hand, trying not to aggravate the scab. Evelyn had scolded him for not see-ing the doctor. Her love for him ran deep, like the deep-rooted Sugar Maples found at high elevations and exposed to high winds. Their limbs are often lost to the elements, but the trunk remains firm and sure. Their marriage had weathered a few rough storms but nothing like this. It was difficult dropping her off at the station; conversely, that emotional moment seemed tame compared to what had hap-pened within the last few hours.

The itch on his forehead diminished as a headache intensi-fied. He massaged his throbbing temples in a circular motion with his thumbs, pressing deeply to penetrate the ache. His rambling thoughts settled on his tenure as sheriff back in Ohio, to a time when he participated in the hunt for the Lindbergh child. He joined a pos-se of sheriffs who combed the country searching for the little boy. A truck driver accidentally found the child, lifeless along the roadside, discarded like a paper bag. When it was over, those rough and tough law enforcers broke down and cried. He pushed away images of Evelyn, tied up and blindfolded, alone and frightened. He clung to the idea that her disappearance was nothing more than her hitching a ride to the next bus station, for anything else made no sense whatsoever. But he'd not rest until he found her, and that included looking at every conceivable angle of possibilities.

He suddenly realized he'd succumbed to an old habit: grinding his teeth. Was it the intense headache that instigated the grinding, or was it the grinding that triggered the headache? The chicken or the egg syndrome brought a momentary smile. Evelyn generally made him aware of this unconscious tendency. A flash of her frightened face sent a shudder through his body.

Desperation initiates a plethora of emotions: anger, determination, fear, but sometimes capitulation and lethargy. A surge of resolve shot through his soul. He had found Miss Ann when she had gone missing last year; he would find Evelyn. How? He didn't know.

Waiting. He wasn't geared for this, but he was not in charge. He sought ways to distract from the anxiety. Resting his forehead in his open palms brought some relief. The warmth? Was it reminiscent of his mother's tender touch, etched deeply in his psyche? He'd developed this specific maneuver while he was sheriff in Ohio. While sitting at his desk, pondering a difficult case, he always rested his forehead in his open palms. Deputies accused him of napping, which he didn't deny, for it was a subtle way to pray in a hectic environment. His clouded thoughts needed the breath of Jehovah to part the prevailing waters and bring clarity and direction.

Another hour passed.

Sheriff Flin's snoring rattled the otherwise quiet office, ending Harry's reflection. He ran his fingers slowly through his thinning hair and massaged his stiffened neck muscles. Inactivity was sometimes the right tactic, at other times tragic. Knowing when to act and when to be patient could be a split-second, life-determining decision. A vision of little Eddie's lifeless body suddenly clouded his resolve. A melancholic moment seized him. What if he could not find her? With little Eddie, he was simply too late. The thought seemed unbearable.

Harry pressed his fingers tightly against his ears to drown out Flin's snoring. Though a good cop, Flin was wired with a lower voltage than Harry, but he could get the job done. Eventually. The "eventually" part worried Harry. Time was ticking away, and time was what he needed most right now. He had to get the Buffords to talk.

More than likely someone other than the Buffords was behind the plot, and he had a hunch who that would be. If he stirred the pot long enough, Cutshaw and Jenkins would simmer to the surface. Those were the only two with whom he had any beef. The Buffords were probably paid, bribed, or somehow coerced to stalk and nab Evelyn. They headed north and then backtracked through Shenandoah County and back into Rockingham County. Somewhere along the way they … no, he would not go there. Evelyn was resourceful, a survivor. She would have outwitted them. Their alibi wasn't as airtight as they thought, and given the chance, he would get the truth out of them. He had to be careful as to not overstep his bounds with Flin, who toed the line when it came to investigations. The head dunking in cold water for the Buffords was a stretch for Flin, but necessity is the mother of invention—or was it anger overriding reason.

Where else could Evelyn be if not abducted? If they kidnapped her, what did they do with her? She could be tied up in an abandoned shed or cave somewhere in either Shenandoah or Rockingham counties, way more than a thousand square miles of land. But where? And why? What did they want with her? Only one reason made any sense: to get at him they took Evelyn. Was this somehow tied in with the recent discovery of his father's whereabouts? Still, how could he be sure it was his father? Odds were likely it was not; rather, Cutshaw had descended deeper into the quagmire of evil.

Irene arrived at eight so Flin sent her to pick up some do-nuts. The all-night vigil left them exhausted. Flin fell back asleep at his desk. Harry could not sleep.

Irene returned with the donuts. Flin downed three and followed up with two cups of coffee. Harry did not eat. He paced.

With Evelyn's safety—or life—at stake, Harry couldn't chance the Buffords stalling by lying. "Can I talk with them, Sheriff?"

"Talk, or interrogate?" He bit into a donut and wiped the creme filling from his chin with the back of his hand, before resigning to the need of his handkerchief, which he struggled to retrieve from his hip pocket from a sitting position while balancing a donut oozing creme. He stood and jerked the hankie from his pocket and wiped his chin.

"Talk, not interrogate. You can be with me," Harry said. He tried to spare Flin's dignity by retrieving his own handkerchief and wiping his entire face and neck.

"I let slide your caper in Sam's bar last year, Harry. That could have turned out disastrous, and you know it. We're not gonna repeat that fiasco."

"But it worked."

"Could've backfired, so I ain't gonna—" Flin stopped in mid-sentence and grabbed the phone. "Sheriff's Department."

Harry stood and stuffed the hankie back in his pocket.

"When." Flin's concern was obvious.

Maneuvering toward Flin's desk, Harry tilted his head to hear the caller's message.

"Okay. Be there within the hour."

"What?" Harry arched his shoulders and twisted his neck from side-to-side until the joints cracked.

"Bad news. Jack Brady's been shot. Critical. Ambulance headed there now."

"How'd it happen?"

"He had failed to answer some urgent calls from the state house, so a state trooper checked in on him, found him unconscious

135

in that massive library of his. Doesn't Miss Ann work for him, cleaning?"

"Yes, but—"

"I'm afraid she's the number one suspect."

"No way, Sheriff. You know better—"

"They're holding her for questioning."

"That girl would never hurt a flea, let alone hurt another human being. They've got this all wrong."

"Sorry, Harry." Flin placed a hand on Harry's shoulder. "The trooper found her sitting in the room where Brady was shot … babbling incoherently … a gun beside her."

"She wouldn't know how to use a gun, Sheriff."

"Let's hope Brady survives to tell us otherwise. You want to come with me, Harry?"

Harry studied his fingernails for a long moment. "I don't mind waiting here."

"I bet you don't. No way I'm gonna leave you here alone with them Bufford boys, especially now. Come along or let me drop you off at your place on the way."

"I'll go along."

Chapter Twenty-four

The siren wailed as Flin maneuvered the sharp turns twisting up the side of Great North Mountain. He downshifted into first gear as the engine groaned from the steep ascent. Harry glanced out the passenger window, and emotions rushed from the mere sight of the sheer drop over which Brady's car had careened last fall. The brakes to Brady's Studebaker had failed on the s-curve, the result of Jenkins' butler tinkering with the brake line. Brady, quite shaken and badly bruised, had miraculously survived the accident. Harry was pleased to have played an important role in saving Brady's life. His optimism didn't run that high now, for the report of Brady's condition was not good.

The morning sun cast a strobe effect through the trees, creating in Harry a sense of dizziness. Or was it the lack of sleep? Harry glanced at Flin, then closed his eyes and leaned his head against the back of the seat to ease the effect and the escalating throbbing inside his front skull. The car swerved, startling Harry, and he caught the peripheral of a pickup that zipped past. He suddenly realized they were dangerously close to the edge of the precipice.

"Doggone driver." Flin braked as if momentarily considering giving chase.

That was the closest to cursing Harry could recall coming from Flin. Though most accepted the word as slang, short of a swear word, it was one of those euphemisms Harry avoided, since its use replaced a word he would never say. Perhaps he interpreted Paul's reference to abstaining from all appearance of evil a bit too rigid. He wasn't judging Flin, and he held a deep respect for this man, completely devoted to his task of serving and protecting the community. Flin was opened-minded in a bigoted world. And fair. Always fair.

Some of Flin's manners reminded Harry of himself. He had loved his work as a lawman, though it sometimes conflicted with his religious commitment. He'd learned to manage the conflict but not without some regrets. How does the adrenaline rush of breaking up a barroom brawl fit into "turning the other cheek?" He sometimes wondered if moving back to Virginia was more an escape than a thought-out plan. Perhaps he had retired too soon. He couldn't deny that he enjoyed this moment, the energy and intrigue. There was a difference back then and now, for this situation had gotten more personal than he'd ever experienced while sheriff in Ohio. If only things had gone a little differently in Ohio. He impulsively tendered his resignation, mostly from embarrassment over Evelyn's antics on the jailhouse grounds.

That seemed ages ago, and enough time had elapsed since the incident happened that he no longer felt embarrassed. He had told the story a hundred times and laughed every time at his tale. A quirky Mrs. Marshall had complained to Evelyn that their daughter, Doris, had assaulted her defenseless little boy. "My little Jimmy tried to defend himself, but he was no match for that wildcat daughter of yours. Almost scratched his eyes out." Evelyn knew her daughter had been raised among four brothers, and she had learned to scuffle for survival.

Evelyn apologized profusely to the woman for Doris' unruly behavior and assured her she would punish her for such insolence. With her daddy being a public figure, they certainly lived in a glass house, and she had to realize some measure of responsibility. That evening Evelyn confronted Doris, who admitted her misdeeds but defended her action as justifiable cause. "He picked on me one time too many in front of the entire class," Doris argued. To which Evelyn retorted, "Sticks and stones, girl. You can't go around hitting people every time they insult you." Doris clung to her self-defense mode. "He said I was the daughter of a poor jailer. Said that's where I belonged, in jail with the rest of the jailbirds, not in the classroom with other kids."

Harry remained silent as Evelyn took a belt to Doris, which still pained him to think about, and must have left scars in Doris and Evelyn's memories. Doris sulked for hours, but Evelyn made no apology for the whipping. A few days later she saw Mrs. Marshall and informed her the situation had been dealt with by means of a firm hand. "Your son shouldn't have any trouble with my daughter ever again."

Pleased with the outcome, Mrs. Marshall introduced a boy, gawking from behind her, as being her son who had been so dreadfully mistreated. The boy stood taller than Doris by a good six inches and was twice Doris's weight. Evelyn greeted the boy, whereupon, he unwisely displayed a flaunting grin.

"Your little boy seems much bigger than I assumed by your description," Evelyn challenged the smug Mrs. Marshall.

"Are you calling me a liar?" she retorted.

The resulting altercation became Upper Sandusky gossip for weeks, and it remained history until, well, Harry hoped people had forgotten by now. The ladies' circles buzzed about how the young Evelyn Weatherholtz, wife of the county sheriff, thrashed that busybody Marshall woman all over the courthouse lawn. Some joked about running Evelyn for sheriff instead of Harry.

At the time, her actions humiliated Harry. He said little to her about the brawl but served out his term and quietly moved his family to the Shenandoah Valley: far from his humiliation, back to his place of birth and to the native soil that cradled his mother.

Harry corralled his wandering thoughts as the gears groaned under the strain of the incline, until the cruiser completely stalled. Flin struggled to shift the engine back into first, switching between brake and clutch as the car momentarily coasted backward and into the stone-strewn ditch. Flin popped the clutch, and the tires smoked as they re-engaged the blacktop. The combined smell of brake, clutch and tires permeated the car.

Even under the negative circumstances of his departure from Ohio, Harry was glad to be back in Virginia. He could now laugh at the long ago incident of his wife. Things work together for good, he mused, reflecting upon a verse from Paul's New Testament letter to the Romans. Ohio had been good to him, but with all its benefits, it could not compare with the grandeur that engulfed him daily and the tranquility nature afforded. The surrounding George Washington National Forest reflected the beauty of this vast Appalachian wilderness bordering three states. The mountain-view reflected its Creator, and such sights dwarfed life's dilemmas.

The colonial mansion played peekaboo among the trees for the last mile of the ascent. It rose majestically white, nestled among a pine grove that perched on a precipice overlooking the valley. Flin cut the siren, killed the ignition and coasted into the driveway of Brady's newly acquired residence. The crunching of gravel against tires stopped, and the sudden quietness gave a momentary tranquility, which quickly faded with the activity of the investigation. Uniforms of various colors swarmed the yard, going in and out of the front entrance, searching and guarding and gesturing.

"We've got the big boys to contend with, Harry." Flin sighed. "Let's see what they can teach us … or what trouble we can stir up." He chuckled.

Flin's light-heartedness encouraged Harry. The past year he had become a close friend, something many lawmen lacked. Their position often placed them aloof, somewhat self-imposing, for every citizen was capable of criminal activity. It was much easier to arrest an acquaintance than it was a friend, so many kept all but family at arm's length.

They retrieved their hats from the dash and stepped from the cruiser. Harry strolled behind, while Flin headed toward the front door. A cool wind whistled through the towering pines. Such a peaceful place! Harry had seen mansions like this in the wealthy farming community of Upper Sandusky, Ohio, but none of them compared with the stunning scene that loomed below him, shrouded by the dense morning mist. And now another crime has shrouded the peace of the valley. Would it ever end? None of this made sense. Who would shoot Jack Brady? And why? He was such a likable man. And why this at the same time Evelyn went missing? Were the two related? Coincidental? Not likely.

Harry caught up with Flin, who had stopped to chat with one of the state troopers, and they proceeded toward the front door. "Ugly thing, ain't it," Flin said as he lifted and dropped the brass clapper of the grotesque gargoyle staring at them from the massive oak door.

A state trooper swung open the door and greeted them with a firm handshake. The trooper stepped aside and waved them in. Their footsteps on the oak floor echoed in the giant foyer. They paused and observed the splendor of the wood-paneled walls and ornate ceiling craftsmanship.

"Brady's done moved uptown." Flin scratched his jowl as he gawked at the surroundings. "Too bad about this."

"Probably got this one figured out for you, Sheriff." The trooper tucked his thumbs inside his pistol belt. "I imagine we'll find her fingerprints all over the gun."

Teary eyed and frightened, Ann appeared in the hallway, head bowed, lead by a trooper. He nudged her onto a settee pushed against the back wall of the foyer. A large, framed painting of Judge Jenkins hung on the wall above her. The front top of her ripped dress hung loosely. She did not look up, but rocked incessantly, her hands—obviously cuffed—behind her back. Harry wanted to rush to her, to kneel at her feet and tell her it would be okay. He wanted to reprimand the trooper for his sternness to her, to justify any action she had done, to herald to the world that this young woman was as innocent as any child. His years of police work over-rode his personal emotions. He could only stare at the pitiful scene before him, wondering, not so much about Miss Ann's guilt—for he knew she was innocent of any crime—but about Jack Brady's secrets. What had he done to cause this tragedy? A political assassination attempt? Or was he just the victim of a random criminal activity? A robbery gone bad? Worse yet, considering the torn dress, had he done something bad to Miss Ann?

A month ago Harry would not have imagined any of this. His biggest concern was the delivery of a new blade for his rebuilt sawmill. He'd planned a productive spring preparing for Miss Ann's house-raising. All this—his supposed father showing up, Evelyn kidnapped, the Buffords in jail as suspects, Brady shot—was too coincidental for it not to be somehow linked together.

Chapter Twenty-five

Evelyn struggled to stay awake. She'd seldom left Bud's side, and never under adverse circumstances. They'd always worked through their differences, generally talking through the problem, or at least she talked. Bud generally remained silent but mentally engaged. He'd never gotten the last word in any argument. Evidently, he'd come to realize a last word from him generally started another argument with her. Bennett blood from her daddy's side boiled in her veins: hot and hasty. Her temper was not a slow boil; it heated instantly, and try as she may to prevent it, it spewed over incessantly. She'd long ago given up on temperament alteration; hers was generally a temperament altercation. She was what she was, and Bud knew.

She now realized her rash decision to visit family in Ohio lacked timing. It was not the pull of family that lured her. She was a Jonah running from her situation, and deep down she knew that wasn't good. Bud had never refused to take her to Ohio, and this time she had denied him the opportunity to see his family, all because of her impetuous decision. All she had to do was give him a couple days' notice—for he couldn't leave the farm abruptly, without planning for the animals—and he would have taken her.

The bus wreck jolted some sense into her, but evidently too late. Twelve hours had passed since the wreck. Where was Bud? If there had been any way she could have anticipated this, she would have acted otherwise.

Surely by now, he would have heard about the accident. Perhaps he'd gone to make peace with his father, if that was possible. Had something happened to him? If not, why didn't he come?

She wiped at the dried blood on her wrist.

Were the others okay? Had they noticed her disappearance? Did Bud even know? Then again, after another one of her impulsive acts, did he even care?

Chapter Twenty-six

Incessant voices babbled on and on. Were they speaking to him? None of the voices sounded familiar. Were they friends or foes? He tried to inject his thoughts, but his lips wouldn't cooperate. Perhaps hand gestures would help. He tried. Why could he not move his arms? A weight held him tight, like a magnet to a metal table, and held him unyieldingly. He shivered underneath what seemed a thin blanket. Please … someone … anyone, can I have another blanket? The thoughts were there, but the words would not come out. He must get free from the bands that held him fast. Intense pain shot through his chest with each breath. Surely they were wondering what had happened. He struggled beneath the blanket, trying to loosen the restrictions on his arms. If he could free his arms, he could communicate what had happened.

Shallow and infrequent breathing relieved the pain. He momentarily opened his eyes. There were three of them: two armed, but one wearing a doctor's uniform. He understood the doctor, but why the policemen. Were they guarding him? Why? Was he a prisoner or being protected? He had to get free, to explain, to warn them.

Tiredness crept in like shadows at twilight. Soft lights beckoned to him, pulling him upward. His spirit hovered, lighter than the magnetic pull that fastened his body. He floated cloud-like and effortlessly slipped from the straps that harnessed his body, as easy as the white, silky, filament of the milkweed that drifts upon the morning zephyrs. The pain subsided as he spiraled toward the appealing light, and in an instant all became peaceful. Fear loosened its grip, and endless space emerged, inviting and intriguing, cloudless and charming. Fading voices, faint and indistinguishable, acquiesced to chimes in the distance that called in a comforting chorus. The music summoned him, and he cordially complied.

A cloud swiftly emerged, dark and ominous. From the cloud a figure appeared, blurry and nondescript, blocking his path. She held a gun. Neither spoke, but he knew what their silence supposed. And the look on her face, the pitiful and pleading face beckoned to him.

The cloud suddenly vanished and the tranquility exploded into chaos: voices around him, someone barking orders, a stranger pounding his chest. Pain jabbed his chest sharper than the bullet that penetrated his body. The throbbing returned, more intense. Memory, like a misty morning over the mountains, remained vague. He struggled to focus and slowly realized he was in a hospital room, that he was the patient. He further grasped that he had expired and they had resuscitated him. He was glad, for he had some unfinished business regarding his house cleaner. He must not die, not now, not like this.

Chapter Twenty-seven

The ceiling lights blinked twice before the room went dark. A flash of lightning momentarily silhouetted images on the far wall, immediately followed by a boom that rattled the building and sent heads ducking. Rain overflowed the gutters, cascading down the side of the building and across the windowpanes. The wall-clock showed seven in the morning, but it looked pitch black outside.

The jail had gotten crowded overnight: two suspected kidnappers, one suspected attempted murderer and a couple drunken blacks who'd gotten in a knife fight down in the bottoms. There was a sixth inmate that concerned Harry the most. He was a suspicious character whom they couldn't identify because he carried a fake drivers license. A deputy had pulled him over for speeding, headed north just outside of town, and he refused to give his true identity. He'd called for an attorney and a bail bondsman. They'd have to release him shortly or book him for some offense other than speeding and driving without a license.

"This ain't good, Harry," Flin's elevated voice competed with the rain pounding the roof, "Evelyn missing and now attempted murder by Miss Ann. I don't like locking her up this way any more than you would. Neither do I want to believe she shot Brady any more than you do." As an afterthought, he added, "But I suspect her prints are on that gun. I assume there's good reason on her part, but no matter what, a black woman shootin' a white man of Brady's status is a conviction for sure in Shenandoah County. She doesn't have a mouse's chance in a snake pit." Flin paced as if Harry was the jury and he was giving a summation.

Large raindrops pelted the windowpane and formed multiple streams that coursed the outer glass and pooled on the window ledge. Harry unconsciously traced one of the streams, then wiped away the water seeping through the cracked seal and into the inner ledge. He turned abruptly. "There are logical explanations for prints on the gun, without her being guilty."

"Such as?"

"The gun was laying there and she picked it up when she found Jack lying in a pool of blood."

"You're suggesting suicide?"

"Not necessarily. An accident. An intruder. Her story makes sense. She instinctively picked it up without giving thought to consequences."

"And you think a jury of twelve white men will believe that?"

"Let's find the real culprit, then they won't have to make that decision."

"Don't talk down to me, Harry. My deputies are all over this, and we have the state boys involved. It's not like we're not doing our job."

"I know, Sheriff, but I'm tired of being cooped up in this office without progress."

"Comes with the job. Investigations take time. You, of all people, know that."

"Then let's go on what we already know, beginning with Ann. She's never lied to me, not once. Why would she start now? And motive? Sheriff, where's the motive? Brady had given her a job. Helped shed her of Cutshaw. No need under the sun to kill him."

"You've got some good points, and …" he studied his fingernails, "one thing really concerns me, and that's the torn dress. Maybe some kind of self-defense alibi … but I can't perceive of Jack Brady doing anything to harm her. I always felt he was a good fella, that Jack. Still, it's unlikely that'd fly with a jury. Prosecutor will beat that with his hands tied behind his back and sittin' in a corner wearing a dunce's hat. She's in a heap of trouble, Harry, no matter how you look at it. I'm sorry for you … for her … for Jack." Flin lowered his voice as the rainstorm eased.

Harry paced. "Where could she have gotten the gun to shoot him? That makes her story viable. It was on the floor and she ignorantly picked it up, maybe concerned for her own safety. Wouldn't you have picked up a gun if you thought an intruder was still in the house?"

"Good point." Flin dropped into his chair and propped his muddy heels on the desk.

"And what about the fellow in the back … fake license … refusing to identify himself … showing up around the same time someone of Jack's position was shot—?" Harry argued for reasonable doubt.

"You're suggesting a hit man? Why would anyone want Brady dead? And who?"

"Judge Jenkins … Cutshaw … someone he's prosecuted … shall I go on? Prosecutors are the most popular sort for retaliation by criminals. You've been in this business long enough to know that, Sheriff."

"Yeah, but Brady's a pretty likable guy around here. I doubt anybody's gunnin' for him. And the evidence we got points toward Miss Ann, not an outsider. Unless Brady survives and clears her name, she's our number one suspect, Harry. No two ways about it, a jury will convict her without battin' an eye. You was a sheriff and you know good and well that's how it works. She has no alibi, and the torn dress is not a defense for a black woman unless she was raped or something, and she hasn't indicated that at all. No sir, her torn dress is just more proof she shot a white man because she was just mad at him. He probably got a little rough with her 'cause she didn't sweep the floor like she was paid to do ... or something like that. And Brady was not just any white man; he was an important man."

Harry was losing the case rapidly. He closed his eyes to concentrate. "Is it just a coincidence that Evelyn turns up missing, and Ann is entrapped in a murder attempt within a twenty-four hour period? Or could it be a deliberate plan concocted by Cutshaw and Jenkins? You know those two haven't forgiven Brady for ending their malicious scheme. And Evelyn could be a pawn for them to get back at me, or you. It's no secret around here that you and I have become friends ... of a sort." Harry paused to allow Flin time to digest his ramblings. "And there's something else I haven't told you." He opened his eyes to discover a dozing Flin.

The rain had stopped and a sunbeam illuminated the mud on the bottom of Flin's boots.

Harry nudged the boot. Flin stirred.

"There's something else I haven't told you." Harry's elevated voice brought Flin's boots slamming to the floor.

"What?" Flin tossed him an irritated look.

"I received a note from Cutshaw suggesting my father is alive and hiding out in the mountains where he's been all these years. Never died in prison as we were told."

"That's a far-fetched story."

"If bribery could breach the Wall of China, it could certainly penetrate a state penitentiary."

Flin tossed a pencil across the room. "Is that what my stopping Cutshaw and checking his mileage was all about? You think he's behind all this?"

"Yes ... at least partially ... he and Jenkins. Something's going down right under our noses, and we can't see it. Why not let Miss

Ann go until you sort it all out? She's frightened, and she doesn't deserve this. Plus, she's not a flight risk."

"I beg to differ, Harry. We 'bout never found her last time she took off, and—"

The back door to the holding area opened and Deputy Tom March barged into the office waving a small piece of paper. "You need to take a look at this, Sheriff."

"What you got?" Flin asked.

"A photo of a black woman and her little boy. We found it in Ann's dress pocket. She says it's her mother and brother, and she confessed to taking it from a book in Brady's library. That's where Brady was shot, in his library. Right?"

Harry retrieved the picture before Flin uncoiled his legs and got up from his chair. The lad certainly resembled little Eddie, and the woman resembled Miss Ann, but older. He handed the photo to Flin.

Flin studied it, flipped it to the backside, then held it underneath his desk lamp before returning it to his deputy. "Enter this into evidence, March."

"Yes, sir."

"Evidence is stacking up, Harry. What would a picture of Ann's brother and mother be doing in Brady's library? That has to be her mother, since it looks just like 'er. And she's confessed to taking it. Why else would she steal it? You wanted motive. Then here's motive and more motive."

"But why would she confess to taking the photograph if she was guilty of shooting Brady? She would simply have claimed it as her own. Doesn't make sense. Too many unanswered questions." Harry rubbed the graying stubble on his chin.

"Sorry, Harry, but our Ann girl might have asked Brady some tough questions, like why he had a picture of her momma and little brother. And evidently, he didn't give her answers that satisfied. You wanted motive, Harry. How about anger? Revenge?" Flin sighed.

"Deputy March, I'm headin' over to Grandma's Kitchen for a bite to eat. When Irene gets here, have her get Miss Clara Clayborn on the phone, from over't the prosecutor's office, and see if the new prosecutor is available. He'll want to hear about this."

Chapter Twenty-eight

The cane offered him some relief as each limp shot penetrating pain from his knee to his hip socket. He dropped a briefcase with a thud onto the hearth. The lid sprung open, and papers scattered onto the floor. Cursing, he whacked the wall with the cane before tossing it atop the mantle. Clinging to the mantle with one hand, while clutching his knee with the other, grimacing, he slowly lowered himself to a squatted position, his bum leg outstretched to one side. He snatched up some of the papers and wadded them loosely before spreading them onto the charred grates. He struck a match and blew gently on the smoldering paper until flames caused him to jerk his face away. He fell back onto his seat and settled into a routine of scanning each paper before wadding and tossing it into the flames.

His salary wasn't the greatest, but it beat lounging in a filthy jail any day of the week. His was a past of guarded secrets; perhaps that was why he delighted in concealing secrets for those to whom he felt indebted. He paused and stared into the flames shooting up the flue. With a sense of satisfaction, he wiped at sweat beading his brow.

A paper caught his attention. He studied its contents before double folding and tucking it into his suit coat pocket. He couldn't suppress a smile. One never knows when he may have to stand alone in defense against accusations. An ace up the sleeve is always comforting for a man whose everyday life is a gamble.

He struggled to his feet and limped to the library. The book was removed from its normal place on the shelf, but he found it on the shelf just above. He anxiously flipped through its pages. Nothing. He turned it sideways and held it by the spine, shaking it erratically to remove inserted items—again, nothing. Once more he leafed page by page, but the picture was missing. He tucked the book under his arm, walked back to the fireplace, and started to toss it into the flames. Instead, he placed it inside a pocket of the briefcase.

The eastern skyline slowly loosened its eclipse of the sun, and the golden sphere rose like a hot air balloon over the horizon, erasing the shadows from the greening valley. He shielded his eyes with his hand and soaked in the scenery. Breathtaking, even after a thousand times! It elicited a memory of a sunrise in another time and a distant place.

He closed the door behind him, clicked the lock and tossed a smile toward the gargoyle. "Goodbye, ole chap. I'll probably not be seeing you again. Keep a proper guard over the place." He slipped the key into his pocket and walked the familiar path to the cliff's edge. As he stared across the valley, on second thought, he retrieved the key from his pocket and flung it into the abyss.

Chapter Twenty-nine

"Miss Compton, may I use your phone?" Harry eased into the metal chair beside her desk. He had declined Flin's offer for breakfast at Grandma's Kitchen. Food was the farthest thing from his mind. Flin had left him at the office with strict instructions not to bother the Buffords.

"Of course you may, just as soon as you start calling me Irene, instead of Miss Compton. We've worked together for what … going on over a year now, and you're still calling me Miss Compton?"

"Old habit, I suppose."

She slid the phone across the desk.

"Thank you, Miss … I meant Irene."

She smiled. "Not that difficult, huh?"

Flin returned. His mood much improved. "Did you contact Clara?"

"Yes, sir. Prosecutor can see you tomorrow after lunch. Made a pot of fresh coffee."

"Thank, you. Think I'll have some."

Harry withdrew a piece of paper from his wallet and studied it before dialing the number. Holding his hand on the mouthpiece he said, "I've got to get someone to feed the livestock. They're

155

probably feeling abandoned—Yes, hello. Pastor Carnahan? This is Harry Weatherholtz." After a brief pause, he continued, "I hate to trouble you, but I have a situation that needs some attention, and I thought you might send up a little prayer for me and also direct me to someone within the parish that I could hire to do an errand." He repositioned himself on the metal chair. "No, I'm okay, but Evelyn is missing—"

Flin tried to appear as not eavesdropping as he poured coffee into an oversized cup and dialogued with a deputy. Irene studied her nails and offered no input into the discussion.

"You what?" Harry leaped to his feet. He closed his eyes and lifted his face toward the ceiling. He replaced the phone and sat down. The chatter in the room grew dreadfully quiet. He held up an assuring hand to the glaring faces.

"What's going on, Harry." Flin plopped his cup onto the desk, splashing coffee onto his hand. "Ouch!"

Irene grabbed a tissue box and rushed to the rescue.

Harry sighed as he scratched his whiskered cheeks. Then he wiped at the tears streaming his cheeks. "Can you believe it?"

"What," Flin asked.

"Evelyn's home. Safe."

Chapter Thirty

Harry rushed into the living room and tossed his hat onto the sofa. "Evelyn?"

She appeared sheepishly in the kitchen doorway. "Where in the world have you been? Breakfast is cold."

He stared at her, speechless.

She smiled. "I missed your silence, so I just got off the bus and hitched a ride home. It's a long story, but the bus wrecked just outside of town, I guess just long enough to clear my head. I hitched a ride with the—"

"Carnahans, not the Buffords."

"The Buffords? What are you talking about, Bud?"

"It's a longer story than yours. No one knew where you were. We thought the Buffords had kidnapped you. They're in jail. I come close to. …" He pulled her close and hugged her tightly.

She gently pushed him to arm's length. "The Buffords? Kidnapped? Are you losing your mind, Bud?"

"No, I'm thinking clearer than I have in a long time. Remember that song and the story we heard the other day on the radio about the poor fella down in Oklahoma whose wife had left him, and the DJ kept playing his words over and over."

"You picked a fine time to leave me, Lucille? What of it?"

"Well, it sounded a bit sappy at the time, but I think I know just how that fella felt. Except, now I realize you didn't really leave me. I can't imagine. … " He leaned his head against her shoulder and breathed deeply.

"Bud Weatherholtz, what's come over you? Never heard you be so sentimental in all my years married to you. Guess I should leave more often." She pulled away. "Oh, my, you're bleeding again. You've got to get that sore checked. And you've bled all over my good dress."

"Sorry." He wiped at the red spot on her shoulder."

"I'll do that." She snatched the handkerchief, touched it to her tongue and dabbed the blood spot.

"I'd best go feed the livestock." He picked up his hat and started for the door.

"Not till you've eaten something yourself. I'll warm up the food while you attend to that sore on your forehead."

He wiped his forehead near the right temple, and blood gushed into his hand. Evelyn grabbed the handkerchief and pressed it against the wound, but the blood soaked through and ran down his face.

"Dear Lord," Evelyn said. "Something's bad wrong, Bud."

An instant queasiness brought saliva to his mouth. He knew what was coming next. He stumbled toward the bathroom, but the room spun, his knees buckled and he fell hard against Evelyn. They toppled onto the floor.

Chapter Thirty-one

Paramedic John Cushman climbed into the converted '56 Ford Sedan and settled into the jump seat beside the patient's wife. He put pressure on the wound just above the right temple and changed the four-by-four-inch gauze every couple minutes. A pile of soaked gauze reflected too much blood loss, which caused the blood pressure to drop dangerously low.

The wife balanced a navy blue vinyl purse on her lap as she wiped at blood splotches on the front of her dress. She seemed to favor her right arm, a large bruise just below the elbow. He offered her a reassuring smile.

"How'd you get that bruise?"

"He fell against me, and we both hit the floor hard. Tried to brace my fall with my arm."

"We'll have the doctor take a look at that. Your husband's bleeding is my biggest concern right now. You say it was just a sore that broke open, ma'am?"

"It was scabbed over. He's had it a long time, but its never bled like this."

"What's his first name again?"

"Bud … I mean Harry … nickname's Bud."

"Harry, can you hear me? I need you to stay with me. Harry … Bud … you hang in there. We're taking you to the hospital. Your wife … Mrs. Weatherholtz—"

"Evelyn."

"Evelyn is with me in the ambulance. Squeeze my hand if you hear me."

"He just started bleeding and collapsed. I know it's just a sore, but I didn't know what else to do. It wouldn't stop bleeding and when he passed out—"

"You did the right thing, ma'am."

"I don't drive so I was lucky a neighbor stopped in who went and called you."

"That's why we're here. Any past medical history I should know about?" He folded the blood soaked gauze and reached for another to replace it.

"Heart trouble. Had a heart attack."

"When?"

"Last year."

"Is he on any type of medication?"

"Blood thinner."

"Warfarin?"

"Yes."

"That's probably the explanation for the bleeding." He shook his head.

"Not good medicine?" Evelyn asked.

"I'm not saying that. It's okay for what it's designed to do, but in some cases it works against us, causing excessive bleeding."

He had seen this multiple times before. Approved for medical use in 1954, Warfarin had worked well for patients who had suffered a stroke or heart attack. It worked as an anticoagulant to thin the blood and prevent clots from forming. Ironically, the primary ingredient was a poison first discovered in spoiled animal feed, where it existed naturally in plants, specifically sweet clover. Manufacturers originally introduced it to the market as a rat poison, but the concept took a medicinal twist in a research center at the University of Wisconsin. Warfarin got its name from an acronym for the foundation that funded the research: Wisconsin Alumni Research Foundation, thus "Warf" with a medicine-sounding ending. As most medicines have side effects, Warfarin had to be monitored, for it sometimes caused excessive bleeding. This particular case could just be the bleeding sore, but internal bleeding was always a concern. That was a call he couldn't make, but the doctor would order tests.

"Hey Pete," he yelled to the driver through the opened sliding window, "radio Shenandoah Memorial and tell them they may need a coagulant ready. He's on Warfarin. Losing a lot of blood from an old wound."

The monitors revealed concern: the blood pressure was plunging, while the heart rate accelerated. He didn't want to alarm the wife, but time was critical. The patient's ashen face revealed wrinkles of the years. What was his occupation? Probably retired. She appeared much younger. What was she thinking with that stern facial feature, stringent posture, clasped hands and faraway stare? He wanted to offer a reassuring touch, but he didn't want to give false hope. The medical world dealt with realities.

"Is he going to be alright, Mr. Cushman?" Her question startled him.

"Almost there," he said. "He'll be in good hands at Shenandoah Memorial."

She didn't respond.

The siren whined a forlorn tune, not unlike the taut strings stroked slowly by an Appalachian fiddler. Certain sounds of the Shenandoah play a somber and lonely tune: the midnight whistle of a distant train; the chant of a whip-poor-will on a warm, moonlit night; bagpipes at a Virginia military ceremony. The siren, though meant to alarm, was one of the loneliest sounds, for it always alluded to sorrow and pain and death. Cars pulled onto the brim, and folks stood attentively alongside the road and on front porches. Wondering.

The driver cut the siren as they turned into the entrance to Shenandoah Memorial. A couple attendants dressed in white scrubs rushed from the emergency room to meet them.

Cushman hopped from the ambulance and gave the attendants a subdued greeting as he handed the clipboard to the female. She studied the information and glanced through the open door at the patient. "This is interesting," she whispered. "We already have another patient named Weatherholtz. Old enough to be this one's father."

"Name's been around a long time in the valley. Just sign at the bottom, you take charge and we'll be on our way."

He handed her the carbon copy, tossed the clipboard onto the ambulance floor and extended his hand to help the wife from the ambulance.

"Thank you." She feigned a smile.

"Best of luck to you and the husband."

He helped unload the gurney and watched as the entourage of white uniforms disappeared behind the double doors. This job was done; he would now go to the next. His life as a paramedic was sometimes rewarding and sometimes full of despair. This particular run was a tossup.

Chapter Thirty-two

"We'll have another Norfolk on our hands if we don't handle this right, Sheriff."

"And just what do you suggest is right, Mr. Mayor?"

"We don't want them civil righters marchin' our streets and sittin' our food counters suggestin' we think we're better'n them. We have to be cautious regarding their rights, but we don't want 'em thinkin' they got entitlements they don't. We are all equal but separated by certain God-given privileges. You understand what I mean. 'Course I don't have nothin' against them personally. I fought alongside them in the war, but we all have got to know our place in society. It was God who decided birthrights, and we can't change it."

Mayor Tom Schaeffer had barged into Flin's office at the eight o'clock shift change, and he had changed his political position half a dozen times within the hour. Flin had dealt with the mayor in several situations, but he had never seen him as adamant as he was regarding Miss Ann's incarceration. His reference to Norfolk was the special three-judge panel of Federal District judges that declared the policies of Senator Byrd's Massive Resistance as unconstitutional. Their finding ruled that this was simply an attempt to circumvent the laws that prevent public school segregation. Some public schools had closed their doors to avoid desegregation, with the idea of private education, which eliminated education for most black students. In 1956, one of the Stanley plans policies of the state prevented state funding for any integrated school, and the governor was given the authority to close any school he desired. A three-member Pupil Placement Board determined where each student attended school, their decision mostly based on color. It brought down the wrath of the NAACP in Virginia. The Jim Crow ship had run aground on Virginian soil.

"You can relax, Mayor, for I'm denying no one their civil rights, white or colored." Flin struggled for calmness, yet firmness was necessary when dealing with Schaeffer. "I'll let her go the moment the prosecuting attorney or a judge says such. Until then, no rights are being violated according to the law, and I'm sworn to uphold the law."

"I know that, Sheriff, but I also know them rights-mongers will be breathing down our necks, making us look like we're doing something wrong."

"Are you suggesting I release my prisoner?"

"Course not. I never said that. Still, unless you've got sufficient proof you'd best consider letting her go free. Maybe see if she might have relatives she could visit up north till this thing blows over."

"As much as I like this girl and would love to release her, we have evidence enough to hold her for attempted murder."

"Not trying to tell you how to do your job."

"Appreciate that, Mayor. So what are you suggesting?"

"I'm just saying—"

The door squeaked open, and the local black pastor entered. Flin had known Pastor Harris for years, a nice man. But lately, he had become vocal regarding the civil rights of the local blacks. A distinguished looking man carrying a black leather attaché case followed Harris. His dark—with gray pinstripes—double-breasted suit spoke of a newcomer and of significance.

"Here we go," Schaeffer whispered as he muffled a cough. "Tried to warn you."

"May I help you, gentlemen?" Irene's greeting seemed overly friendly for her generally matter-of-fact reception.

"I'm Pastor Harris from the local AME church."

"Thought I recognized you, Pastor," Irene responded. "Nice to see you again."

"And you are?" Harris asked.

"Irene Compton."

"Nice to meet you, Miz Compton."

"You here to see Miss Ann, I presume?"

"Yes."

"Good to see you, Pastor Harris. It's been a while." Mayor Schaeffer marched quickly across the room, his hand extended.

"Nice to see you again, sir." Harris' resonating voice commanded attention.

"Sheriff Flin and I were just discussin' how this situation with the … with Miss Ann is so terribly tragic. We're doing everything we can to get to the bottom of things. May I ask who your associate is?"

"Dedrick Shelton." The distinguished man spoke for himself.

"Mr. Shelton. A delight to meet you." The mayor shook his hand.

"Thank you, sir. And you are?"

"Tom Schaeffer … Mayor Schaeffer … Tom. I assume you're not from around here. I tend to know most everyone, being mayor and all."

"No, I'm not from here. Actually, this is my first time ever in Woodstock. A lovely little town you have here, Mayor."

"Well, thank you, sir." After an awkward silence, the mayor continued. "So, you're from?"

"Washington."

"D.C.?" Schaeffer asked.

"Yes. Pastor Harris contacted me."

"An attorney, I presume?" Schaeffer continued, his voice quivering.

"Yes. Bradford, Pearson and Shelton." He withdrew a business card from his pocket and handed it to the mayor.

"Oh, I see." Schaeffer studied the card for another awkward moment. "Well, I have to be going. Got a busy day ahead of me. Sheriff Flin will take care of any requests you might have. If ever I'm up your way maybe I can stop in and say hello." He studied the card again and slipped it into his suit pocket. "Nice meeting you," he called over his shoulder as he exited the building.

"Nice man, Mayor Schaeffer … maybe a little talkative but a nice fella," Flin said, as he broke the uncomfortable silence and strode across the room. "Sheriff Flin at your service. Nice to see you again, Pastor. Miss Ann will be pleased to see you. Welcome to Woodstock, Mr. Shelton."

Shelton handed Flin a business card. "Thank you, Sheriff. I'll be representing your prisoner, Miss Ann. Her full name is Mary Ann Shaver, I believe."

"My congregation took up a collection and retained Mr. Shelton to represent her. I'm sure you understand, especially since she was terribly mistreated for years in the welfare system, not to mention her brother's killer wasn't served justice in this county just last year. Every individual has a right to fairness, no matter the color of their skin. Don't you agree?" Harris' words seemed sharp.

"Certainly." Flin studied Shelton's business card. "In all honesty, gentlemen, I want Miss Ann to have the best legal representation possible, and I'm glad you and your congregation are assisting her." He hesitated as he studied the business card. "My only concern is the five initials on this business card: NAACP. I want to be upfront, for this case isn't about race, this case is about someone breaking the law by shooting another person with the intent to wound or kill. That's all. Nothing more; nothing less."

"I understand your position, Sheriff, I really do. Still, you have to appreciate mine." Shelton opened his attaché case. "I believe all men should be treated according to the law, so I have some questions regarding the arrest, and I'd like to know the grounds on which you are incarcerating my client?" Shelton pulled a legal notepad from the attaché case and retrieved a pen from inside his suit pocket.

"She's the prime suspect in an attempted murder, and not just anyone, it was our former prosecutor, Jack Brady. That's reason enough to hold anyone."

"Did you read the Miranda Rights to her?"

"Yes, well not me personally, but I'm sure a state trooper did."

"Name please?"

"I don't know, but I can get that for you."

"Please do. Did she confess to the shooting?"

"No, at least not to me."

"Weapon?"

"A .25 caliber handgun."

"Hers?"

"We assume not."

"Whose?"

"We're working on that."

"Witnesses?"

"State trooper found her with the wounded body in the room. She was holding the gun, no, the gun lay beside her."

"Did anyone see her actually holding the gun?"

"No."

"Fire the gun?"

"No."

"Did she offer any explanation?"

"Not at the time, just some babbling."

"Babbling? Was she in shock?"

"Not sure. Perhaps. She was rocking back and forth and … you know … babbling about something."

"Did you offer her any kind of medical treatment then or since?"

"Now listen, I'm not the one being accused, Mr. Shelton."

"And I didn't intend to do such. You yourself said you wanted her to have good legal representation. That's what I'm trying to do. So, just answer my question. Did she receive medical treatment?"

"No."

"Why not?"

"Not sure but probably should have."

"Because of the babbling?"

"Yes … and. …"

"And what?"

"The top part of her dress was torn … like it had been ripped by someone."

"You're suggesting she may have been defending herself against an attacker?"

"Possibility."

"And you didn't have her examined for physical evidence?"

"I already answered that."

"Why didn't you seek medical attention for her?"

"It all happened so fast, and the state troopers were so convincing with their investigation."

"Have you been questioning her since you brought her in?"

"Some."

"Did she ask for a lawyer?"

"No, sir."

"Did you suggest one?"

"No, sir. But I don't have to do that if her rights have been read."

"I have one final question."

Flin breathed deeply and exhaled deliberately, trying to get his pulse rate to slow. Shelton's pause gave him some relief.

"Are you privy to information that Miss Mary Ann Shaver has been diagnosed as retarded?"

He'd never had a heart attack, but he imagined the spontaneous jucies rushing through his endocrine system could easily trigger one. The truthful answer to the question, as it was asked, was more than enough to exonerate Ann; it was more than enough to incriminate him. And Harry Weatherholtz. And Jack Brady. Why was he holding a young woman in custody who had been classified by a county judge as being retarded? It was one small bit of evidence he had forgotten about, primarily because he knew she was not retarded. But knowing and forgetting are two different items. Ann should have been treated differently than the common prisoner, but she was being held—by him—in the common jail area. He suddenly regretted not pushing harder for an indictment against Jenkins and Cutshaw. Harry and Brady had convinced him otherwise, and he agreed to the termination of the grand jury. He vividly recalled Brady's explanation, "It's a dead-end road we're taking and bumpy to boot." At the time it seemed the right thing to do. Now, like a loosed rabid dog, it had returned to bite him, perhaps ruin him. He could lie, but he had not gotten his job and earned his good reputation by lying. And he would not try to keep it by lying. Still, he didn't want to implicate Harry and Brady.

"I asked you a simple question, Sheriff."

"No, Miss Ann is not retarded. I can vouch for that, and a dozen others can, too."

"That wasn't the question. My question, sir, is about privileged information. Are you privy to information that Miss Mary Ann Shaver has been diagnosed as retarded?"

"I heard something to that effect."

"And you put a babbling young woman, whose upper dress had been torn, and whom you had information suggesting retardation, into your jail without any type of medical or mental evaluation? Care to elaborate?"

"No, sir."

"I suggest you release your prisoner into my legal custody."

If Harry Weatherholtz was here, perhaps this might not have gone so badly. If he'd only listened to Harry and released Miss Ann, this inquisition might have been avoided. A trip to the Weatherholtzs' place might calm his worrisome thoughts. And one of Evelyn's biscuits with sorghum would be mighty tasty. He was starting to lose his taste for sheriffing.

Irene knocked a book from her desk. Shelton turned. "And you'll be called as a witness to this conversation, Miss Compton."

"Don't drag her into this, Mr. Shelton. Pastor Harris, I don't know what to say. It isn't how it all sounds. You know I've been in Miss Ann's corner all along," Flin pleaded.

Pastor Harris showed no sympathy. He'd always been very respectful, even helpful in dealing with the colored community. Had the NAACP folks brainwashed him? Was he misinformed? Was the civil rights movement emboldening a hidden resentment? Or has he seen through the years too much mistreatment of his own kind, and it has boiled over inside his soul?

"Sheriff Flin, I strongly suggest you release Miss Shaver." Shelton replaced his pen inside his coat pocket and placed the legal pad back inside the attaché case.

"I can't do that, sir, not without a court hearing."

"Why not?"

"I believe she shot Mr. Brady. I'm holding her for attempted murder. You'll have to go through the legal channels to get her released. With the extent of her crime, I doubt any judge in the commonwealth will release her; further, I doubt you'll find any grand jury in Old Dominion that will exonerate her at this point."

"So this case is about race. You've made it a civil rights case by your blundering investigation, insistence on incarceration and admittance of previous knowledge of retardation regarding my client. You leave me only one option: see you in court, Sheriff Flin. I'd like to visit with my client now."

"This way, sir."

"On election day, Sheriff, if I were you, I'd make sure my name wasn't on the ballot. On second thought, don't even consider that, for a convicted felon can't be sheriff," Shelton said.

Flin couldn't think of a thing to say as a rebuttal.

Chapter Thirty-three

Pastor Harris had paid Dedrick Shelton with the offering he had collected from his small congregation. He was worried it was insufficient to cover any extended legal expenses, but Shelton didn't seem concerned. Shelton had prepared for more than a hearing. He wanted to make a lot of noise. He was known to quote from the American Revolution. This time it was "the shot heard around the world" quotation he had garnished to fit the occasion. Indeed, he had rallied the troops for the cause. He, Dedrick Shelton—a modern day Paul Revere—shouted out the warning to his brothers. Pastor Harris had acquiesced to his request for a rally at the courthouse, but Harris wasn't sure this was the right approach. He wanted to put pressure on the legal system designed to protect the freedom of all, but he didn't want to make enemies. That could backfire on his parishioners.

Still, this was much more serious than a simple colored girl's rights; this was about a white political figure who had been shot, supposedly by a colored girl. This was national news, not local gossip. And the evidence was strong against her, especially since a state policeman found her in the room with a discharged gun. Harris was worried and couldn't help being so. The girl needed all the help she could get.

Youthful chatter filled the room as a dozen excited teens gathered in what doubled as the pastor's study during the week and a classroom on Sunday. Some sat on battered, folding chairs, while others sat on the pine knotted floor, or squatted with their backs resting against the wall.

Dedrick Shelton assumed Pastor Harris' desk chair, smug and confident behind the gray metal desk. The chair was a cast off from the newly opened Stonewall Jackson High School in neighboring Quicksburg where Harris worked as the school custodian. The chair had not made the cut for furniture good enough to be in a new school building. Harris sat on a worn, orange-velveteen chair facing the desk, thumbing through a picture album Shelton had shared, pictures of recent mistreatment of coloreds around the country.

The Bible says to "judge not," but Harris couldn't help but perceive Shelton as smug and confident, even if that assumption was considered judging. He'd always viewed those two features as the antithesis of Christ's inaugural sermon. But lately, he'd battled an inner struggle regarding Christ's teaching: particularly the meek inheriting the earth. That was a joke in the valley, where his kind hardly owned more than a shack. Meekness and submission had gotten his church parishioners nothing but abuse and disdain from the community. Shelton seemed the exception. He had an office in D.C., drove a fancy car and carried a wad of money in his expensive three-piece suit. Did these come about because of a previously meek and submissive nature, or did he fight to gain what he had? Was his confidence a product of his possessions, or did he acquire his possessions because of his confidence? Or was he just a lucky one? Whatever, that wasn't Harris' concern, especially now; his concern was a scared black girl in a white man's jail. He stared at a photograph in the picture album: Rosa Parks when she was booked into the Montgomery jail. What were her thoughts? Was she scared? Meek? Or just too tired of discrimination to care about what happened to her?

"Nice nameplate." Shelton's comment surprised Harris. Shelton ran his fingers across the wooden nameplate that set on his desk.

"Thank you."

"Samuel Harris. Samuel's a good Bible name. Stood against evil, even in the face of the High Priest, Eli. Beautiful piece of wood. Walnut?" Shelton studied the wood.

"No. It's called purpleheart."

"Really? Never heard of it."

"One of the hardest woods in the world." Harris repositioned himself on the overused chair, a yard sale purchase. He had planned to repair the tear in the arm; he resisted the temptation to try and hide the rip from Shelton.

"Interesting." Shelton picked up the nameplate for a closer look. "I can see a hint of purple. Native timber?"

"No, not grown in North America. It comes from the tropical rainforests of Central and South America."

"But purchased locally?" Shelton checked the bottom of the nameplate as if to discover its history. His interest surprised Harris.

"No. This piece came directly from Brazil."

"And how did you come about it? I ask because I'd love a nameplate made of this wood."

"My grandfather acquired it from his father who worked the forest. He was one of the four million or so slaves imported from Africa to Brazil. Of the total number of African slaves brought to the Americas, around forty percent were sold to masters in Brazil. Slavery wasn't abolished there until 1888, the last country in the western world to abolish slavery. Sorry for the history lesson, which I'm sure you already know."

"History's my favorite subject, next to current events."

"Anyways, that's when my grandfather came to the States. Brought this piece of wood with him, one of his few possessions."

"Wow! And priceless to you?"

"No one's ever made me an offer." He chuckled.

"With a story like that, I may." Shelton replaced the wood and resumed his work.

Harris wiped perspiration from his forehead. Some of the girls fanned themselves with wooden-handled cardboard fans, compliments of the Jackson, Hausher, and Clangdon Funeral Home. Theirs was the most prosperous desegregated business in town. Death seemed to equal the playing field for most. His young daughter had asked him, "Daddy, is there a separate place in heaven for black kids?" He tried to explain the equality of heaven, to which she responded, "Then why do I have to go to a separate playground down here?" He wanted to offer a plausible explanation, but nothing came out right. That's when he made a decision to fight against injustice. His decision wasn't about himself; it was more for her and young women like Ann.

A stack of poster board sat on the corner of the desk, along with a stack of rough-sawed wooden handles to which the poster boards would be stapled. A Bostitch staple gun sat on top of the stack of poster board. Pastor Harris had purchased it, also at a yard sale, but had never had an occasion to use it. The Bostitch name came from a combination of the city of Boston and "stitch," though the company had recently moved to Rhode Island. Harris was a connoisseur of trivia, never passing up an opportunity to read. Mostly he read the discarded magazines in the break room at his job at the school, or from his Bible.

"Could we get a window opened?" Shelton barked.

A young male rushed to the task. "I need a stick to prop it open," he yelled, pointing to the stack of handles.

Another boy darted to grab one of the handles, but Shelton snatched it up and tossed it toward the window.

"Thank you, sir," the youth said, as fresh air filtered into the room through the open window.

"That's much better. Thank you, son," Shelton said, as he wiped his brow with a handkerchief. "Let's go ahead and get started. First of all, I want to express gratitude to Pastor Harris for opening his church and office to us." He paused until the applause stopped. "Secondly, thank you all for accepting the invitation to meet with me. You are truly a part of the making of history in your community." More applause. "The equal but separate policy of the southern states offers privileges only to those in charge, in essence, rendering equality a moot point for the minority. We are here to challenge that, but we will do it on the shirttail of a more pressing issue: that of the unjust incarceration of Mary Ann Shaver. Now, let's get down to the business at hand. What we will do tonight—"

"Mr. Shelton, could we first offer a word of prayer for our endeavors?" Pastor Harris stood.

"Of course, Pastor. Thank you for reminding me." Shelton stood, pushed his chair back from the desk and acquiesced to the request with a gracious hand gesture toward Pastor Harris to lead in prayer.

"Please," Harris extended his hands to the ones beside him, and each followed suit, forming an irregular but unbroken prayer circle, "let's pray together." After a long pause, he continued, "Dear Lord, we humbly ask Your presence in this meeting. …" The unrehearsed prayer began slow and in his resonant baritone. Others joined in with an affirming word during the thoughtful pause that preceded each new sentence. The content of the prayer climbed like stair steps to a higher cause. Each step carried a set cadence and increased in volume until a concluding "Amen!" punctuated the final ascent. A momentary silence descended but quickly faded into a dozen affirmations of "amen" and "hallelujah" and "glory."

"Thanks, Pastor." Shelton quickly returned to the agenda. He held aloft a stick and poster board and explained, "Our picketing the jail won't necessarily cause the sheriff to release Miss Shaver, but it will bring attention to the national cause of civil rights. Our task tonight is to prepare our signs and work on a strategy of protest. We'll work in teams of two, creating and assembling the placards. Any questions or comments."

"We dare not stray from our main purpose," Harris cautioned. "More than anything else this is about Miss Ann's defense and ultimate freedom. That's why our church parishioners gave money."

"Of course." Shelton dispersed papers to eager recipients. "We must keep the young woman's situation in the forefront. And we'll do this by picketing in front of the jail. On these papers are sample slogans we need to paint on the poster boards. Use powerful words like *freedom, equal rights, integrated schools* and *now*. Use the red markers to highlight these words."

Harris scanned the young faces. Enthusiasm and resolve broke forth with hope, like the sun interrupting a rainy day, but something else shown through. Something other than hope, and that concerned him. It was a bottled anger, seething, like water drops on carbide, ready to explode into revenge. They gravitated to Shelton's rhetoric, but Harris felt uneasy. Jealous of Shelton's influence? Perhaps he wished to be more influential in their lives, but that wasn't jealousy. What was his concern? They seemed aloof, like he might no longer be on their side. No one had said such to him, but their faces reflected their unspoken words. The harsh treatment they received at the hands of the community pushed them further into despair, and despair stopped only with either resignation or action. They were inclined to the latter. At times, his sermons taught that identifying with the pain of Christ was a Christian virtue. Other times, he challenged the idea of segregated schools, pointing out that the colored schools were dilapidated, overcrowded, lacking libraries and understaffed. He could never see equality in schools as long as the blacks were not allowed to attend the schools of the whites. Most tax dollars would be funneled to the schools for whites. That wasn't the only anxiety that plagued his daily thoughts. Ever since the drowning, he couldn't get the image of the young Eddie Shaver out of his head; it haunted him at night, thinking that the child's death was the result of sheer hatred and negligence by a foster parent. The funeral for the lad did something to him; it made him want to push back. The hypocrisy of the community galled him to the point of … was it revenge? No, he hoped not. Action? Yes, it was a call to action. He held back his anger that day, but the sight of that little fella in the casket emboldened him to speak publicly for the first time regarding the discrimination of blacks. He received a couple threats shortly after the funeral. The sermon still reverberated in his mind: "Master Eddie was God's child. He was God's child, like Jesus was God's son. Both were born in a foreign land. Both were born into humble means. The difference being Jesus came to save the lost communities of the world, while young Eddie, he come into the world lost, needing his community to save him. In the end, no one did. Master Eddie went to sleep in hunger and poverty, but he awoke to a banquet supper, golden streets and timeless days in that land of no nights. Engraved on the gates to that city are the names of the twelve apostles and the names of the twelve tribes, but on the gates of that city there are no signs that say, 'Colored folks not allowed.'"

Since that day, countless times, he had injected into his sermons the idea of equality and hints of agitation against the community oppression. He was treading on thin ice. How would his family survive if he lost his job at the school?

Some of these young faces were present at little Eddie's funeral. Few things had changed since then. Day-to-day mistreatments and the neglected crime against an innocent lad had driven them to this point. He was partially the cause of their action today, and maybe he was to blame for such action. His leadership had brought Shelton to Woodstock. His intention was to obtain a proper defense for Miss Ann. But had the purpose become sidetracked? Was Miss Ann to become the sacrificial lamb for a greater cause? By bringing in Shelton to the situation, his actions cast a shadow over Sheriff Flin and Harry Weatherholtz, the very two people who had defended Miss Ann against Cutshaw. Now he was sacrificing their reputations and futures for the sake of one of his own. Lines of the concerned and compassionate toward the cause of the colored community were being blurred with the bullies and oppressors. The words of the Apostle Paul came to mind: "If it be possible … live peaceably with all men." How much was possible? Where did the line of peace stop and conflict begin? "Servants, obey … your masters … fearing God." Did the apostle actually promote slavery, or had the white man used unfairly the Holy Script for selfish gain? He was convinced of the latter, though he tried to balance civil rights with Christian liberties, the latter being a gray area even in Scripture. "Forgive seventy times seven," Jesus said. But how many times do you turn the other cheek?

The smell of paint and permanent markers permeated the room. Shelton had brought the chisel tipped markers from D.C. The young people had never used them before, so they bartered over who got to use the markers instead of a paintbrush. The markers, invented in '52 by Sidney Rosenthal, another of Harris' trivia knowledge, were much easier to use than spray paint and letter templates. The assembled placards lined the walls of the office. Shelton hovered over the students like an art teacher mentoring a prodigy: proud but challenging. As Harris became more an observer, what began as an exciting journey had dwindled into ambivalence. Where would the journey end? Were there any true winners? And who would the losers be?

Their task accomplished, the young people left, their expressions reflecting satisfaction. Shelton lingered, studying the placards in silence. The evening ended abruptly with a handshake.

"See you at the rally, Pastor." Shelton tipped his black brimmed Stetson. He was a looker. The silk band and green feather accentuated his flamboyancy.

Harris assumed Shelton's silence, broken only by his subdued parting words, mirrored concern regarding his resolve. He hoped his stout handshake absolved any doubts Shelton had about his intentions.

Harris removed the stick that held the window open and contemplatively exited the church. The sun slipped quickly behind the Appalachians. It painted a multifaceted coloration of gray, pink and puce, punctuated with a golden hue over Great North. Such a masterful sunset, controlled by the infinite God he served, never became commonplace for him. The star maker! The peace speaker! Yet he was poor and troubled. A dozen thoughts traipsed seemingly uncontrollably. He loathed the doubts that buffeted his soul. Why could he not be more certain about what God required of him as a Christian, like Shelton? From a child, he had memorized the Scripture, which effortlessly and frequently popped into his mind. "He hath shewed thee, O man, what is good; and what doth the Lord require of thee, but to do justly, and to love mercy, and to walk humbly with thy God?" Another verse from the Bible corralled his thoughts. He contemplated the meaning. Three things God required, none of which resembled rebellion. In contrast, Micah had peacefully preached under the leadership of three kings. The first two were wicked, and Micah's message of righteous living did not move them. However, the decisions of the last, Hezekiah, brought a revival of righteousness to the land. How did this Bible example apply to his situation? Could it be fairly applied to a colored man's condition in a white man's world? Did God require it of him? Harris had followed a few generations of peaceful black preachers, but still, the black man lived oppressed under the Christian, white man's rules. Was his message from the pulpit relevant or merely inciting rebellion?

Chapter Thirty-four

Thirty-year-old surgeon Randal Swartz studied the patients' charts. Each day, and every case carried its routines and its challenges. The past twenty-four hours were without exception. He'd operated on three patients representing about three generations, all male. Each of the patients lost a substantial amount of blood. He had one transferred to the University of Virginia Hospital in Charlottesville in hopes they could save his life. No amount of money could be more rewarding than saving a life, and no amount of money could compensate for the anguish in losing a life. He had confidence in the Charlottesville's medical team, having done his internship there. He'd spoken by phone directly with his old professor, the chief surgeon at the university hospital, offering any info he could about the patient.

Swartz found the historic Charlottesville area to be quite intriguing. It was home to three presidents: Jefferson, Madison and Monroe. Jefferson had forever left his fingerprints on the community. He built his personal residence on a summit a few miles from downtown, thus the name, Monticello, of Italian origin meaning "little mount." Jefferson also designed the Rotunda on the university campus, patterned after Rome's Pantheon. It housed the university library, including the eight thousand books Jefferson had purchased

181

for the school library's upstart. In 1895, a fire swept through the Rotunda, but students were able to rescue some of the books, along with a life-size statue of Mr. Jefferson.

The school of medicine on the Charlottesville campus opened its doors in 1825, the tenth medical school in the United States. Jefferson recruited its first and singular professor, an Englishman, Doctor Robley Dunglison. The university hospital opened in 1901 and shortly afterward created a training program for nurses. The nursing program developed into the University of Virginia School of Nursing about five years ago. That's where Swartz met his wife. She was a student at the university and a resident of the community. This drew them as often as possible back to his alma mater while his wife spent time with her folks. But being the only surgeon at Shenandoah Memorial kept him busy night and day, with little time to travel very far from the small town of Woodstock.

The second of the three patients had an old-wound, skull penetration. The projectile had severed a superficial blood vessel in the temple area, causing excessive blood loss. The surgery went well, but the loss of blood caused Swartz concern. He needed to speak directly to the patient regarding the details of the wound. The wife's knowledge seemed sketchy at best. The patient's name also caught his attention: Weatherholtz. It was a name he was familiar with, but he had never before met a Weatherholtz.

The third patient suffered from a tumor in the lower left lung but also a pulmonary embolism. He had been brought in suspecting pneumonia, but the symptoms were that of the embolism. The tumor, undetected, would have eventually killed him, so the embolism had actually saved his life by causing the tumor to be discovered. Interestingly, his name was also Weatherholtz.

Two surgeries on two patients in the same day with the same name proved intriguing to Doctor Swartz. The Weatherholtz name was well known in the valley, and it was a name that particularly stuck in his mind. The Minnie Weatherholtz murder, the subsequent manhunt for her husband and the eventual acquittal of the same was still a conversational piece in the valley. It especially involved Doctor Swartz' grandfather, a valley physician in the latter part of the nineteenth century and into the twentieth. It was a scene he tried to forget but was forever etched in his memory and passed along in family conversations. The details of that damp February morning two generations ago still surfaced in family gatherings.

He snatched up the Weatherholtzes' charts and headed toward the post-surgery wing. He eased open the door and stepped inside. The sound of beeps and hisses never welcomed him, though they did not frighten him. He had emotionally detached himself from the suffering. The elder Weatherholtz had done remarkably well considering his condition. A ventilator covered most of the patient's face. His wife sat in the corner, dozing.

"Mr. Weatherholtz?" He tapped the patient's shoulder. "I'm Doctor Swartz."

The wife stirred.

"Hello, ma'am. How's he doing?"

"Bout the same, I suppose."

"A mighty sick man. You got him here just in time. Another few hours and I doubt I could have reversed the situation. We'll continue to monitor his vitals, get him back on his feet and hopefully, with the good Lord's help, get him home in a few days."

"Thank you, doctor."

"Any questions?"

"How long you think he'll be here?"

"Hard to say. He'll probably need to go to a rehab facility before he can go home."

"What do I do 'bout gettin' him there?"

"We'll take care of that for you. The only thing I'll need is consent from him, or you if he's unable to give consent."

"Don't think I have any objections."

"Okay. I'll get out of here and let you rest. You've had a long night. It's good to meet you, Mrs. Weatherholtz."

"Who?"

"Mrs. Weatherholtz."

"That's not my name."

"Sorry, I assumed you were married."

"We are, but our name ain't Weatherholtz. We're Halls."

"I'm sorry, but he told the intake nurse his name was Elmer Weatherholtz ... though she said he seemed somewhat confused. Were you not there when he checked in?"

"Yes, but I ... I can't read or write none ... so I stepped out so he could do all that ... 'specially since he was able to talk. Embarrassing not being able to write and stuff."

"I understand, ma'am. No need to worry. We'll have to correct the information on his registration."

"Thank you for doin' that. Can you do it without me?"

"I'll let the nurses know and they'll get it corrected. You don't worry about it."

"Thank you."

"I mean that, Mrs. Hall. No worrying. You okay?"

"Yes."

"I've got another patient to check on. Interestingly, he is a Weatherholtz ... that is unless he's given us the wrong name." He laughed.

"Not Harry Weatherholtz?"

"As a matter of fact, it is Harry." He glanced at his chart. "Harry Thomas. You know him?"

"I've heard of him ... only other Weatherholtz I know. Owns a sawmill ... that's probably how I remember 'em. My man was into loggin' and we could have met him."

She appeared to weigh her words. Her consternation seemed obvious. Why?

Chapter Thirty-five

The hospital door burst open. "Good morning, ma'am. I'm Doctor Swartz. I think we met yesterday."

"Yes. Good morning, Doctor Swartz." Evelyn used her fingers to substitute for a comb as she tried to straighten her lopsided hair.

"How's our patient today?"

"Ready to go home," Harry said, as he pulled himself up and slid his legs over the side of the bed. The doctor seemed a mite sanquinish for such an early hour

"I'd prefer you decide that for him, Doctor. He's a bit headstrong." Evelyn smiled.

"We'll give that request consideration, but one thing I've learned while doctoring is to never get involved in domestic disputes." He laughed. "How are you feeling, Mr. Weatherholtz?" He studied the chart.

"Better. Much better. What happened to me?"

"That's what I'd like to talk about." He placed the chart on the foot of the bed and pulled a small clear container from the pocket of his suit coat. "Any idea what this could be? It's a piece of metal about one centimeter long ... that's less than half an inch." He handed the container to Harry.

Harry turned the container in his hand, studying the contents. "Any hints?"

"I removed it from your skull during surgery."

"From the sore?"

"Yes. Any explanation?"

"Well, I did receive a shrapnel wound in the war. I thought it got removed, but the wound has festered up and scabbed over many times through the years. Never gave it any thought that shrapnel might still be there."

"Makes sense. I assumed the wound was old, but I needed some explanation. A blood vessel ran near the injury, and evidently, when you scratched the sore, you caused the shrapnel to perforate the vein."

"I've fussed at him for years to get that checked." Evelyn snatched the container from Harry's hand and stared at the slither of metal inside. "This little piece of metal almost killed him twice. But he'll be okay?" Her face revealed her concern.

"Well, I'd like to think so, but the male skull is only about a quarter of an inch thick, so the shrapnel did penetrate the skull. That's my concern, primarily that infection could set up inside the brain. Have you ever had any difficulty processing thought?"

"Don't think so," Harry said.

"Do you agree, Mrs. Weatherholtz?"

"Yes, I think he does fine."

"Were you hospitalized for the wound?"

"Not really. I went to a makeshift infirmary for medical attention and they released me back to normal duty. I did get a Purple Heart out of it."

"I salute you for that, sir."

"Thank you. Now, back to my question. When can I go home?" Harry asked.

"If you don't run a fever for twenty-four hours, I'll dismiss you. In the meantime, I have a personal question. Are you related to Minnie Weatherholtz who was killed here in the valley over fifty, maybe sixty years ago?"

The question surprised Harry. He stared at the doctor, speechless.

"You don't have to answer, but I'm just somewhat curious. My grandpa talked a lot about that day."

"February 4, 1896. She was my mother."

"I assumed such. So sorry. And your father, whatever happened to him? Grandpa discussed the tragic event but he never—"

"He died in prison a year later."

"Please forgive me for being so personal, but there are two reasons I ask. One, my grandpa was a doctor at the time of your mother's death. He was called upon, but of course, there wasn't anything he could do to help. I'm sorry, I shouldn't be intruding upon your personal life—"

"It's okay." This was the most Harry could recall of talking about his mother's death to anyone other than Evelyn. "I'm interested in anything you know about that day. It's difficult to recall the details, me being a child. What else, if anything, do you know about my parents?"

"Just that my grandpa used to mention it ... every winter he'd say something about that winter day when the young Weatherholtz woman got shot. That's about all I know."

"Did he, your grandfather, ever mention my father?"

"Just that he wasn't convicted ... due to a legal technicality."

"Did your grandfather have an opinion about my father's guilt?

"From all he knew and heard, he said your father was 'as guilty as sin.' Pardon me for the bluntness."

The sights and sounds flashed before Harry. His heart accelerated at the explosion of the gun. In slow motion, he reached for his falling mother.

"I'm sorry, Mr. Weatherholtz. I shouldn't have—"

"No. Perhaps I need to talk about it."

"Wasn't there two sons?"

"Yes, me and my brother."

"Grandpa said one of the sons was with her when it—"

"That was me."

"Sorry. I can't imagine. Grandpa said you were just a small lad."

"I was five. It seems so long ago … it remains like a fog to me."

"My second reason for being so nosy is that a patient down the hall identified himself as Elmer Weatherholtz, but then his wife corrected him. Wasn't Elmer your father's name?"

"Yes, but like I said, my father died in prison."

"Anyway, as strange as it was, his wife said his name is Elmer Hall, so we'll get that corrected. He was probably just hallucinating … just coincidental he thought Weatherholtz was his name."

"I assume he is from around here," Harry asked.

"I really didn't discuss that. I'm sure it's in his admission papers, but of course, that's confidential, so I can't—"

"Understandable." Harry traced the outline of the bandage that covered his temple.

"About how old is the gentleman down the hall?" Evelyn straightened the covers at the foot of the bed.

"I'd have to look at his chart to be exact, but I'd say eightyish."

"Is his wife staying with him, poor fella?" Evelyn removed a hatpin and repositioned her hat.

"She was there when I left them a few minutes ago."

"I hope he's okay. Must be hard on the wife." Evelyn picked up her purse.

"Yes. I think she's been the primary caretaker for him at home." He scribbled on a notepad.

"I'll be back tomorrow, Bud. I've got a few chores stacking up, including some of yours. Thank you, Doctor Swartz."

"Nice to meet you, ma'am." He reached out his hand and shook hers. "We'll take good care of your husband."

"Nice to meet you, too, but I wish under different circumstances," she said.

"I get that a lot, but I fully understand. We'll get your husband fixed up and back home as soon as possible."

"How're you getting home, Evelyn?" Harry asked.

"I've made arrangements with the pastor's wife to pick me up. She could be waiting. Pastor Carnahan is at a conference in Richmond. That's why he hasn't visited you. Thank you, Doctor."

"My pleasure, ma'am."

"Goodbye, dear. I'll probably not come back tomorrow, but the day after I should be able to get a ride and visit." She touched his shoulder gently and left.

Harry knew where she was headed, but he could not stop her, nor was he sure he wanted to.

"Would you mind taking some deep breaths for me and let me check your breathing?" Swartz uncoiled his stethoscope.

Harry braced himself with his hand on the nightstand. The Gideon Bible remained on the stand where Evelyn had placed it. She had read to him that morning from Genesis. Isaac had two sons: Esau and Jacob. One sold his birthright for a bowl of soup, assuming life without the father's blessing was still better than death. The other justified selfish actions in obtaining the blessing of the father, for the blessing seemed imperative to him. Those two conflicting concepts never concerned Harry. A dead father could offer no blessing.

"Breathe deep and hold, please."

It seemed more than a coincidence that a man down the hallway, about the age his father would be, could hallucinate about his identity, thinking himself to be Elmer Weatherholtz. Had Cutshaw told the truth? Was the man he went to see on the mountain the same one in the hospital bed a few doors down? Still, he could not bring himself to believe the man was his father. He did not want the man to be his father. And if by some strange fate it was his father, he wasn't sure he could ever accept him, not after what he had done. And if he was his father, all these years of abandonment complicated the issue even more.

"Breathing seems fine, Mr. Weatherholtz. Your heart rate is a bit elevated. I noticed on your chart a history of heart problems. Let me check your blood pressure. Try and relax."

If it was his father, did Hurley Cutshaw bring him to the hospital? He needed to find that out. Cutshaw's motive would be selfish at best. How did Cutshaw know the man? Were they together in some kind of deal? He certainly could not believe any action of Hurley Cutshaw was untainted. If Hurley knew Harry was in the hospital, it would be just like him to connive some plan such as this. Was this part of Hurley's outlandish scheme to try and get him to accept the deal he'd placed on the table?

"Pressure is elevated. We need to watch that. Are you allowing yourself to be anxious? Worrying about anything?"

"No more than usual."

"Best to remain calm. Worrying never changes anything for the good. It's a fool's bed partner."

He withheld the urge to ask the doctor why the man was in the hospital. Evidently, surgery, since Dr. Swartz was a surgeon. What kind of surgery? At his age, he may not survive. If the man was his dad, he had survived for years without any contact with his sons. If he could get by without them that long, he could get by alone now. He has a wife; let her care for him.

"I'll check back tomorrow and make a decision about your release. I need to visit some other patients now."

"How is he doing, Elmer Hall?" Harry had not processed the question, it just came out.

"Not well. Lung surgery. A tumor. Rough on an eighty-year-old with chronic emphysema from years of smoking."

Was it his dad? If so, after sixty years, he was finally under the same roof with the man who murdered his mother. Was the man dying? He felt no sympathy, and he did not want to. "Revenge hath no sweetness," somebody once said. Who was it that said such? They weren't completely right, and they certainly didn't have a father murder their mother.

Chapter Thirty-six

The nurse at the front desk didn't bother to look up from her paper-work. He limped quietly along the hallway, reading the homemade name tags on each door. The judge's door stood ajar. Glancing left and right at the empty hallway, he slipped quietly inside and gently pulled the door shut. He stared down at the shell of what used to be a robust man, but the last few months had stolen his health. The sheet rose and fell with each erratic breath. A pillow over his face would end this emotional enslavement.

Few understand the pain experienced when another controls his fate, in this case by sheer manipulation of a past that must be concealed. Even imprisonment doesn't necessarily surpass in anguish the pain associated with incarceration by mental bars and emotional chains. Ironically, resignation to a prison sentence eventually relieves the caged felon, and he enjoys a measure of freedom even behind lock and key. This is not so for the one blackmailed by the deeds of the past, with the constant fear of losing his freedom. His torment has no end. It continues indefinitely under the looming intimidation of the extortionist who threatens to reveal his true identity and past deeds, unless he continues to serve his every whim.

"Who's there?" Jenkins stirred.

"Just me, sir."

"It's about time you showed up. I've been wondering how things have progressed."

A knock on the door stopped the conversation. The door eased open. "Oh, sorry. I didn't realize you have company. Would you care for a snack, Mr. Jenkins?" A nurse's aid pulled her snack cart into the room.

"Not now, but you can raise my bed," Jenkins demanded.

She adjusted his bed. "Tell me when."

"There. No, up just a little. There!"

His demands secretly angered Pratt, but he made sure such did not show. "Thank you, ma'am," Pratt said.

"You're welcome. Just let me know when you'd like something, Mr. Jenkins, and I'll be back. You know where the call cord is located." She retrieved the cord and placed it in his hand. "There."

"Not a lot of good this thing does. Nobody ever answers."

"Sorry about that, sir. I'll see what I can do to improve efficiency around here. We're a little short-handed with … one of our workers gone."

"The colored girl?"

"Yes."

"What happened? She quit already?" Jenkins tossed the call cord aside.

"I heard she ran into some trouble with the law."

"Just as well without her. Never liked her kind."

"I'll check in on you later."

Jenkins hesitated until the door closed. "Did you have something to do with that, Mr. Pratt?"

"Indirectly, I suppose. I had to shoot Brady."

"You what?"

"I had to shoot Brady." He pulled a chair next to Jenkins' bed.

"Something went wrong with our plans?"

"I didn't realize Brady was home. Came into the room out of nowhere. Left me no option, sir."

"So you shot him?"

"Yes, sir."

"I'm not sure that was the wise thing to do."

"Right or wrong, I shot him."

"Is he dead?"

"Barely alive, but he'll die, sir."

"Did he see you?"

"Yes, but I'm not sure he recognized me. I was in the shadows. Left me no choice but to shoot him."

"It's just as well. He knew too much. Did too many things against me, became too independent. He got what he had coming, though I believe he would have come around for us in a squeeze. How'd the girl get involved?"

"She was in the house. Cleaning. Of course, she heard the shots and found Brady lying on the floor. She went into shock instead of calling for help. I heard a state trooper found her with the gun by her side, right where I dropped it, sitting near the body. Stupid girl. I'm sure her prints are all over that gun. I was wearing gloves."

"So they think Cutshaw's wench did it?"

"Yes, sir. She's in jail."

"Two birds with one bullet. Good job, Pratt." Jenkins laughed.

"Thank you, sir, but it took two bullets. As you blokes say, one for good measure."

"And the papers? Did you find them?"

"Had to go back for them later, after the law left, but yes, I did, sir."

"You destroyed them?"

"Yes, sir. Burned them in the fireplace."

"All of them?"

"Of course, sir. What use would I have to keep them?"

Jenkins did not answer.

"What's next, sir?" Pratt stood.

"This changes things. With Brady out of the way and all the records burned, we no longer have reason to keep that Elmer fellow around."

"The elderly man you mentioned, the one in the mountains?"

"Yes. He could prove to be a liability if the law ever got wind of him, my past relationship with him."

"Seems he and Cutshaw have become pals," Pratt said with a smirk.

"Not a good team. Their blunder could do damage."

"Shall I eliminate the old man, sir?"

"Do I need to answer that?" Jenkins' agitation grew.

"What about Weatherholtz? Shall I snuff him out?"

"Too much killing could arouse unnecessary suspicion. I think we've neutralized his influence. Let's leave him be for a while. We'll see. Maybe he'll fade away, and if he doesn't, we'll deal with him. He's blocked our progress for too long, and we're not going to put up with it if he persists."

"And Cutshaw? Is he useful to us anymore?"

"Perhaps. Our ace in a hole if we should need him. What do you think?"

"I think he'd squeal like a stuck pig if he got in a jam, sir. I can eliminate him easily, and no one would care."

"Later, if we need to. I don't want Sheriff Flin snooping around his place. Not yet, anyway." Jenkins closed his eyes as if in thought.

Pratt waited unto he stirred. "What about Cutshaw's demands? Such a boorish chap. He's demanding to reclaim custody of that little fellow the system took from him, and he'd like another girl, too, to help around his house."

"Is our man in place, Judge Arthur Caldwell?" Jenkins smiled. "Art and I go back a long way."

"Yes. He moved into his office yesterday and will serve on the bench starting next week. Taking over all custody cases."

"I'll give him a congratulatory call today. I need him to stop by for a little chat. I think he can satisfy Cutshaw's request for a child or two. On your way out, have that girl come back. I'd like a little snack to celebrate our good fortune."

"One thing more. A civil rights lawyer from D.C. just got into town, representing the black girl, I presume. He's holding a rally in Woodstock, demanding her release, stirring up the black community, mostly the youth."

Jenkins slammed his fist onto his food tray, sending a cup of water flying across the room. His face flushed as a string of expletives and disdain exploded from his mouth, until stopped by a coughing spasm. A nurse rushed into the room.

"You okay, Mr. Jenkins?" She lifted his head and repositioned the pillows.

"I'm fine." He shoved her away.

"Aren't we a little feisty today? Didn't your momma teach you manners?" She slightly scolded him.

"Sorry, ma'am," Pratt apologized, wiping water from his coat sleeve. "He'll be okay in a jiffy."

"Call if you need anything." She picked up the cup. "I'll wipe up the water when you've finished visiting."

"Thank you." Pratt paused until she closed the door. "Anything else, sir?"

"Time to call in reserves, the men in white would be best for this job."

"Consider it done, sir."

Jenkins yawned and closed his eyes. The room grew quiet except for his heavy breathing. Pratt waited, wondering, contemplating. *I could end this once and for all. Why do I torture myself so?*

"Mr. Pratt?" Jenkins stirred.

"Yes, sir."

"Don't do anything you'd regret."

"What do you mean, sir?"

"In my last will and testament, I have a paragraph about you." Jenkins paused.

"Me, sir. Why would you mention me in your will?" The thought of being left something in Jenkins' will surprised him. He never expected someone as cruel as Jenkins was in life to be kind in death. Perhaps all these years of servitude had paid off.

"If I die of natural causes, you are to inherit a nice income, but if I die of suspicious causes, you are to receive nothing. All determined by my estate attorney. Further, if my death is of a suspicious nature, I have instructed him to reveal the contents of a certain lockbox of which you are not apprised. Pray that I die of natural causes, Mr. Pratt."

"You think of everything, don't you, sir?"

"Right down to my last breath, Mr. Pratt." Jenkins closed his eyes and positioned his hands—his fingers intertwined—behind his head. Satisfied.

The sinister smile shot adrenaline throughout Pratt's body. He closed his eyes and breathed deeply, then exhaled slowly, contemplating his options. He repeated the routine several times before speaking. "I'll stay in touch, sir."

Jenkins didn't answer. The menacing smile remained.

Pratt removed a paper from his pocket and slowly unfolded it.

"What is that noise?" Jenkins' ominous facial features turned into concern.

"Insurance papers, sir. Insurance papers in case our partnership should ever dissolve."

"Why you little—"

The door opened suddenly.

"You have some mail, Mr. Jenkins." A different aid entered. "I'm sorry. I didn't realize you had—"

"No problem, ma'am. I was just leaving. See you, sir."

Pratt slipped from the room, leaving the door ajar, and limped toward the front entrance. He refolded the paper and slipped it into his suit pocket. He had some unfinished business to take care of. He had to stay a step ahead of Jeremiah Jenkins or he would be a dead man, or worse, he would be back in a London prison.

Chapter Thirty-seven

Pastor Harris walked in the front of the march. He took the full impact of a raw egg from someone along the crowded sidewalk. It looked like half of Woodstock's 2,000 citizens showed up to protest the protesters. Harris pleaded for calm when those around him wanted to retaliate to the insults and slinging of objects. "To break rank is to abandon our purpose," he shouted repeatedly. "This is not about us; it is about Miss Ann." They arrived at the jail without a major disaster. Dedrick Shelton joined them on the jail steps, apologizing that he had pressing matters that prevented him from making the march.

The rally lasted until Flin and some deputies, along with Shelton, escorted Miss Ann from the jail. They followed the entourage to the courthouse where she would meet with the judge. Harris joined Shelton inside the courtroom for the arraignment. Scheduled for nine o'clock, the concern of the sheriff's department over the protesters had delayed it by an hour. Harris' heart ached for the frightened Miss Ann as she answered the judge's questions in a voice barely above a whisper. Shelton repeated her answers for the judge. "Not guilty, your honor." Shelton compensated for her timidity with his flamboyant style, which seemed to irritate the judge. This concerned Harris. The formalities ended, and Sheriff Flin, along with a deputy, escorted Ann out the courthouse alley and back to the jail. At one point Harris thought Flin had looked his way as if to say things would be okay. Flin had been kind and fair to the black community in the past.

The rally at the courthouse started at noon. Most bystanders had already lost interest and went about their business. The occasion went better than planned. Reporters from three TV stations, and one national reporter from D.C., showed up to film the event and interview the protesters. Shelton had arranged for some white civil rights advocates from the D.C. area to join in the protest, adding clout to their cause. The best thing that could have happened did happen: a group of ruffians counter-protested.

Deputies kept the two groups apart. In his non-partisan stand, Sheriff Flin had made some enemies on both sides: too soft on crime and too harsh against citizen's rights to protest. The cameras focused on the German Shepherd on the scene. No one bothered to ask whose it was, and therefore, no one explained it was the local pet that traveled from house to house begging leftover biscuits. The deputies evidently didn't consider how it might look having the dog hanging out with them.

Mayor Tom Schaeffer made his typical buffoon appearance. He defended his political career as one focused on equal rights. He desperately tried to whitewash the reporter's accusations that the Woodstock schools lacked equal opportunities for whites and blacks. He defended the Virginia Commonwealth's concern for the education of all her children—black and white. Ironically, he lacked knowledge of Margaret Douglass, of Norfolk, who a hundred years prior had been arrested and imprisoned for a month because she taught free colored children how to read and write. The question regarding this lady momentarily stumped him, but he recovered by expressing his personal belief in Ann Shaver's innocence—calling her that girl—but had no knowledge to substantiate such. He concluded with a sincere expression that he was praying for her family, and he went blank when the reporter asked whom that might be.

Shelton stole the interview with his civil rights diatribe. He focused on the state's attitude about black students' education. He associated Woodstock with the typical small-town mentalities in Virginia that were against equal rights. He mentioned the Montgomery bus boycott, Recy Taylor and Emmett Till, but he said nothing about the drowning of Eddie Shaver, and he said little about Miss Ann's innocence. That disappointed Pastor Harris, but he realized Shelton's view of the big picture took precedent over their local concerns. Nothing seemed gained, but nothing lost. At least he hoped so.

Chapter Thirty-eight

Harry Weatherholtz was blessed with the antidote for fear: action. He slipped out of bed, donned his pants and tucked in his hospital gown. The room spun as he gathered up his belongings, including the bloodied shirt he'd worn to the hospital. He sat on the edge of the bed and let his head clear, then stuffed the items into the brown shopping bag Evelyn had left on the windowsill. With the paper bag under his arm, he slipped his jacket across the other arm, eased open the door and surveyed the hallway. A minute later he paused at the door of Elmer Hall's room. He had to find the answer to this puzzle. Who was this impostor, and what was he up to? And why?

A woman sat in a chair next to the window. He assumed she was Elmer's wife, but her blond hair, made into a single braid and coiled into a bun, made her appear much too young to be the wife of the disheveled man shivering underneath the blankets. Perhaps she was his daughter.

She saw him. He started to turn away.

"May I help ya?" She rose slowly and walked toward the door.

He stared into her quizzical face. She was probably the woman he saw through the window of the cabin. The blond hair was deceptive, but up close, her wrinkled brow, sunken cheeks and weak, raspy voice revealed a much older woman. He glanced again at the frail body in bed. Who was he really? Another pawn of Cutshaw and Jenkins?

"I was looking for someone … for my father. Wrong room. Sorry."

"This is Elmer Hall's room."

Her demeanor seemed fraught with hopelessness. The desperation on her face tore at Harry's heart. Two elderly people alone at life's end. Had they a friend in the world? If this was his father and his stepmother, was there no responsibility he bore? But deception has its payday. How do you trust a life of deception, even when life has come down to the end?

"Sorry to have disturbed you, ma'am."

"Who's there?" The man stirred. His voice was weak and seemed pleading.

"I have the wrong room, sir. Sorry, ma'am." Harry tipped his hat.

"No problem." She followed him to the door.

Harry quickly walked away. Years of sheriff work honed his ability to separate emotion from reality and even to corral the emotions of reality. If the man was his father, he was a criminal, having escaped prison. If he wasn't his father, he was an impostor, a liar and a schemer with Hurley Cutshaw. Either way was not good, and it was criminal.

Most men would have succumbed to an emotional decision. Harry sought only truth, and truth trumps emotional judgments. He found a public phone in the lobby, placed a dime into the coin slot and dialed.

"Sheriff's department. How may I assist you?"

"Miss Compton … Irene, this is Harry Weatherholtz. Is Sheriff Flin available?"

"He's out on patrol, Mr. Weatherholtz. If it's urgent I can radio him."

"Yes, somewhat urgent. If possible, have him meet me at the front entrance of Woodstock Memorial."

"Will do. What are you doing at the hospital, if you don't mind my asking?"

Harry hesitated.

"You there, Mr. Weatherholtz?"

"Yes, sorry. Stopped to visit an old acquaintance." It wasn't a lie, but he knew it bordered on such. A half-truth got Abraham of old into hot water with a pharaoh. He breathed a prayer of repentance, just in case.

"Anyone I know?" Irene asked.

"I wouldn't think so."

"Sheriff Flin should be there shortly. I'll call him soon as I hang us."

"Thank you, Miss … Irene."

Chapter Thirty-nine

Harry refused to operate out of emotion; he had to have the facts. The man in the hospital might be his father, but he had to have the proof. He would not fall for Cutshaw's manipulation. He hated to drag Flin into this cat-and-mouse game, but Flin was involved from the beginning. He would be upset if he found out he had been left out of the loop. Plus, Harry didn't have his car. He couldn't send word to Evelyn, for she would disapprove of him leaving the hospital until the doctor released him. He'd be home before she came back to visit, and hopefully, he'd have some answers by then. Now, if Flin would only go along, he might be able to dig up some facts.

A nurse passed by and gave him a second glance. Harry smiled and hoped she didn't recognize him. He certainly didn't want to lie, but neither did he plan on spending another day in the hospital. She continued on her way without an inquiry, and Harry sighed.

He exited the front entrance and leaned against the side of the building, somewhat winded but determined. A good half hour passed before he waved at Flin as the cruiser entered the hospital drive. Flin pulled alongside the curb and Harry quickly fell into the passenger seat, breathing heavily. He hadn't realized how weak he was.

"Thanks, Sheriff." Harry tossed the grocery bag and his coat into the back seat.

"Anything for my friend. What's in the bag?"

"My laundry."

"Couldn't this have waited?"

"For the loss of a nail, Sheriff."

"I know, I know ... a shoe ... a horse ... a battle was lost. This had best be important, Harry. I had to leave a deputy in charge of keeping a two-block distance between a dozen or so hooligans and a group of black folks protesting Miss Ann's incarceration. Did you know Harris and his church were holding a protest rally? And that big-shot lawyer from D.C. is leading it."

"No. I hadn't heard."

"Is that a hospital shirt you're wearing?"

Harry didn't answer.

"What's that bandage on the side of your head for? You been in a fight? What's goin' on, Harry?"

"Lots. I had a minor surgery to remove a piece of shrapnel."

"Shrapnel?"

"Yes, shrapnel. But that's not important right now. I'll explain later. Remember the note I received from Cutshaw suggesting my father is alive and hiding out in the mountains?"

"And I don't believe a word of it. And if I did it wouldn't change my mind about Miss Ann shootin' Jack Brady. I'm sure that's where this is leading."

"One move at a time, Sheriff."

"Whatta you mean?"

"We got ourselves a puzzle to solve, and the only way we're going to solve it is one puzzle piece at a time. I've got one of those pieces, and we need to see if it fits."

"Another wild goose chase, Harry?"

"I don't think so."

"What is it?"

"I found the cabin where my father has supposed to be living all this time, but of course I don't necessarily think he's my father."

"So."

"The man that lives in that cabin is in the hospital right now. His cabin is empty, so let's take a little drive up the Blue Ridge and check out his cabin for some clues."

"Without a warrant?"

"Don't need one."

"So you're now a legal expert?"

"No, but I know a little about law enforcement. His cabin is on government property. So the inhabitants are squatters. We're just checking out who might be trespassing on government property, and why. We're … you're a government employee, so you have a right to check on what belongs to the government. You tell me, is that breaking the law?"

"Well, since you put it that way, it makes more sense. Point the way."

Chapter Forty

The car skidded sideways when Flin braked hard at the gravel road's abrupt end.

"Must have taken a wrong turn somewhere," Flin said. "We've plum run out of civilization."

"We walk that trail from here." Harry pointed toward an opening in the underbrush.

"How far?"

"A good way, but you'll enjoy the scenery."

"How in the world did you find this place?" Flin stared across the vast valley.

"Logged some for the government in this area some years back. Had a general idea of where a squatter could be living. It matched the mileage you tricked out of Cutshaw. You'll need your jacket up here. It's a little cool at this elevation." Harry reached into the back seat and retrieved his denim jacket.

Flin opened the trunk and retrieved his brown sheriff's jacket, a 12-gauge shotgun and a box of slugs. "I feel safer with this against a bear." He propped the shotgun against the bumper and retrieved a Smith & Wesson .357 Magnum he had wrapped in a towel.

"Here, stick this in your waistband." He handed Harry the gun. "Ever used one of these beauties"

"Sure have. Nice gun."

"Those tire tracks look fresh. Actually two sets of tracks." Flin started to bend down and check but had second thoughts. The air was thinner at this elevation, and his breathing was heavy. "No more than a couple days old, I'd say."

"Right on, Sheriff. And do you recognize them tracks?" Harry asked, pointing.

"Yep. Only person I know who uses studded tires all year round is Hurley Cecil Cutshaw." Flin shook his head. "That man's a mess."

"These tracks could mean he's the one who gave Elmer Hall a ride to the hospital," Harry said.

"Who's Elmer Hall?"

"The man pretending to be my daddy." Harry slid the pistol into his hip pocket. "We'd best get going."

Flin tucked his jacket under his arm and placed the shotgun on his shoulder, barrel pointing behind him and tilted skyward. They walked a good fifteen minutes side by side in silence. The trail exited the trees into a breath-taking panorama of the valley.

"Ever seen nature any more beautiful, Sheriff?"

"Lived in this area all my life but never took the time to enjoy God's green earth. This has to be one of the most beautiful places in the world, Harry. If nothing else comes from this trip, it's still been worthwhile, just to see all this."

Harry pointed toward the eastern hemlock that hugged the north slope where the wind whipped their droopy tops. "It's hard to believe that those giants could ever vanish, but if we don't change some of the ways we do things, you're seeing the last of the hemlocks in this part of the country."

"Hard to imagine that ever happening." Flin shook his head in disagreement.

"Mark my warning, Sheriff. Too many folks can't appreciate nature until it's gone."

"Hope you're wrong." Flin propped the gun in the fork of a sapling and donned his jacket. "How much farther?"

"Not far, but the worst is still ahead." Harry started out again. Not hearing Flin's footsteps, he turned. Flin stood looking across the valley. What was he thinking? Had he never passed this way before? Harry waited until he caught up.

They followed the incline of the muddy path for several minutes. Harry paused, his breathing laborious. He glanced at Flin, whose complexion had paled. "Tough going this high up." He wiped beads of sweat from his brow. "You okay," Harry asked.

"A bit winded, but I'm okay. What about you?"

"I'll make it. The loss of blood took something out of me."

"You never did finish why you was in the hospital. How'd you get shrapnel?"

"Oh, that … I started to tell you but got sidetracked. From the war. A slither of metal was still in my head."

"I'll be. Whoever heard of anything like that? And after all these years." Flin cupped his hand to his ear. "What was that? Sound's like it's coming from over there."

"Last time I was up here a bear and her cubs walked right past me." Harry smiled.

Flin removed his gun from his shoulder. "I'm scared of a bear more'n I am a convict."

"Spending too much time in the city, Sheriff. Need to take some time off and do some camping."

"There it goes again," Flin said.

"That's called a hungry dog, Sheriff. He's been left alone a few days now without food. Would you happen to have a biscuit or something on you?"

"Not hardly. I'd have eaten it myself if I did?" Flin chuckled.

"I just happen to have a little something." Harry pulled a piece of toast from his pocket. "Hospital food. Left over from breakfast. Thought we might need it."

They rounded the boulder and saw the dog sitting near the cabin door. He growled as they approached. Harry tossed the bread away from the front door, and the dog immediately vacated his sentinel.

"It won't last long," Harry said as he sprinted toward the door.

Luckily, the door was unlocked.

"What are we looking for, Harry?" Flin placed his gun on the table and circled the small room.

"Anything to prove that Elmer Hall might be Elmer Weatherholtz."

"And what might that be?" Flin asked as he opened a cabinet door.

"It could be an old letter, a picture of him with a member of my family or a newspaper clipping he's kept. You'll know a clue if you see it. We'll have to search his personal stuff."

"If'n you'd mentioned it, I could have gotten a search warrant. Made this a little more legal."

"And if we got a search warrant we might as well have announced our arrival to Cutshaw, Jenkins and whoever else is on Jenkins' payroll."

A half-hour search turned up nothing of significance. Disappointed, Harry sat on the makeshift bed and studied the room. There were no obvious hiding places, and it seemed unlikely there were concealed places in the crudely laid logs. There was no electricity and no running water. There were no conveniences of any sort; rather, the cabin displayed only bare necessities.

"You've been at this a long time, Sheriff. Let's think about this for a moment from your years of expertise," Harry said.

"And that's basically what I've been doing the last half-hour, Harry. There're no clues here at all."

"True, nothing we've found here tells us anything we need to know, but that's a clue within itself. Don't you think?"

"What are you gettin' at?" Flin rubbed the nape of his neck and turned in a slow circle, as if he might be missing something.

"We need to ask another question, Sheriff."

"And just what might that be?" Flin's patience was reaching its endurance mark.

"What's missing in this room?"

Flin contemplated the question. "You tell me."

"The past."

"What do you mean, the past?"

"There's nothing in this entire cabin that speaks of the inhabitants' past. No pictures, no letters and not even a Bible that could reveal names and dates. Common items in any home in all of Shenandoah County. So what does that tell you?"

"Tryin' to hide a past."

"I think you're right, Sheriff." Harry stood and slapped Flin on the shoulder.

"Then you know what that means?"

"What?" Harry asked.

"This Elmer Hall could well be your daddy."

Harry did not respond. His own deductions had proven something he didn't want to even consider, let alone admit.

Chapter Forty-one

The rally had started at the steps leading to the front door of the jail and ended on the courthouse lawn, and like many a revival service it resembled, the meeting kept on going. Upon Flin's absence, the deputies argued as to the time the rally started and should end. In the heat of discussion, they allowed the rally to continue even after the allotted hour. They did so especially after Shelton had used a few legal terms they'd never heard of. The young people seemed harmless enough, and Sheriff Flin wasn't answering his radio, though they'd sent him a dozen distress calls, so they decided to do nothing. In doing nothing, they risked their boss' wrath, but at least they would not be going against the legal rights of the marchers. That's what concerned them, for civil rights were gaining a lot of attention lately.

Shelton stood on the top step and gave a rendition that sounded more like a revival preacher than a D.C. lawyer. The marchers shouted back at him and waved their poster boards like they were tambourines or some other instruments of worship. Or weapons.

Cutshaw's blood boiled. He had gotten a call from Jenkins. It angered him how demanding he could be, but he had gotten the job done. He observed the rally from his pickup parked across the street at an expired meter. He tuned his new CB to the sheriff department's frequency and eavesdropped. Irene sure was a sassy one. He was enjoying this new toy: no more guesswork as to what was going on in the sheriff's department. He thumped his thumbs against the steering wheel, glancing occasionally down the street. Jenkins would be pleased with his ingenuity.

They arrived right on time, the dozen clansmen he had rounded up, hiding beneath the bed sheets of mothers and wives. And they followed the cross of the white man's savior, shouting slogans of pride and partiality. But they didn't have placards; they were armed with ax handles, tire tools and homemade blackjacks.

Chapter Forty-two

Pratt paused in the hallway of the Shenandoah Memorial emergency room. A couple-dozen or so bleeding black youth and too few medical staffers filled the room and overflowed into the hallway. Several adults had arrived and cradled sobbing girls, and they pinned together torn blouses and skirts. The silent demeanor of the boys seemed a combination of anger and fright, as some paced and others sat, cupping their foreheads, rubbing bruised limbs and wiping bloodied noses. Drying blood dulled the sheen on the finished terrazzo, hiding the multiple colors of the polished Virginia aggregates that gleamed just below the surface. A custodian sloshed a mop and diluted the blood. He mopped up the stained water and squeezed it into a yellow bucket. After repeating this a couple times, he shook his head and wheeled the bucket into a janitor's closet adjoining the emergency room. He quickly returned with a "wet floor" sign and placed it in the center of the room before returning to retrieve a fresh bucket of water.

Shelton pressed his blood-soaked suit jacket against the side of his head and walked among the youth, offering words of consolation. Like a military sergeant, he directed nurses to the more seriously wounded. A deputy stood ambivalently in the doorway, his right hand resting on the butt of his pistol, and the thumb of the other looped on his belt-buckle. It wasn't clear if he was protecting the innocent or guarding those whom he considered criminals.

With all the ruckus, no one seemed to notice Pratt as he slipped beyond the double doors leading to the patients' rooms. He paused at the empty nurses' station, snooped over the counter and found the information he needed. He scooped a stethoscope from the station and draped it over his shoulder, then followed the signs directing visitors to the rooms of the twenty-five-bed facility. Finding the room he sought, located conveniently at the end of the hallway, he looked both ways and quickly slipped into Elmer Hall's room.

Chapter Forty-three

Evelyn sipped coffee while Harry dunked a freshly baked, molasses cookie into his cup. He held it there a few seconds, then bit off the soggy part and dropped the rest into the cup. He spooned it out and finished it off before repeating the same with another. He said little as he contemplated the past couple days and what he knew as fact, fiction and some things he wasn't sure about. The contents of the letter Hurley had given him from his supposed father seemed authentic. But Hurley was one not to be trusted even with truth, for there would be a catch to it. Elmer Hall, if indeed the elderly man in the hospital was Elmer Hall, was about the same age his father would have been if still alive. He assumed the Elmer in the hospital was the same person who lived in the isolated cabin he and Flin had visited.

Some things didn't make sense. Cutshaw was promoting the old man as being Elmer Weatherholtz, but his wife insisted his name was Hall. But Elmer had checked into the hospital under the name Weatherholtz. Doctor Swartz had confirmed that. Had Elmer used the fake Weatherholtz name purposefully because he was in cahoots with Cutshaw? Or could he actually be Elmer Weatherholtz and the hallucinatory condition caused him to unconsciously reveal his true identity?

Could he be escaped prisoner Elmer Weatherholtz—aka Elmer Hall—and have hidden out all these years in the Blue Ridge? Most anyone living in that area would have been considered squatters. The land was within the Shenandoah National Park, though it was a known fact that a few folks still lived in the park. These were mostly loners who didn't take to having to sell their land and move into civilization. Some who sold their land to the national park project had received permission to reside there until death. Was that the case with Elmer Hall? If Elmer Hall was his father and had escaped prison, he certainly would want to keep his past identity secret. Living in isolation in the mountains would have helped to do so. The contents of the cabin lacked a past, suggesting an activity that needed concealment. Had his father … no, not his father, rather, had Elmer Hall been one of the landowners who got lifetime permission to stay on the land? But all this seemed too far-fetched. All of this was probably another ruse concocted by none other than the ornery Hurley Cutshaw.

The ordeal had opened up old wounds: wounds that consumed. If only there was some way to identify Elmer Hall, he may be able to get to the bottom of this and go on with life. And Miss Ann could certainly use his undivided attention with her situation.

"If only I could figure out this Hall fellow's true identity." Harry pushed back his chair, strode across the kitchen, placed his cup in the dishpan and stood for a good while gazing out the window.

Evelyn interrupted the silence. "You could just find this Elmer fella and tell him you've come to kill him for murdering your mother. If he isn't your father, I think he'll come clean quick enough." Evelyn chuckled. Harry turned but showed no expression. "Sorry. Bad idea?"

"No, you're probably right. I do need to pay him another visit."

"Another visit? Bud, did you stop in his hospital room?"

"Just momentarily, but I didn't identify myself. And how about you? Did you identify yourself when you stopped by to visit them when you left my room?"

"No."

"So you don't deny the visit?"

"Why should I?" Evelyn chided. "I'm a free moral agent … proved that by my recent, short-lived trip to Ohio." She chuckled at herself.

He turned back toward the window in contemplation. After a long silence, he turned to her. "Do you think he's my father?"

She seemed to study the dregs in her coffee cup. "How should I know, I was only there a few moments and mostly spoke to the wife."

"But you must have some assessment. Do I favor him? Did they act guilty? What did your gut say? Anything?"

Harry's elevated voice surprised her, but he wasn't angry, just emphatic. Evelyn realized he valued her judgment and that pleased her. She was not just an outsider watching the drama. Hers was a key role. She was tied up in this mess, drawn as taut as the bailing twine that holds fast the corn shocks in the late fall.

"I could only feel sympathy, Bud … that poor lonely woman and her pitiful husband. I wish you could feel some sympathy. What if it is your father? You know you used to feed every tramp who came by the jailhouse." She paused, as if waiting for an answer. "You did it because you would have wanted someone to feed your father if he was wandering around the country penniless. You said so yourself. You always gave consideration to the rumors … that he bribed officials, got out of prison and took on a new identity. Now the possibility is staring you in the face, and you're closing your eyes and refusing to respond."

"It's just too far-fetched to believe that after all these years he's alive. Even if he was my dad, he wouldn't recognize me, not after sixty years."

"And what does that matter?"

Harry paced, stopping at every window and peering out as if the answer might be out there somewhere. "But he isn't my dad."

"And how can you be so sure?"

Harry did not want to answer that question. After a long pause, he turned to Evelyn. "You were right. I need to ask him point blank who he is, and if he says he's my father, I need to threaten him within an inch of his life for murdering my mother. If he's a fake he'll come clean. Not a bad idea, Evelyn."

Surprised, she set her cup hard onto the table and coffee splashed onto her hand. "I was just teasing, Bud. Surely you knew that. And that'd land you in jail for sure, and even Flin won't be able to rescue you."

"But what else will work?"

"You've got to use your brain and not your brawn. Surely you can come up with something that can identify this Elmer. What about fingerprints? Your dad was a criminal. He would have been printed."

"No, because fingerprinting didn't catch on in the states until about 1903. We were somewhat behind other countries in technology."

"And you found nothing in that cabin that could have belonged to your dad?"

"Nothing. And even if I had found something, I was only five or six when he went to prison. I wouldn't remember anything he ever owned." Harry rubbed gently at the edge of the bandage, frowning.

"Are you in pain, Bud? I think you should go back to the hospital. Doctor Swartz warned of infection."

"No, it's not pain. This bandage is itching me like crazy. But I think you're right. I need to go back to the hospital and pay another visit to my pretend dad."

"And do what?"

"I think I have an idea that will identify him as fake or real. It's time we end this charade. And I need to return the hospital shirt I borrowed, before Flin arrests me for stealing."

"I'll go with you. Give me time to change into something more respectable."

Chapter Forty-four

They stopped at the receptionist's desk to pick up a visitor pass and confirm Elmer Hall's room. As they walked past a cleaning lady, Harry tossed the hospital gown onto her cart.

"Conscience clear now that you've returned the gown." Evelyn patted him on the shoulder. "Now do us all a favor and try not to do anything that would spoil that good feeling."

Harry loved to laugh, but lately, there seemed to be nothing humorous about life. With Jack Brady shot and likely not going to make it, and with Ann accused of the crime, and languishing in jail, laughter seemed inappropriate. And how do you respond to a dying man pretending to be your father who was supposed to have died in prison some sixty years ago? How do you make sense of a letter from that man expressing he'd left you an inheritance? The latter was certainly hogwash. And if there's a shred of truth to the letter, there's Cutshaw trying to use it to coerce you into turning a deaf ear to the resurgence of child abuse in the valley. But as gloomy and confusing and disgusting as events were, Harry couldn't suppress a chuckle at Evelyn's comment.

Evelyn was a stern woman, but sometimes her comments were hilariously funny. He wasn't sure she was trying to be funny.

Perhaps it was the contrast of the situation at hand, and her light-heartedness to it all, that made her comment touch his funny bone so. And this was far better than having her run off to Ohio.

"What's so funny?" Evelyn slapped him on the shoulder.

"You are, Evelyn."

"I don't get it. By the way, just what is your plan to identify your father?"

"I'm going to use your suggestion. You've told me exactly what I need to do."

"Which is—?"

"I'm just going to walk into the man's room, introduce myself, tell him the story as Cutshaw has related it to me and see if he claims it's true, that he's my father."

"His claiming to be your father still doesn't solve the mystery. You know you're not going to threaten to shoot him."

"No, but if he sticks to the story that he's actually my father, then I have one more question to ask him."

"He can just tell a lie, so I don't see how questioning solves anything."

"You will when you hear my second question."

Their footsteps on the terrazzo echoed throughout the long hallway.

"And what is the question?" Evelyn's impatience kicked in.

"You'll know soon enough. Here's his room." Harry knocked gently on the door and waited for an answer. Silence. He rapped on the door a couple more times before slowly opening it. "Hello."

The patient was gone.

Chapter Forty-five

Winston Pratt mapped out the route to Charlottesville. His unfinished business was becoming easier by a twist of fate. With Elmer Hall and Jack Brady out of the picture, he would have only two more individuals standing between a fortune and the freedom for which he pined: Cutshaw and Judge Jenkins. He liked Harry Weatherholtz, and unless necessary otherwise, he'd decided to let him live. But Weatherholtz would have to stay out of his way, which he hoped would happen. Jenkins had warned him it was best to avoid any more suspicious activity, especially with Weatherholtz being close friends with the sheriff. The death of Weatherholtz might just be the straw. Still, he would not spare him if necessary to get his way.

He had not considered that the judge would leave him an inheritance. Then again, the judge didn't have any relatives to speak of. Who else could he have left it to? The judge wasn't a genuine philanthropist; he had begrudged every humanitarian cause to which he had ever given a dime. His financial gifts were only to remain in the graces of the important folks. Yes, he had given a lot of money for that singular reason, but he had held back much more. Now some of that money would become Winston Pratt's. Or was that Sir Winston

Pratt? At least that's what he'd be called back in London. What great news! Could he ever go back? Perhaps under his American identity.

Jenkins trusted Pratt only because the judge knew his past and knew the past needed to ever remain secret. The judge had kept the secret these past twenty years, and surely he would take it with him to his grave. Though he had skimmed from Jenkins' income, he still had very little money without Jenkins' resources. Now all that was about to change. His biggest challenge was how to eliminate the judge without it hinting of foul play, and then he would just sit back and wait for probate court to write him a check.

He definitely had to eliminate Hurley Cutshaw. The man was privy to too much information that could throw a cog in the wheel of his world of deceit. And Cutshaw seemed to have turned rogue lately, befriending Elmer Hall in a manner that bespoke of treachery. Cutshaw's demise would probably be welcomed news by most in the valley; at best he would not be missed. No one would cry foul when he was found dead. *Death by Natural Causes* was what the valley newspaper would read somewhere in the back section. Not so with Judge Jenkins, for he had influential friends in high places who would scrutinize any questionable report. He had to plan and perform well for the judge's demise. He had to remain Jenkins' loyal butler to the very end, but he did not want the end to be a drawn out affair. He wanted it over now. But how?

Chapter Forty-six

Tubes dangled from stands as if they had been jerked from the patient's arm. The crumpled and bloodstained linen, along with a bloody pad on the mattress, created more questions than answers. What had happened? Where was the patient? Was he okay? Harry could only speculate that, again, he was minutes—maybe moments—too late. He was too often too late. For his momma. For little Eddie. The lad's face brought a flash of memories. Regret. Blame. Anger. If only he could forget that face, still, evil men will triumph if good men remain aloof from the struggle. John Mill was right: Bad men need nothing more to accomplish their ends, than that good men should look on and do nothing.

Harry had never run from duty. He fought in the Great War, his only regret being the loss of so many innocent lives. His sons took up the cause in the second great war, as all five opposed that merciless beast reigning in Germany. All five returned home safely, but oh the price many families paid! The right cause usually carries a heavy price. Only God knows what the outcome would have been had not America abandoned its isolationism policies adopted after the first Great War. The expansive two oceans had naturally created some sense of security, but even that failed in the west. Emperor Hirohito sent Admiral Yamamoto and his fleet on a preemptive attack that prompted Roosevelt's *Day of Infamy* speech. That necessitated the sending of troops across the Atlantic to push back the Nazis and island hopping in the vast Pacific to stop the Japanese Empire's advances.

"May I help you?"

"Ah, yes." Evelyn stood in the doorway. The woman standing in the hallway behind a janitor's cart awaited her response. "We were hoping to see Elmer … Hall."

"He's probably the man that got transferred to another hospital."

"Is he alright?"

"Not sure. They sent me to clean the room he was in."

Harry spun on his heels in renewed hope. "Do you know which hospital?"

"No, but I can ask for you, if you like."

"Thank you, ma'am. We'll check ourselves," Harry said, as he brushed by Evelyn and headed for the nurses' station.

****

The information given them by the nurse elicited mixed emotions. The patient in room twenty-five had been transferred to the University Hospital in Charlottesville. Harry hadn't visited the historic town in years. He clutched the steering wheel and occasionally checked the speedometer as he drove in silence. He squinted at the unfolded Virginia state map on the bench seat between him and Evelyn. Reading glasses were on his list. He adjusted the sun visor and glanced at her, catnapping. He adjusted her visor and she stirred.

"You're awfully quiet." She peeked in the mirror and adjusted her hat.

"I assumed you were asleep," Harry responded.

"No, just enjoying the quiet ride. You okay?" she asked.

"Just thinking."

She tilted her head against the headrest and closed her eyes. She seemed to know when he needed silence.

Harry seldom verbalized his feelings, for they seemed too elusive. After forty years of marriage, she had become accustomed to his frequent bouts of silence. Early on, she had tried to help him talk through his doldrums, but eventually, she came to realize nothing she did or said corrected his melancholic moods. He was glad she accepted him the way he was, though he wished she understood. Since he could not explain his bouts of depression, he certainly did not expect her to understand. He assumed it came from the childhood trauma. How many children had witnessed the murder of their mother at the hands of their father? How many children lost both parents in the same day? He wasn't on a pity party; rather, he truly cared for any child who had to be raised without a parent. His grandmother had done a decent job raising him and Lawrence, but she had died when he was still in grade school, leaving them to fend on their own. Even so, they'd done well for themselves. The army had been good for him, but in spite of his accomplishments, Harry struggled against a sense of incompleteness. Was it a carryover of childhood without a family? Had he retired too soon? He wasn't sure.

What he knew for sure was that this mental bout had existed from childhood. Grandma Biller, when he lived with her, never talked about his daddy, as if he never existed. She'd hurried him and his older brother away to Ohio shortly after the murder. It seemed to be out of fear for their safety, for his father had escaped from jail previously. Perhaps she feared he would escape again and harm the children. Or did she do it for personal reasons? To get even with his father for killing her daughter? If so, it was successful. He'd spent a lifetime estranged from his father's family. Being back in Virginia seemed to compensate somewhat, but that, too, seemed perplexing. He sometimes felt like a stranger in a foreign land? Now, something even more confusing was added to the fray: a father, absent some sixty years, wanting to reconcile. Why now, after all these years, did Elmer want to meet with him? Then again, he didn't know for sure if Elmer was his daddy. And how was Elmer connected with Hurley

Cutshaw? That in itself was enough to incriminate him and reason to keep him at bay.

Perhaps he wouldn't have to deal with any of this, for death seemed imminent with Elmer. Evidently, there were some complications from the surgery, and the doctor had ordered him rushed to the university hospital in hopes of saving his life.

Why did he not feel any pity for Elmer? Was he heartless? Or worse, full of hate for the man? Why no emotion for a man who may be his dad? Then again, would he ever find out for sure if the man was or wasn't his daddy? After these many years, perhaps that was best.

"How are you going to find out, Harry?"

"Find out what?"

"Whether or not the old man is your daddy? You said you had a plan, a second question."

"A poem," Harry said.

"A poem?" Evelyn's perplexity was obvious.

"Yes. He used to recite a poem to Lawrence and me. He wrote it down and gave it to Lawrence, who after the murder threw it away, but I got it from the trash. I still have it."

> *Tall and straight without a flaw,*
> *Weathering cold and thaw,*
> *None could equal this towering giant,*
> *Until it met the crosscut saw.*
>
> *No one mourned trees hauled away,*
> *Regret none dared to say,*
> *Until a logger solemnly sighed,*
> *We cut the last Hemlock today.*

"I never knew that. But how does your having a copy of a poem identify Elmer as your father?"

"I'm going to ask him to recite it."

"Interesting plan."

The hum of the engine and incessant whine of the tires seemed out of sync, like an orchestra warming up: different keys, tunes and timing. The mind has a way of trying to synchronize the dissenting composition. Such is a difficult task and senseless.

"Bud!" Evelyn's nails gripped into his forearm at the sound of a blaring horn.

"Sorry. Daydreaming, I guess." He had drifted across the centerline.

"You need to be more careful." She released her grip.

The discordant music returned. Charlottesville signs appeared along the way. A billboard advertised the university hospital, alongside one promoting the newest Holiday Inn, still five miles out.

"One thing concerns me about your plan." She picked up the map and attempted to duplicate the original folds.

"What is that?"

"He's in his eighties. What if he knew the poem and has just forgotten it?"

"I've thought of that." Harry tapped his thumbs against the steering wheel.

"And?"

"Then he isn't my dad."

"How so?"

"If he can't remember a poem he recited a hundred times to me, then he can't remember anything about me. That poem was the only positive connection I had to him. If he can't remember it, he didn't care enough to keep me alive, just like he did my mother."

Chapter Forty-seven

"And what's the nature of your visit, sir?" The state trooper guarding the door held a clipboard in one hand and the other hand rested on his gun holster.

"Friends. We've been longtime friends."

"I've orders not to let any unauthorized person into the room."

"I see. And I can only assume my name is not on the list. So could you tell me how Mr. Brady is doing?"

"To the contrary, Mr. Pratt, your name is on the list. That is your name, Pratt?"

"No. You must have me mixed up with someone else, sir. My name is—"

"Pratt. Winston Pratt. And as for Mr. Brady's condition, he is doing quite well, and he's been asking about your whereabouts."

"I don't understand. You have me mistaken for someone else."

Pratt bolted and almost ran into a trooper who rounded the corner with a gun pointed at his chest. He lifted his hands in surrender. That's when he noticed the blood, but it was too late.

"You've been a busy man, Mr. Pratt. How'd you get that blood on your cuff?"

"I'd thank you, sir, if I can call my lawyer." If only he had washed the blood from his sleeve.

"That is dried blood, isn't it Mr. Pratt?"

Pratt refused to answer. The dried blood on his cuff was a detail he generally would not have overlooked. Things did not look well, but he still had an ace up his sleeve.

Chapter Forty-eight

He felt the good Lord had endowed him with the virtue of patience. While sheriff back in Ohio, he had never drawn his gun on anyone. In fact, he seldom carried a gun. His deputies were good for the gun toting. He preferred the man-to-man talk, which generally worked well. His six-three frame, and solid build, worked wonders in calming many a criminal. In his youthful years, he'd scaled Chimney Rock near Cootes Store, and he did a headstand on the summit to punctuate the event. The locals still talked about it. Still, his stature added a challenge to some men, especially when they'd had a little too much to drink. So, he'd had his share of senseless fights, and he'd never backed away from a fight. Though hating to admit it now, he even enjoyed a scuffle once in a while back in the day. As a young man, he had fought his way across the country, leaving many an opponent lying flat on his back. Though of a kind nature, he knew prizefighting was for keeps. A couple blows to the head had taught him that. He learned that you show no mercy while your opponent is standing, but after the knockout, he'd gladly help his opponent to his feet and kindly shake his hand. His boxing career paralleled his day job of wielding a sledgehammer on a railroad gang. Such conditioning prepared him for the sheriff's job, for the physical labor had made him a formidable foe to any lawbreaker.

He prided himself in calm. Evelyn sometimes chided him for inactivity regarding things that perturbed her. But lately, things seemed to change. He had become way too impatient. Little things accelerated his heart rate. People, ordinarily considered his assets, seemed a necessary nuisance. Today was no exception. His patience wore thin quickly when the receptionist insisted that Elmer Hall, Elmer Weatherholtz, or anyone near that name had not been transferred from Woodstock Memorial to the Charlottesville Hospital in the last twenty-four hours. The nearest person fitting their request was a lady expecting a baby that had arrived from Woodstock.

He'd somewhat enjoyed working alongside Sheriff Flin during the previous summer. It brought a sense of purpose that retirement had lost. But the present situation was escalating out of his control, and he found himself having to fight back his anger. Was he getting too old for the stress? The frequent sharp pains in his chest offered some concern. He hadn't told Evelyn. Could his heart take another episode of tragedy? As Evelyn negotiated with the receptionist, he remained silent. Her stubbornness could sometimes create a stalemate. Negotiating through tragedy had been his responsibility all these years, but she was doing fine, so he remained silent.

"Then would it be possible to see Mr. Jack Brady?" Evelyn asked as she placed a calming hand on his fist that rested firmly on the receptionist desk.

"Can't see him unless you're from the governor's office or someone really important. They got him under lock and key to protect him from another assassin's attempt. The same man who shot him before evidently showed up to finish the job." The receptionist eagerly shared the latest news in detail.

Harry and Evelyn huddled with the receptionist as she shared what to them was great news, something they hadn't had much of lately. The story unfolded like new linoleum being rolled across a kitchen floor, transforming bare and ugly planks into a floral arrangement of multiple colors and patterns. Jack Brady had come out of his coma, had identified the man who shot him, and the state police nabbed the criminal when he came to finish his job. "They are questioning the man in some hospital room right now. Security guards have been sharing confidential information right and left." She smiled as if proud to be in the inner circle of the gossip.

"That's wonderful news, ma'am," Evelyn said, as she retrieved a white, laced handkerchief tucked inside her belt.

"And that's not all. You say you're from Woodstock?"

"Near there." Evelyn gripped Harry's hand.

"News crews are headed there now. This means that colored girl they have in jail for the murder is not the murderer after all. Can you believe what a change of events?"

"Sure is wonderful news." Evelyn daubed her eyes with her handkerchief.

"Y'all must know the girl?"

"Yes! Yes, we do!" Evelyn said as she patted Harry's shoulder. "Thank you, ma'am, for some good news."

"Sorry about not being able to help you find your friend. But why don't I make a call to Woodstock Memorial to try and find out what has happened? There must be some sort of mix-up."

"Do you know the name of the man they arrested?" Harry asked.

"Some British fellow, Patton or something like that. I think that was his name."

"Maybe Pratt?" Harry asked.

"Yes, I think that's it. Some man who used to live in the house before Mr. Brady bought it. Must've been angry about losing his home, or something. You know him?" She held up her hand as if asking for silence. "Just a moment, I have Woodstock on the line."

A commotion occurred down the hallway. Cameras flashed as a sea of uniforms moved quickly toward the main exit. Harry's eyes locked with those of Winston Pratt, who smiled, but not a do-you-remember-me friendly smile. It was eerie. How strange! He called out to Harry. "I have something that will interest you, Harry Weatherholtz."

It seemed all the state troopers turned to look at Harry as they hurried Pratt out the front door. It's a wonder they didn't haul him in for interrogation.

"What's that all about?" Evelyn asked.

"Not sure. Awkward though." Harry had the chance meeting with Pratt at Twelve Oaks but had never talked with him. "What would he have that would interest me?"

"He's gone missing." The receptionist held the phone aloft.

"What do you mean?" Harry asked.

"Your friend at Woodstock Memorial was never transferred here like you thought. He has gone missing. Completely disappeared. They can't find him anywhere."

How can that be? The nurse at Woodstock Memorial definitely said he was transferred. But now he's missing? Harry wanted to grab the phone and start an interrogation. Someone had messed up. Who? How? Why? Nothing made sense.

The convoy of state police cars exited the parking lot. In one of those vehicles, Jenkins' henchman evidently held some dark secrets. "What could he have that would interest me?" Harry said to no one in particular.

"You know him?" The nurse stared at Harry.

"Sort of. Thank you, ma'am, for your help," Harry said, as he nudged Evelyn and they started for the exit.

"What's that all about," Evelyn asked.

"I'm not sure what. ... " Harry's words trailed off as his mind raced. Did Judge Jenkins have Pratt shoot Jack Brady? Why? Would Pratt squeal on Jenkins? Evidently, Pratt was much more than a butler. Jenkins was still ruling from his sick bed. What else had Pratt been involved with? Harry's only connection to the judge was his involvement with Hurley Cutshaw and Miss Ann. What was Jack Brady's association with the butler? He hadn't the faintest idea. Jenkins? Jack had facilitated Ann's freedom from Cutshaw, which angered Jenkins. Miss Ann was cleaning Brady's home, which used to be Jenkins' home, of which Pratt was the former butler. Did that anger Jenkins? Pratt? Or both? There had to be some kind of connection with all this. Perhaps Pratt's comment, though bizarre, was a corner piece to an otherwise complex puzzle. He had to somehow visit with Pratt.

Chapter Forty-nine

A throng of the Negro community gathered in the courtyard of the centuries-old Shenandoah County courthouse, a Greek Revival structure built of native limestone. The crowd lined the sidewalk, and a few folks spilled into the street. Cars slowed and tempers flared as drivers maneuvered their vehicles around those lingering in the street. The rally cry for freedom was not new to Woodstock. One of the first, if not the first rally in Woodstock, was during the War for Independence. Like this present rally, a minister, Peter Muhlenberg, headed up the cause.

Reverend Muhlenberg's legendary actions were told and re-told in and around Woodstock. His history began in Pennsylvania, where his father encouraged him to enter the ministry. As a pastor in Woodstock, he made the citizens very proud. Though he moved on, his good reputation remained, but it also went with him. The people of Pennsylvania affirmed that when they sent a marble statue of him to The National Statuary Hall Collection in the United States Capitol Building. It arrived in Washington D.C. in 1889. And the people of Woodstock never forgot his good deeds, for there was talk of a second statue of him being erected on their courthouse lawn.

Of Muhlenberg's five years in Woodstock, his most famous sermon proclaiming "A time to pray and a time to fight," whether true to text or embellished, is forever etched in the hearts of Woodstock residents. Depending on who's telling the story, the details vary, but generally the account crescendos with the good reverend casting aside his clerical robe to reveal a military uniform of the colonial army. A group of Woodstock patriots answered his battle cry and followed him from the valley to form the 8th Virginia Regiment. They joined Washington in the fight against the redcoats and tyranny. Today's emotions were as high as those of almost a century and three-quarters ago. A mass of men, women and children pressed jubilantly toward the courthouse steps. These legendary steps were laid to the specifications of the architectural design of the same man who drafted the Declaration of Independence, Virginia's own Thomas Jefferson. But that independence, holding that all men are created equal, did not apply to the Negroes, neither then, or the present. Now, another lawyer had mounted those courthouse steps to recall the words written by Mr. Jefferson. Ironically, he was the descendant of slaves, and he was free, and he was willing to demand equality for all. He was somewhere inside the courthouse, welding the sharp sword of Jefferson's constitution. This crowd awaited the outcome. They had prayed for Ann Shaver's release, and they had fought for her freedom through a peaceful demonstration, even though some paid a price at the hands of the clansmen. Now the battle was all but over, and they had won. The county judge was making it official. Any minute now, Ann would walk out of the courthouse a free woman.

With a slight resemblance of a miniature White House, four round and towering columns supported the two-story front portico of the Woodstock courthouse. The weather vane atop the courthouse cupola showed an east by west wind moving into the valley from the Blue Ridge. It was a beautiful spring day. Tufts of clouds resembled an artist's slight wisp of a brush across a bold blue canvas.

The chatter momentarily silenced when a deputy slowly opened the double-wide door to the main entrance, and a cheer erupted as Sheriff Flin, Dedrick Shelton, Pastor Harris and a smiling Miss Ann exited the building. They stopped on the porch, waving to the exuberant crowd. Ann stood between Shelton and Pastor Harris; they held her hands aloft in victory. The crowd roared its approval, clapping, shouting and whistling, while some did a hallelujah jig.

A block away, behind a line of police tape, and loosely guarded by a couple deputies, a subdued and smaller swarm of men stalked the courthouse audience. Some probably carried their hoods in their pockets. They had little regard for justice and a whole lot of disgust for the black man. Why? They'd never considered any logic to that question. That's the way it's always been, the way it is, the way it's supposed to be. The boundaries have always been so. Some things are predestined, so you don't question, reason, or doubt. You accept. The sooner the black man realizes this the better off things will be for him. How'd the apostle say it? Be content with whatsoever state you are in. Don't fight against nature and God. These men are not a praying crowd, though they use the Bible when it supports their cause. Their mentality is to continue on with that which has always been and should always be: rules they made up without any consideration to those whom the rules affect.

From across the street, Harry and Evelyn observed both crowds. They were generally for the underdog, and they were thrilled that Ann was free, again. This time they celebrated from the sidelines, for it was not their intervention that had won Miss Ann's release. They lingered, wondering whether Ann scanned the crowd, looking for them, but mostly out of concern because of the irate crowd a block away.

Miss Ann was fortunate to have Reverend Harris on her side. He had cared enough to jeopardize his future. He stepped down from his pulpit and went into action on her behalf, just like Reverend Muhlenberg fought for freedom. Was he aware of Reverend Muhlenberg's story? His lore had survived time, but his philosophy seemed lacking in some aspects: time to quit praying and a time to start fighting. Is that what he meant? Muhlenberg abandoned his pulpit to take up arms. And he won. Then again, maybe his philosophy was not advocating the abandonment of prayer for fighting. Perhaps it was both simultaneously—praying and fighting—that works. Reverend Harris and his congregation had done both, and they were certainly pleased with the outcome. Surely Reverend Muhlenberg knew about both—praying and fighting—for he somehow survived the winter at Valley Forge.

Evelyn shielded her eyes from the sun. "Let's go home, dear. She'll stop by to see us. I'm sure she missed us." She slipped from the back of the crowd.

Harry hesitated. "Wait for me at the car. Be there in five minutes," he called to her.

Shelton took the microphone, and cheers erupted from the crowd. He allowed the applause to last a bit longer than necessary before he raised his hands, signaling for quiet. The cheers slowly subsided. "Victory at any cost!" The crowd roared again. "Victory is not the winning of a single battle; victory is the destination of a long and continuous struggle. So we haven't really won." The jubilance quickly turned to contemplation and low murmuring. He was a master of mood setting. "The battle isn't over; it's only beginning. It will never be over, at least this side of eternity, as long as mortal men reign. But never forget, the battle is the Lord's, and we are the Lord's children." He turned preacher and the jubilance returned. "And our Savior Himself was more black than He was white." Contemplation returned. They were not accustomed to such statements, had really never considered such. Reverend Harris had never ventured that far into Christology. He mostly preached the significance of the crucifixion.

Harry reflected upon his own speech of last year's local Independence Day celebration. "Democracy should be written in characters of living light … the doctrine of divine rights of kings should have met its death thrust with the great war … under the serene skies and shining stars of that glad future, there should break forth again the song ushered in by the Savior's coming: 'Peace on earth, goodwill to men.' The passions of war should have subsided, and prejudices should have been dethroned … the sacrifice made on foreign soil by so many of our young men, shouldering their rifles in defense of our great country … these men who gave up every opportunity in life and bared their chests to shot and shell and defied disease and death that this country might survive in all of its original integrity."

He had taken the speech to memory. Since last July the folded copy made his wallet a mite fat. He wasn't sure why he memorized the speech, and he certainly didn't know why he carried it in his wallet. The contents were mere diminishing words on deteriorating paper. The war to end all wars failed to bring lasting peace. He'd come home to a hero's welcome, but history has a way of being repetitive. Seventeen million deaths—including civilians—wasn't quite enough to cause men to beat their swords into plowshares. So his five sons joined the thousands of G.I.s who repeated the cause globally in a Second World War, the death toll more than doubling the first Great War. Following World War II, with Europe weary of bloodshed and busy rebuilding, a new kind of war developed. Relationships between the United States and the Soviet Union chilled. This cold war eventually flowed over into Korea, when the Soviets prevented a UN resolution for a democratic Korea. China stretched its muscles in support of a communist Korea, sending another wave of G.I.s across the Pacific. The UN forces, led by his old hero, General Douglas MacArthur, fought a back and forth battle, gaining and losing the same ground over and over. Advancing and retreating across the 38th parallel finally ended with a consensus for a demilitarized zone to separate the factions. This agreement divided family and friends, and perhaps they will forever be separated. The war never formally ended, it just lost significance as the Geneva Conference of '54 focused more on the French colonial war in Indochina. Only God knows how that will end up, and how many young lives will be snuffed out, as the United States already has military advisors on site … probably a repeat of Korea.

He had fought in the Great War for twenty-two months, was wounded eight times and bore scars to prove it. He kept his five citations and medals for bravery in his footlocker. It seemed the badge of courage was something you shouldn't wear on your shirt. Honor and courage is a principle by which you try to live, not parade. Were there black veterans in this crowd? He should know them by name, should shake their hand and congratulate them. They had fought for the same cause he did in France and the Rhineland, in the heat and the cold. Over 200,000 black men had crossed the Atlantic to fight and labor in a war for European freedom. If he'd had any prejudiced sentiments against the black community, he had shed them during the war. But the black soldier returned home to a nation engaged in Jim Crow antics in the south and job limitations and discriminations in the north. They helped win a measure of freedom for a foreign people, but that same freedom eluded them at home. The Emancipation Proclamation ended slavery in principle but not in practice.

As much as he hated to admit it, Shelton was right. The war goes on. How did Jesus say it? "Wars and rumors of wars" … to the bitter end. Yes, the war goes on. Miss Ann is free but free only from jail. She's still held captive by a system, a system that protects and promotes and preserves its own kind. It is a system that operates from fear and therefore cannot trust those who are different. What if the shoe was reversed? What if the black man dominated? Was that what his race feared? Retaliation? Was that a possibility? Would a change of power change the way power works? "Love your enemy" was Christ's antidote for a world of peace, but it's a pill too few are willing to swallow.

Dedrick Shelton is the black folks' hero. Place him on a pedestal alongside Muhlenberg. He prayed with them and he fought for them. They followed him and he led them to victory. Now he'll go on to another battle, leaving the black community in Woodstock with a fleeting sense of victory. Who can tell what enemies he's stirred? How many more innocent Miss Ann's will be unjustly incarcerated, raped and beaten? How many more little Eddie's will be harmed, even killed, and the truth white washed by the system.

All wars are not fought with bullets and guns and grenades. There is the war within, the battlefield of the mind, the soul struggle. That is his war, a war that has gone on and on and on. And when the war seems to have subsided, a forgotten splinter of the past festers and sends poison into the heart and mind. He thought he'd long ago forgiven his father for killing his mother. And now a stranger shows up, claiming to be his father, wanting to reconcile, and it seems the hate he'd had for his father had never gone away. Like a sapling shooting up from the stump of a felled tree, the anger resurfaced. He could well forgive the man if he wasn't his dad, forgive him for the pretense, the lies and the scheming. He'd forgiven worse before. Why could he not forgive this stranger if he is his father?

"Let it go," Evelyn had said. And he wanted to do so. That wasn't the problem, letting go. The problem was an elusive feeling, like an itch you can't reach. Or phantom pain. Some of the soldiers, who lost limbs in the war, had it. How do you correct something that bypasses the senses? After all this time it should be behind him. Was it his pride that kept it alive? Or an excuse? Someone to blame for unrealized dreams? When do you draw a line in life's shifting sand and determine from here on I am responsible for me? Here I take up my life, play my hand and no longer blame someone in my past.

Then again, was he angry at his father for his mother's sake. Perhaps that was the real issue and seemed justifiable cause for anger. To forgive the murderer of his mother seemed to somehow say it was okay. He wrestled with this in dreams most of his life. The dreams he could shake, but a real person stepping out of the past and into the present, claiming to be his father, was different. Much different.

The smell? Soured clothes. It got his attention before the familiar voice said a word. He turned into the face of Hurley Cutshaw, who seemed to have stepped out of nowhere.

"I got just one word for you, Weatherholtz. Murderer."

"What do you mean?"

"Either you deal with me or you are a murderer. Your old man will be dead inside of a week if you don't cooperate."

"Is that a threat?"

"No, reality. You're painin' him to death."

"What is that supposed to mean?"

"He's grievin' over you refusing to see him."

"And my visit with him will fix sixty years of his neglect?"

"Not just help fix an old man's broken heart, but if'n you co-operate, it will take care of some other important issues that concern you and me."

"And how do I cooperate?"

"Two things … simple as that. One, back off. Quit playing nigger protector. Be the Christian you claim and turn the other cheek. And the other, go see your ole man. He refuses doctor's help unless you come see him. You've got a day to think on it and give me your word, otherwise, he'll be a dead man."

Harry hesitated.

"One day or I'll take him to where you'll never find him."

"Where is he now?"

"Over't the Twelve Oaks Home."

Harry hesitated. "Twelve Oaks?"

"Your ole man and Jenkins were closer than you care to 'cept."

Harry stared into the shifty eyes of Cutshaw. Years of dealing with criminals taught him the art of hiding emotions. You had to keep the criminal guessing, never give him the upper hand, but Cutshaw's comments angered him … go see your father or he'll succumb to death … insinuating death from grieving. How ridiculous! Not that he expected any less of the man who claimed to be his father … who, if so, was a criminal. It wouldn't surprise him if his father was associated with Jenkins … birds of a feather.

"Not that your ole man cared that much for Jenkins. They were just … in dealings together." Cutshaw was an agitator, and he drew lines to his advantage.

"Why now, after all these years? What does he want from me?" Harry felt anger toward Cutshaw, but Cutshaw wasn't really on trial. This had gone way beyond his feelings toward Cutshaw. This was about himself and a phantom of his past. He needed to face his fears, and his heart ached to know the truth.

"That's a question you need to ask your pappy, not me. He's the only one knows for sure why. 'Course he had his reasons, but something I'd never do, 'specially not to my own."

Harry did not like Cutshaw's tone, his choice of words and certainly not his insinuation. For some, the accepted illusion of the present is sometimes safer than the unknown truth of the past. Where did he stand regarding his father? "I'll think about it and let you know." He stuffed his hands into the hip pockets of his khakis. There was no way he would shake on a deal with Hurley Cutshaw.

"One day, Weatherholtz, I'll give you just one day. And don't bring no law with you." Cutshaw jabbed a finger at Harry, turned abruptly and slipped into the crowd.

Harry didn't need one day to decide. He had already made up his mind.

Chapter Fifty

"I was thinking about the time one of the tramps attacked Doris," Evelyn said. "Gullible, that's what she called you, Bud." Between sips of coffee, Evelyn awaited his response as she stared at him over the rim of her dusty pink, depression cup—a gift from him—that she deeply cherished.

Harry lived with a few regrets: this one bothered him the most. Early on in life, he made a mistake in judgment, which he felt brought a breach in his relationship with his only daughter. It happened while he was sheriff in Ohio and the family lived in the apartment over the county jail. He furrowed his brow as Evelyn brought up the long ago incident.

Harry didn't realize his error until Doris was grown and the mother of four daughters. She had become quite religious and sought ways to share her faith, so she submitted a story to a Christian magazine. In the story, she related the account of having been accosted by one of the transients whom he always allowed to mill around the jailhouse. The story, *A Tramp Invaded My Castle*, shared her remembrance of the account, her terror in having barely escaped the attacker and her trauma in wondering what could have been. Indeed, the apartment in the circular tower over the jail was his daughter's imagined castle, but he had failed to properly protect her. It wasn't that he was slothful, for he was generally busy in his office across the jailhouse lawn in the upper level of the courthouse. But though a few hundred feet away, he had not properly protected his only daughter. To complicate matters, Evelyn busied herself cooking for the inmates and couldn't always have close oversight of their five children. So the tramps felt liberty to sometimes wander into the family apartment.

"I know I was preoccupied in showing kindness to the tramps. I should have believed her." He paused. "In my mind, each of those transients was my dad traipsing across the countryside in search of his next meal. When in reality they were all either too lazy to work or else touched in the head in a way that removed them from reality. I should never have endangered her the way I did, but somehow I thought that if I was kind to others, perhaps someone would be kind to my father if he was alive somewhere. I refused to accept the idea that one of the tramps I gave food and shelter would attempt to harm my daughter. 'You're imagining things again, Miss Doris,' is what I told her. She must have thought I didn't care."

"At the time, she did, but time is the healer of wounds. Gullible is how she perceived it in later life, not unkindness."

"Either is unacceptable. I could never have forgiven myself if one of those men had—"

"Water under the bridge, Bud. I brought it up only because of what is happening now. Stick to reality. No matter what Cutshaw or anyone he's involved with says, they are up to no good. Don't allow your emotions to interfere with truth. It's truth that will set you free, not pandering to what might have been."

"Thank God I've had you to balance me through the years … and now to help me wade through this mud hole."

"I can't go on with this, Bud. I'm done with Cutshaw, with Jenkins, with the old man, with … done with it all. You'll never know the truth from these men, for their entire lives have been a lie. Just don't allow gullibility over what might be, to interfere with what is, what you have, what you know to be true."

"It's strange how emotions work, how he was so disappointing to me, but through the years I've still missed him."

"Your father?"

"Yes." He paused and swirled the last of his coffee, studying the dregs that had escaped the percolator. "And now ... refusing to see the man that claims to be my father. Has hate won out?"

"I'd not call it hate ... maybe accepting reality ... protecting yourself against deception. ..."

"But what if—"

An unfamiliar car pulling into their long driveway interrupted his sentence. Could it be the family from up north coming for a visit? Maybe they'd purchased a new car. That always brought them for a visit. Harry's spirit's immediately lifted in anticipation.

Chapter Fifty-one

The car stopped at the end of their drive. Evelyn shielded her eyes from the evening sun dropping over the Alleghenies. The cool evenings had given way to a Shenandoah spring, free of the fog that often shrouded the mountains. "I think it's Annie," Evelyn said.

Though Harry wished very much to see his family, Evelyn's comment was not a letdown. Disappointment and joy balanced each other.

The car slowly backed out of the drive and pulled away, its occupants waving at Ann as she walked alone down the drive. She had changed from the first time she stepped foot onto their front porch: forlorn and unkempt, pale and emaciated, with disheveled hair protruding from a dirty, red bandanna. And frightened. They had never seen anyone as terribly frightened. Not so now. She wore a neatly pressed black and white dress, with matching slippers. Most notable were the smile and sparkling eyes.

"Hello, Ann, dear. I told Bud you'd be by."

"Evenin', Miz Evelyn." They embraced.

She turned toward Harry. "Mistuh Weatherholtz."

"Nice to see you, Miss Ann." He cupped her hand in his own and held it gently. She had lost a few pounds, but her smile had not diminished.

"Had supper?" Evelyn asked, ever the mothering type.

"Yes, ma'am. Just wanted to stop by and say hello … maybe ask a favor or two, and. …"

After a long pause, Harry prompted, "And what favor do you need from us, Miss Ann."

She hesitated.

"Here, have a seat," Evelyn said, as she picked up a rumpled throw, folded and placed it on the arm of the sofa.

"Shore's good to be free again." She sighed. "Learn't something though. I knowed it wus bad living in Hurley Cutshaw's house, but I never knowed just how bad afore now. It wus worse than being in jail."

"We're so sorry, Miss Ann." Evelyn sat beside her on the sofa, gently patting her clasped hands.

"We did everything we knew to do to get you released sooner. Nothing we did or said worked, not that Sheriff Flin didn't want to release you." Harry sat in the oversized armchair opposite them. "Your church family really stood beside you. Evidently, their prayers worked."

"It's a miracle Jack Brady survived, for him and you," Evelyn said. "Things looked pretty bad … oh, enough of that talk. Let me get you something to drink. Coffee or tea?"

"Maybe just some water would do."

"What is it you need us to help with?" Harry asked.

"I may have lost my job at the nursing home, unless—"

"I'll speak to them," Harry said.

Evelyn returned with a glass of water.

"Thank you." She paused. "Don't know where I'd be without y'all." She smiled apprehensively. "Don't quite know what to do 'bout Mistuh Brady's house. I guess he'll need my help soon's he gets out of the hospital."

"And I'm sure the Carnahans are excited to have you back," Evelyn said.

For a long moment, the room grew quiet. Ann fiddled with the glass of water, tracing the *Waterlily and Cattails* pattern with her finger. Did the cattails remind her of that tragic day? Its designer called the color Golden Iris. She had no way of knowing that spraying a metallic liquid on the hot-pressed glass created the shimmering marigold color. Her world was small, so it did not include men like Harry Northwood and Frank Fenton, renown for their glasswork. Unlike most her age, she had never attended a carnival, where the glassware served as prizes for ring toss and a dozen other games. Nor had she been able to purchase such from the five-and-dime store, though it sold for pennies. But her small world had been harder than most, for it had been filled with slave labor and men like Hurley Cutshaw.

Evelyn sat beside Ann and cradled her head on her shoulder, softly stroking her hair. It was a moment that quite possibly had never happened before. Then again, what was her home like before she was placed in foster care? Was it one of abuse and neglect, or did she have a loving mother whose utter poverty created the necessity for social assistance? Whatever, such assistance landed Ann in the care of Cutshaw. What really happened to her mother?

"I don't mean to pry, Ann," Harry broke the silence, "but do you need to talk about what happened at Mr. Brady's place?"

"I suppose I should. It wuz really frightenin' finding Mistuh Brady layin' on the floor … bleedin' … thought he wuz dead. Didn't know what to do. Stay? Run? Shouldn't have picked up the gun but didn't know if whoever shot him wuz still in the house and all. Course I wuz already confused after findin' the picture of Eddie and my mamma stuck in a book in his library."

"That was the picture they had as evidence against you?" Harry asked.

"Yes. Suppose I shouldn't have told 'em where I got it."

"Truth's always best." He glanced at Evelyn. She tossed him her live-what-you-preach look.

"Strange how I found the picture. Wuz dustin' the books and realized that by lookin' at the pictures of people I recognized—like General Lee and other important people I knowed by their faces—I could sound out the letters of their names. Mistuh Brady first showed me how to do that, to sound out letters, so I studied a few of the books with faces I knowed and wuz ... I wuz actually almost readin' when I lost track of time and had to work faster to catch up. That wuz when I dropped this book and out fell the picture."

"Could you tell what the book was about?" Harry sat on the edge of the chair.

"That wuz one of the things I wanted to ask you. I could tell some of the letters, like I said, by the names of the faces on the book ... like Lee ... so I figured out part of the word on the front of the book. I can show you if I had a pencil and paper."

"I've got that right here." Evelyn pulled open a drawer from the end table, retrieved a pen and notepad and handed them to Ann.

She slowly scribbled the letters: R E V E N G E, drawing a line under the V. "I figured out the first letter was the first letter in Robert E. Lee's first name, so I could make that sound. Three of the letters were in his last name, so I figured out the next sound. This letter," she pointed to the N, "is the letter in my name." She pointed to the G. "General ... General Lee. So I could say most of the letters. But I can't make out this one letter." She circled the V with the pen.

"That's a V, Miss Ann, as in victory, but not victory. The word is revenge," Evelyn blurted out. "Must have been a book he kept of people he wanted to take revenge on, or had already taken revenge." She paused. "But why Annie's family, Bud?"

"I doubt it was a personal revenge on Ann's family, just people in general. Did you look at any other pictures in that particular book?" Harry asked.

"No. Heard Mistuh Brady comin' and put it back on the shelf."

"I'd say it contained records and pictures of Negro orphans and those born to single mothers. Jenkins had a deep-seated hatred for black kids of single parents," Harry said.

"How do you know that," Evelyn asked.

"Jack Brady told me the story. Judge Jenkins' great grandfather, worked as an apprentice for a lawyer by the name of Anderson. Anderson had no children, so he decided to adopt the young Jenkins. He even planned to leave Jenkins his business and his wealth. The Civil War erupted and Anderson joined the Virginia militia. He was killed toward the end of the war. That cut Jenkins to the heart, but then something else happened that added fuel to the fire. Jenkins thought Anderson had adopted him. He filed to inherit Anderson's property, only to find out that not only had the adoption not been processed, Anderson had a living relative. It was a Negro boy born to one of Anderson's slaves, and fathered by Anderson."

"How'd Brady know all this?" Evelyn questioned.

"Judge Jenkins showed him a copy of the affidavit from his great grandfather, that set the young slave lady free. In it, he also set free her child. But not only that, in the affidavit he confessed to being the father of the child. After the Civil War, the young woman obtained a lawyer from up north who filed for inheritance rights on behalf of her illegitimate child. She won. Jenkins—even with old man Anderson's intentions—inherited nothing—"

"But that was so long ago," Evelyn broke into the conversation.

"He allowed hate for the Negroes, especially the illegitimates, to drive him. The young Jenkins worked night and day for the next few years to save enough money to finish his education and to establish his law practice. His efforts paid off. He left his fortune to his only son and also passed along his hate. His son used his fortune to mint a prominent name in society and passed his wealth, influence and hate to his son, Judge Jeremiah Jenkins. For years, Jenkins has used his position as judge to carry out acts of hate against the Negros in this valley."

"How do you know all this, Bud?" Evelyn asked.

"Jack Brady did the research, just last year. He got to wondering how Cutshaw could end up in foster care … what kind of vetting was done … who was responsible for the decisions? He found out dozens of illegitimate children were placed into questionable homes. And each of the cases was presided over by Judge Jenkins. Evidently, the book was a record of all his victims. That was his revenge."

"So that's why Mistuh Jenkins been so mean to me at the nursing home," Ann said.

"I'm sorry, Annie," Evelyn said.

"Wuz he connected with Hurley Cutshaw?" She looked directly at Harry.

"Yes," Harry said.

"Did he place me and Eddie in Cutshaw's care?"

"I'm afraid so."

"You knowed all along?"

"Not at first." Harry weighed his words.

Harry, Flin and Brady had discussed whether to pursue charges against Cutshaw for little Eddie's drowning and against Jenkins for his devious court rulings. There was weak evidence to prosecute Cutshaw, just Ann's word against his, and Ann had fled the courthouse before her grand jury hearing. Still, Brady did his research and challenged Judge Jenkins by presenting the facts. Though Jenkins confessed to Brady, he challenged that he'd win in court. That's when Brady offered him a compromise, a compromise that would end the corruption, but would not tarnish Jenkins reputation. The three—Harry, Brady and Flin—decided to accept Jenkins' resignation instead of pushing for prosecution. Why? Jenkins was right. He would have won in court. But more so, they did not want to drag Ann through the mud of the judicial system to lose in the end. She was free of Cutshaw, so they had obtained their goal. Further, Harry had wondered, if he pushed to prosecute Jenkins and Cutshaw, could that have implicated Brady in some form of complicity. His family had been close to Jenkins. They associated in the local blue-blooded circle … had worked together in the judicial and political system … Jenkins promoting Brady in the system. Jenkins would probably have seen to Brady's demise. Harry wasn't sure just how involved Brady was in the corrupt system, or whether he was involved at all. His was only speculation. It didn't seem prudent to needlessly tarnish Brady's reputation, especially since he was the one who stood up against Jenkins and the white supremacy in the valley. Brady, alone, challenged Jenkins, demanding his resignation.

Weighing all the evidence, they had agreed it best to not pursue charges against Cutshaw and Jenkins. Now Harry faced this dilemma. Could Ann comprehend these complications that motivated their decision? She continued to stare at him.

"We decided it best for a number of reasons, but mostly we felt it best on your behalf to drop the issue after Jenkins resigned his position," Harry said.

Ann studied her hands for what seemed too long before answering. When she looked up, the expression on her face told him it was okay, even before she spoke.

"You did right, Mistuh Weatherholtz. I'd not stand a chance against them in court. I couldn't even face them in court. You knows I run away from that court hearin' instead of facin' them." She reflected, staring into the distance.

"It was a complicated decision," Harry said. "I'm sorry you had to find out this way."

"You're a brave soul," Evelyn said.

"Wuz scared out of my mind but blessed with good friends. I's blessed again since Mistuh Brady lived or I wuz headin' for the state farm. The good Lord shore must be watchin' over me. And you all, too, been watchin' over me. I wuz wonderin' though, you bein' a sheriff afore, do you think my mama is still alive? They let me keep the picture." She pulled the photograph from her pocket and handed it to Harry.

Harry stared at the picture of a mother holding the hand of her small lad, perhaps days before he was snatched from her life forever. He could relate. He felt the hand of his mother holding his, the sway of their hands in rhythm to their steps as they walked the path together … for the last time. The explosion of the gun. The anguish. The beads of water glistening on the face of little Eddie lying on the ground, his eyes staring skyward, fixated with that last terrifying moment. What were his thoughts? He relived the heart-wrenching funeral. Annie's parting words to her brother as she bent over the casket. He mentally scanned the faces of the crowd. If Ann's mother was alive, why was she not at the funeral? Did she not know? Or didn't she care? How did the prophet say it? "Can a woman forget her sucking child, that she should not have compassion on the son of her womb?" But women sometimes do forget … somehow turn their backs and walk away … choosing a substitute … alcohol … pleasure … consumed with self … or defeated with life. Even the old prophet said it was so. "They may forget." What was the situation with Annie's mother? Not just once, but twice she lost a child. Why wasn't she searching for them? Or was she? Wasn't searching very hard if she lived in the same county, or close by. How could he share such with Annie? Her hopes have soared again, only to be dashed by another tempest. Such hopelessness, were it not for the prophet's conclusion, "Yet will I not forget thee." That's the secret for Annie … developing a relationship with Christ. It's the sure safety net for life's devastation. He'd tried to live his faith before her, but he'd never really talked to her about God. She had her own church. But he and Evelyn had become influential in her life. Had they somehow failed her?

"If she's alive, can you help me find her?" Ann's plea interrupted his wandering thoughts.

"Sure, Miss Ann, whatever we can do." He suddenly remembered Flin's mentioning of the colored woman who'd been beaten. "A spitting image of Miss Ann, only older," was how the sheriff described her. Harry hadn't given it much thought at the time. Ann's request moved it to the front burner.

Chapter Fifty-two

Cutshaw had calculated incorrectly. He assumed Harry would turn his head regarding his childcare scheme. His leverage was the threat of revealing the whereabouts of an eighty-year-old escaped convict. The plan unraveled in a day when Harry had single-handedly found and disarmed the trap. Further, Harry would not surrender his principles even for his father. This left Cutshaw a threadbare chance of resurrecting the good old days of child labor. But with his plot thwarted, Cutshaw still insisted on pushing the issue. Why? What motivated him to continue his quest when all gain was gone? Harry knew there could only be one motivation, greed: the love of money … just like the Bible warned. But how could Harry's meeting up with his father profit Cutshaw? That was the mystery.

Harry's preoccupation caused another long line of cars to form behind his Hudson. He slowed and drifted onto the brim that ran alongside the winding Shenandoah River and waved to the drivers that passed by. He was in no hurry, especially with this mission. The morning sun reflected off the dewdrops clinging to the pine needles of the evergreens. Countless crystal-like sparkles on a thousand trees illumined the hillside and stimulated the senses. A slow drive in the valley normally cleared his misty thoughts, but today the mist lingered like the low hanging clouds obscuring the view of the forest higher on the mountainside.

Fat cows dotted the green fields, fields long ago cleared of the forests that had dominated this valley before the white man came. Harry slowed for a pothole, the lingering evidence of winter vanquished by the colors of spring. A patch of bloodroot, in full bloom, created a picturesque border underneath the shade of a ridge of trees. The multiple petals of the short-lived spring bloom remained, topped by a long stem that rose above the foliage underneath. The moist soil from the runoff of a natural flowing spring nourished this colony of plants. A farmer had diverted some of the spring water into a metal container from which his cows drank. A whitetail deer momentarily looked his way but continued to graze on the flowering plants.

The bloodroot plant was suspect. Native Americans had long ago used the plant for medicinal purposes, but medical studies declared it to be hazardous. It was believed that Dr. John Henry Pinkard, a wealthy black man from down in Roanoke, used bloodroot in some of his medicinal potions. Though both his credentials and his potions were suspect, he was a successful banker and did much good among the black community in giving them loans. How strange a man's life could be so contradictory: a life of prominence stained by the suspicion of reddish sap that flows through the root system of the bloodroot plant! Harry couldn't suppress a smile when he recalled Ann comparing Cutshaw with the bloodroot plant, its pure white bloom appearing innocently above the ground, but full of poison under the surface. Such a man could not be trusted under any circumstances.

Lots of events had transpired since Harry's first visit to Twelve Oaks. He turned slowly into the driveway, braked and put the shift into park. Why should he continue this pursuit? Ann would not be safe at Twelve Oaks now that Jenkins knew her identity. He certainly didn't want another confrontation with Jenkins. Cutshaw's claim that the old man from the mountain was his father had little merit, and Cutshaw would do nothing good for him, so the whole plot was bogus at best and criminal at worst. But the slight chance the old man was his father could be settled with one question. Now that he recuperated at Twelve Oaks, perhaps Harry could end the charade. Still, what good could come from finding out his father was alive. If so, he was an escaped criminal that could be arrested. He slapped the steering wheel and accidentally honked the horn. A blue jay took to flight, circled the vehicle a couple times and landed again in the tree. It hopped threateningly from limb to limb and squawked its familiar "jayer-jayer" sound, from which it got its name. Harry studied the scene and finally saw a female sitting on her nest. "You sure are a testy fellow." To their credit they were a tight-knit family, watching out for their own. Harry had tried to do the same, but the old man in the nursing home, if he was his father, had long ago separated his family and abandoned what remained. *What am I doing here? I should leave.* He threw the shift into reverse and glanced in the mirror but noticed a patrol car had turned onto the driveway. *Why would Flin be visiting the nursing home?*

Harry removed the Colt .45 from his belt and slid it under the seat.

Flin pulled up beside him. "Hello, Harry." Flin's voice was a welcome reprieve to his troubled soul.

"Hello, Sheriff. Have you come to arrest a fugitive?"

"What do you mean?"

"My daddy. Cutshaw says he's staying here at the home."

"You ever gonna learn not to believe anything that ole coot says? And even if it's true, there'll be an ugly motive you don't want to get tangled in."

"I know … just started to leave when you arrived."

"Might as well not waste your trip. Why not go ahead and talk to the old codger and find out who hired him and why? Cutshaw has his hand in it for sure, and maybe Jenkins, but I don't have a clue what his angle is."

"What's your business here, Sheriff?"

"Wanted to see you. Stopped by your place and Evelyn told me you'd headed this way. Jenkins' man, Pratt, has been transferred back to my jail. He knows more than he's telling. I'm sure he'll want to work out a deal to cut prison time. He's not talking to me, waiting for his lawyer, but he asked to speak with you. Not sure what that's about. Just wanted you to know."

"Thanks, Sheriff." Harry paused. "Wonder why me?"

"Not sure but something to think about. Certainly won't hurt. You don't have no beef with Pratt. He might have something worthwhile to share."

"I'll be over there as soon as I finish here," Harry said with a sigh. He just wanted it to be over.

Chapter Fifty-three

Harry tapped lightly on the door.

"Come in." The voice was that of a female.

He slowly pushed open the door. She sat by the bed, gently dabbing the old man's lips with a wet washcloth. His eyes were closed.

"Mrs. Hall?"

"Yes, Vera Hall."

"I'm Harry Weatherholtz. Hurley Cutshaw told me your husband was here. Also says he is my father."

She hesitated. "Yes. He's been hoping you would come by … wantin' to make amends fer what he's done all these years."

"Can he hear us?"

"Not sure. Elmer," she said in an elevated voice, as she tapped him on the shoulder. "Elmer, you got company. Harry Weatherholtz … your son is here to see you."

He stirred but didn't answer.

"Mr. Hall," Harry bent over the bed, "Hurley Cutshaw said you wanted to see me."

Elmer opened his eyes and stared at Harry. His breathing was slow and raspy. "Yes. …" He hesitated and tried to lift his head but

273

seemed too weak. His wife elevated his head and stuffed another pillow underneath. "I wanted to see you before I died … doctor says it's almost over … needed to ask for forgiveness … make sure Cutshaw gave you the letter. Did he?"

"Yes."

"Wanted to try and make amends for what I done to you and your brother."

"And my mother." Harry didn't try to hide his emotions.

"Yes, of course, her too … didn't mean to not mention her … was terrible what I done … but I was drunk."

"I find it hard, after all these years, to believe you are my dad. It all seems too far-fetched … even mind-boggling."

"I understand. It was real bad of me … not to contact you all these years, but I didn't want to go back … back to jail. If I showed up in public someone might recognize me and squeal. You, of all people, being a former sheriff and all, should understand that." He paused and stared away. "Time just got away." He tried to wet his lips with the tip of his tongue.

Vera dipped a cloth in a glass of water and wiped his lips. He lapped the water from his lips and tried to swallow. She elevated his head and placed the glass to his lips. He sipped from the glass and began to choke. A nurse stepped into the room. "He okay?"

The coughing subsided.

"Yes, I think so, thank you," Vera said.

"This your family?" The nurse asked.

"Yes, Elmer's son," Vera said. She smiled. "Come to see him."

"Nice to meet you. Y'all ring if you need something." She slipped from the room.

"I wrote you that letter, thought that was enough to explain and hoped that you'd believe me," Elmer said.

"I'm having a difficult time believing you. You could have gotten that letter somehow … or made up this whole thing … though I don't understand why?"

"Can't prove I'm your daddy other than the letter. You just got to believe me, but then again, you don't have to believe me. Your choice. I understand if you don't." His voice was weak.

"There is a way you could prove to me you're my dad." Harry paused. "There's something you should know that few people ... if anyone other than me, knows."

"What's that?"

"A poem."

"A poem?" His face seemed expressionless.

"Yes. There was a poem my father used to recite to me."

He did not respond.

His silence spoke volumes to Harry. "You don't remember the poem, do you? Or else you never heard about the poem."

The coughing started again.

"I'm sorry, son. He's awfully weak," Vera said.

Harry resented her calling him son. He stared into the face of the stranger. There was nothing about him that sparked any remembrance. There was no feeling for this man other than pity for the cruel death he was experiencing, and the fact that he was a liar even on his deathbed. "I understand. I'm sorry for your ... your pain. I won't trouble you any longer." He started toward the door.

"Hem ... lock." The voice was barely audible.

Harry turned. "What did you say?"

"Hemlock ... we cut the last Hemlock. ..." He closed his eyes. "Sorry ... can't hardly speak ... hope you believe me ... forgive me for. ..." His words tapered to an inaudible whisper.

Harry stared at the helpless man. After all these years, how could this be? Was he supposed to be thrilled—like an adopted child who has just found his birth parent or sibling—that a criminal parent has just come out of hiding? He felt not one iota of delight for his prodigal father. Is a lack thereof a sign of hard-...heartedness? Perhaps, but not because he willed it; it just was.

"What do you want from me?" Harry asked.

"For ... forgiveness."

275

"I think I've done that, years ago."

"Thank you. I hope you can keep it secret that I'm alive … not turn me in."

"I have no intentions of reporting you. Anything else?"

"Your inheritance … in the letter … did you read it?"

"Yes, but I have no way to prove that … just a letter, and even if I did—"

"Please son, if not for yourself … for your stepmother."

Her brown hair, braided and coiled toward the back of her head, somewhat veiled the dingy gray, making her appear younger than her years, but up close the wrinkles were obvious. Her red and swollen gums withdrew from the enamel on the few teeth that remained. Weathered skin revealed years of a hard life. She seldom spoke, and when she did, it exposed her trepidation. Had he taken her from a life of such dearth that living on bare necessities in a shack with a fugitive was an improvement? Or had he held her like a caged animal until she submitted to his controlling nature, like he tried to do with Harry's mother before he killed her? Or underneath her timidity, was there a secret needing to remain hidden? No matter her story, Harry felt pity, for he somehow associated her with his mother.

"How can I help her?"

"Cutshaw has the details … let him handle it. Just verify for him that I am your daddy."

Why does anything around here that's shady always cast a shadow upon Cutshaw? How does a man like him come up with so many schemes? He could make an honest living with his grocery store, but enough never satisfies greed. And greed takes chances that, just as often as not, winds the perpetrator in trouble.

"For her … not me," the old man said. "Please … I'm begging. …"

Harry wanted to say no; he needed to say no, but he could not bring himself to do so. "I'll be in touch."

Chapter Fifty-four

A survey of the small room stimulated memory; it was neutral ground, unlike the holding cells of the incarcerated. Here—though ever so infrequently—the inmates meet with their lawyers, their pastors, their rabbis: always their advocates. No snitches, no recorders, no secrets. Bare the soul and formulate a plan without fear of retaliation from guards or fellow inmates. In another time and place, this was the setting where Harry, as sheriff, often met with inmates. His gentle nature dismantled walls, reasoned with the willing and helped many a petty criminal tell the truth, suffer the consequences and change his ways.

"Not sure why he asked for you, Harry," Flin said.

"Nor I."

The inner door opened, and Winston Pratt entered, followed by a deputy sheriff who guided him with a hand on his shoulder as if he was a blind man needing assistance. Pratt took a seat across the table from Harry and extended a handshake.

"Just give the guard a shout when you're done," Flin said and exited with the deputy.

"Will do, Sheriff." Harry nodded.

The clang of the steel door resurrected his senses to the sounds of the incarcerated: incessant chatter beyond the walls; an occasional shout reciprocated by a dozen others; the smell, especially the smell. His intuitiveness, like riding a bicycle, seemed to return. For a moment it seemed only yesterday he had worked in the law enforcement community in Ohio. He had loved every day on the job. That was when being sheriff was more about law enforcement and less about politics—at least Harry hoped his tenure was such.

"Mr. Harry Weatherholtz, we meet again, sir," Pratt said, "though our brief meeting at the hospital in Richmond was on the embarrassing side for me."

"Mr. Pratt," Harry said. Pratt's steely eyes concerned Harry. In a thousand interviews, he had dealt with such eyes, with nothing positive to report. "You requested to see me?"

"Yes, I did, sir. As you can tell, I am in a precarious position. My boss—shall I say, my benefactor of years—has had to disassociate himself from me, understandably so. So I am on my own … again. Money meant little in the past, for all I needed was more than enough to provide for me. More recently, that has changed, and I find myself in need of a lot of money." He paused and seemed to study Harry. "That is where you come in, sir."

"Mr. Pratt, I have all I need in life to get by, but I have very little money. So I can't—"

"Oh, no, nothing like that, Mr. Weatherholtz. I'm not asking for money; on the contrary, though money is a necessary nuisance for my legal defense, money will help me little where I'm headed."

Another long pause. Harry was unsure of where this conversation was headed and even more uncertain if he wanted to take the journey. "Then what do you need from me, Mr. Pratt?"

"Vengeance, sir."

"I'm sorry, but I don't follow what you're getting at."

"Not vengeance in a sense of breaking the law; vengeance in the sense as a motivator to see that justice is carried out."

"I have no opinion for or against you, Mr. Pratt. I certainly have no vengeance in my heart for—"

"I'm not speaking of myself; I'm speaking of the judge." A sinister smile momentarily appeared, but he quickly suppressed it, awaiting Harry's response.

"Judge Jenkins?"

"The only judge both you and I know personally."

"I still don't understand."

"You will, sir. First, I must have your word of honor that our conversation is confidential."

"Without knowing what you are going to share, I can't make that promise."

"Jolly honorable of you, Mr. Weatherholtz, and that is why I called for you before I met with my attorney. In short, I trust you, your prudence. I know you and Jack Brady had the judge in the crosshairs of an investigation. I assume you chose to drop the case out of prudence, prudence for the sake of that Negro girl, prudence because you knew the case could never be won in a court of law in this county. You were able to manipulate a fine line of practicality without breaking the law. And you forced the hand of Judge Jenkins, making him do something he would not otherwise have done. You forced him to resign. Though he was not prosecuted, you still beat him." He paused, as if suddenly wondering if their conversation was being overheard.

"This is the neutral zone, Mr. Pratt, our conversation is safe, but I still don't understand where we are going with this."

"I'll get to the crux of the matter, or as you say here in America, the nitty-gritty, though I don't quite understand the origin of that phrase. I'm headed for prison, and I've accepted that. I've been identified by Mr. Brady himself and caught red handed trying to finish the job. I do know about the origin of that phrase, caught red handed. It originated around the fifteenth century in Scotland. When caught with blood on your hand and a dead man at your feet, it meant speedy punishment." He paused as if questioning whether or not Harry believed him. "I'm from the old country where the term originated, Mr. Weatherholtz, so I know what I'm talking about."

"Never said otherwise, Mr. Pratt, but I still don't understand how your attempt to kill Jack Brady involves me."

"I'll get to that in a jiffy, just needing to lay the foundation. I'm guilty, and I'm going to jail, but. ..." He paused, as if unsure of his next statement, or unsure if he should share it with Harry. He stared at the ceiling for a good while before resuming. "The extent of my jail term could be diminished with proper evidence submitted. Some sort of a plea bargain, that seems quite popular in America."

"You should be talking to a lawyer, not me."

"I know what I'm doing. I'll speak to my lawyer about all the details, but I am afraid to give him the evidence I speak of. Documents can disappear overnight without explanation. I know for a fact, because I worked for the judge. That is where you come into the picture. My lawyer will know what the documents say, but I want to entrust the actual documents into your keeping. I trust you, sir. I want you to guard the documents until the day they are submitted as evidence in court."

"And what are these documents?"

"You have to promise me, first, that you will keep them safe and present them at the proper time."

"And why should I make such a promise? I hardly know you, and you almost killed a man I consider a friend."

Pratt paused, seemingly not from a lack of words but as if to preface his next statement. Harry had seen drama before. Every prisoner has his backstory that he wants to share, to explain ... to justify his crime.

"You had an interesting person enter your life recently, correct?" Pratt was a manipulator.

Harry did not answer.

The sinister smile reappeared but quickly changed to warmth. "Let me be more specific. An old man claiming to be your father?"

Harry still did not answer. How did this man know such details?

"I know the truth about that old man. Do you believe he is your father? Let me answer that. You have doubts because you have no proof. Right?"

"Yes, an elderly man is claiming to be my father. Yes, I have doubts, but I have some proof that he could be my father."

"What?"

"A poem, he knows a poem that my father wrote."

"I'm not knowledgeable about that, but never mind. I know whether or not he is your father, and I have documents to prove it. You do what I ask, simply safeguard my secrets, and I will give you the answer to your dilemma. A deal?"

"When do you give me the information regarding the man claiming to be my father?"

"When you present to the court the documents in your keeping."

"That is too long. I need to know now."

"Why?"

"The old man is dying. Soon."

"I'm sorry to hear that."

Why would he be sorry? Does this thwart his plans? Or did he just say that out of courtesy for a dying man? Pratt had to be more than a butler. He tends to brandish psychopathic characteristics. He remained unnerved when Harry rejected his deal. His unblinking eyes stare right through your soul. Yet, he has an appealing smile when appropriate and facial expressions reserved when necessary. He keeps his hands flat on the table with no expression, and his breathing remains steady. He had walked into a hospital with a concealed gun to finish a botched job. The man is definitely a psychopath.

Harry stared into Pratt's unblinking eyes. This man is definitely more than Jenkins' butler. And Jenkins is tied into this plot some way. Harry didn't want to be a part of anything he's involved with. But things have really unraveled for Jenkins to distance himself from Pratt. So Pratt is now on his own, playing his own hand. And it is for keeps. But why should he get involved with such a game of chance? How can he make such an outlandish promise to a convict—a promise he may not be able to keep, to a man he hardly knows and who has attempted to kill a government official? Twice. He could appease him. It's an investigative tactic, to make promises with no intentions of honoring. But he was not an investigator. It's his honor being challenged … and why does he need to know who the old man really is? That will change nothing … except perhaps to allow him to die with some measure of peace … which he doesn't deserve … but isn't that a subtle vengeance on Harry's part. Pratt is right … vengeance is a motivator.

"You have the upper hand, Mr. Weatherholtz. I will tell you now, the old man is your father."

He was calculating. Keep the carrot out there. Pratt's was a conditioned criminal mind … lie without batting an eye.

"Proof?" Harry asked.

"Like I said, I'll give you the documents to prove he's your father after you fulfill my request. Not before. Let me know."

"No deal," Harry said.

"Too bad, sir. I'd hoped you would be more reasonable. Thanks anyway." Pratt slowly pushed his seat back from the table, stood and stepped toward the door.

Harry, too, stood and turned toward his exit. It happened in an instant and seemingly with trained skill. Pratt's forearm clasped Harry's neck from behind; a sharp object pricked the skin under his chin.

"Do as I say, Mr. Weatherholtz, and you may live to see your daddy die; otherwise, he'll be the one mourning your death."

Pratt was more than a psychopath. He was a skilled killer. The grip squeezed Harry's throat enough to restrict air but not cut it off completely. "What do you want?" The words came in wheezes.

"I'm going to release the grip enough for you to call the guard. No alarm. Understood?" He squeezed tighter for a moment before relaxing the grip, but he kept the sharp object pressed against Harry's neck. "Now, call the guard."

Chapter Fifty-five

Accordingly, as Pratt demanded, Flin ordered the deputies to keep their distance. He'd instructed another to rip the wires from the CB and phone, just as Pratt commanded. Pratt maintained complete composure but vehemently threatened Harry's life if anyone exited the building before he was gone. He directed Harry to open the hoods to the two patrol cars and remove the ignition coil wire from each. Pratt tucked them into his pocket. Pratt's commands were as calm as a Sunday school teacher instructing her students in prayer, but all the while, the point of the chiv pressed against Harry's neck. He could feel blood soaking his collar.

Once at the Hudson, Pratt hesitated, "This is where we part company, Mr. Weatherholtz. Since you refused my offer, I'll have to make other arrangements to safeguard the evidence I need for my trial, but I do have you to thank for my escape. Give me the car keys."

Harry hesitated.

"Now." Pratt twisted the chiv slightly against Harry's neck.

"They're under the seat."

"Get them. No tricks or I'll slice your throat."

Harry knelt and reached underneath the car seat. In his awkward position, the chiv slipped from his neck. He spun, facing Pratt, who was momentarily distracted, observing the jail. Harry held his pistol deadeye against Pratt's forehead. Blood trickled from a gash made by the gun barrel as it slammed against Pratt's head.

"Drop the blade, Mr. Pratt. Easy does it." The chiv clinked as it bounced off the side of the car and hit the blacktop. "Now, put your hands in your pockets and back up slowly."

Pratt stared at Harry but did as he said.

"Now, ease into the car. That's good … slowly." Harry slid to the passenger's side, keeping the gun aimed at Pratt's head. "Your right hand please." He unbuckled his belt and cinched Pratt's right hand to the steering wheel. "You drive."

"I need the key."

Harry pulled the key from his pocket.

"You said … well, I'll be … you do lie, Mr. Weather—"

"No, I do not. There is a set of keys under the seat, for emergency. Engage the clutch." Harry started the engine … he glanced at the jail, hoping they had obeyed Pratt … that they did not see the exchange of who was now the hostage. He held the gun low, in hopes that no one could see it.

"Where to?" Pratt asked.

"Turn right at the corner and left at the next." Harry kept the gun trained at Pratt's head.

Pratt followed Harry's instructions, as calmly as if he was the chauffeur. They drove for thirty minutes before Harry ordered him down a side road and into a grove of pine trees.

"Now, Mr. Pratt, we need to talk. This time, on my terms."

"I'm saying nothing, sir. I made you an offer and you rebuffed me. The deal is off the table."

"Mr. Pratt, you no longer have a deal to take off the table. I am the only one with a deal. And it only has one option. You tell me the truth about my father, with the proof, and I may keep your papers safe until time to submit them to the court. That's the only deal offered."

"And if I don't accept?"

"I shoot you, here and now, and haul your dead body back to the jail, where I'll tell them how I managed to retrieve my gun from under the seat and shot you. They will automatically assume in self-defense."

"You're bluffing, sir."

"One way to find out."

"Which is?"

"Reject my offer and you die."

Their eyes locked. Neither gave ground. Harry knew he had the winning hand, so he called Pratt's bluff. "Times up!" He pressed the barrel against the side of Pratt's head.

"Okay! Okay!" Pratt threw up his unshackled hand in surrender. He had cracked.

Chapter Fifty-six

"I'll be a son-of-a-gun, Harry. How did you do it?" Flin asked as he stepped from the holding area into the office of the jail.

"Long story, Sheriff. The short of it is luck."

"Or the good Lord above." Flin looked upward.

"That, too," Harry said. "Always good to have the Lord on your side. Can I sit in on the interrogation, make sure Pratt tells the same story he told me?"

"I see no reason why not. He's actually asked for you to be present when he makes his statement. Kind of odd, don't you think? Seems like he'd be spittin' mad at you."

"Yes, kind of odd behavior."

"He did say you threatened his life with the gun."

"And you believe him?"

Flin stared at Harry. "Maybe … maybe not." He paused. "Be here at nine, tomorrow for the interview."

"Why wait?"

"He's called for his lawyer."

"That. Okay, tomorrow at nine."

"I still think it's strange he's asked for you, especially after his taking you hostage and all."

"That does seem strange. But you know criminal minds, Sheriff. They do some of the oddest things."

Chapter Fifty-seven

Harry eased the door open and stepped inside. Pulling the door shut, he paused as the dimly lit room slowly focused. Vera sat by the bedside and seemed not to notice his entrance. The sheet covering her husband's face answered Harry's question. He was too late. They would never have the conversation Harry had rehearsed.

He cleared his throat, and she turned toward him. He felt compelled to say something, to offer some kind of comfort, but words did not come. If he had known the truth earlier, perhaps it would have been different and would not have come down to this moment. Still, he felt no remorse. He had developed tough skin early on; that was how he survived his personal pain without descending into self-pity. And his tough skin dealt with reality, not that he was without Christian charity. He had valued his Christian faith, which had kept him morally grounded, though he felt a tinge of guilt for rebuffing the old man so. Still, he could honestly say he had no animosity toward him. That was good. Surely things had been tough for him, as he had struggled to survive the past fifty plus years living in the mountains, grubbing for basic necessities. Mountain folks were resourceful. They could survive by digging ginseng for a little cash, picking berries and hunting wild game for meat. The downside for the old man was having to look over his shoulder, wondering if the law would ever catch up with him. But worse than his fugitive life was that his primary source of connection to the world was through Hurley Cutshaw. That in itself seemed cruel punishment for any man.

She motioned for him to come closer. Harry gently placed a hand on her shoulder. "Sorry," he said. And he truly meant it.

She said nothing, but her hand against his acknowledged she accepted his condolences.

How had she met him? She said they had been together almost fifty years. Being a good many years younger, she must have been barely a teenager when they met. Had he bartered for her from some desperate family needing a dowry? But the manner in which she cared for him suggested he had been kind to her through the years. Love transcends all social and economic boundaries.

What were her thoughts? Was she reminiscing their life together? If he had treated her badly, surely she would have fled this room in relief. But where would she go? Back to the shack in the mountains? Return to a squatter's subsistence? She could not, nor would he allow it. She would be cared for.

She gently rubbed the old man's pallid hand. How long had she been sitting by his side? The nurses were kind in not rushing the issue.

She looked up at Harry. "He loved you. 'Course I didn't know about you 'cept a few months back. He told me a little about the past. But especially at the end, he wanted to see ya. I could tell. I think he wanted to … to make it right."

The room grew quiet. Harry wanted to bolt … to put it all behind him, but that was what he remembered about his daddy … what he always did … run.

"Sure. I understand. I have no animosity toward him."

"Don't rightly know what to do now that—"

"You will be cared for," Harry interrupted her.

She stared at him, seemingly understanding what he said but doubtful. "How?" She whispered.

"I will help you get the proper assistance offered by the state. There are programs available. We'll find a way." He hesitated. "I know you will miss him, and it will never be the same, but you will learn how to … to cope with … time has a way of healing our hurts."

"You know about hurts, don't ya? He … Elmer told me."

Harry nodded, wondering how much she actually knew about his life. He wanted to challenge her. But why, especially now? "Yes, I know about hurts."

"Don't know what to do about a funeral. Ain't never done this afore."

"The nursing home will help you make those decisions."

"We ain't got no preacher? Never went to church, 'cept when I was young."

"I know a pastor who can perform the funeral. Don't worry about that."

"I ain't got much money."

"The funeral home will work with you and … and I can talk to them."

"Thank you." She paused. "Will you and Evelyn … that's her name, ain't it?"

"Yes, Evelyn."

"She was nice to me when she stopped in at the hospital. "Will y'all be coming to the funeral?"

Harry hesitated but quickly realized her disappointment. "Sure. We'll be there."

"He'd like that."

Chapter Fifty-eight

Sheriff Flin didn't mince words. "Gentlemen, this interview is taking place because Mr. Pratt requested it. His lawyer, Mr. Stahl, is here to advise him. You all know Harry Weatherholtz, and he is also here because Mr. Pratt requested it. Everyone is okay with this meeting as arranged?"

"I don't like the seating arrangement, Sheriff." Pratt stood. "I sat here when I was interrogated before … feels too uncomfortable … here, Mr. Weatherholtz, I'll trade seats with you. Do you mind?"

"No." Harry stood and exchanged seats with Pratt.

"Well, now that that's settled, 'cause we certainly don't want the accused to feel uncomfortable, let's continue," Flin quipped. "Anyone else uncomfortable?"

Attorney Stahl cleared his throat. "I would like to go on record that I have advised my client against this meeting and against having Mr. Weatherholtz present, but he has declined my advice."

"Noted, Mr. Stahl," Flin said. He began to pace. "Now, Mr. Pratt, when you took Harry hostage and broke out of jail, you shared with him some very informative and incriminating evidence both against yourself, Judge Jeremiah Jenkins and Hurley Cutshaw. Harry has related much of your conversation with me, but I need you to make an official statement to the law. First, were you coerced in any way to have this meeting?"

"No, sir."

"In the course of events yesterday, Harry overpowered you and brought you back to the jail where we now hold you on multiple charges, which include attempted murder, a jailbreak and kidnapping. We have made you aware of these charges. Correct?"

"Yes." Pratt glanced at Stahl.

"And we have read you your rights?" Flin continued.

"Yes."

"I have a question I need my client to clarify, for the record." Stahl scribbled on a legal pad as he spoke. "Mr. Pratt, did Mr. Weatherholtz coerce you in any way to give up information that you would not otherwise have done?"

Pratt hesitated, and he stared directly at Harry. This was the question Harry dreaded, but Pratt had assured him there was nothing for him to worry about if he would sit in on the interview. Harry wasn't sure where Pratt's attorney was going with this question? He had forced Pratt to talk. He even threatened his life, so why did Pratt allow Stahl to ask this question?

"No, sir, he did not."

"Thank you, sir. Back to you, Sheriff."

The question now made sense to Harry. The attorney had established no motive on Harry's part other than escape from a hostage situation.

Flin continued his pacing as he thumbed through the small, spiral-bound notebook he kept in his shirt pocket. "You told Harry that the old man, Elmer Hall, was actually his father?"

"Yes."

Flin sat down and thumbed through his notes. "But then you changed your story? Said he wasn't Harry's real father."

"Correct. Elmer Hall is an impostor, but he did know Mr. Weatherholtz's father."

"How?"

"They were in prison together."

"I'll need proof." Flin stood and walked toward the door, as if he was about to end the interview. "Could we get some water in here?" He called to no one in particular.

"I have proof in some documents, plus, you can check the prison records," Pratt said.

"You can be sure I'll check the records, but where are the documents you're talking about?" Flin demanded.

"You don't have to answer that question, Mr. Pratt," his lawyer said. He had come in from Richmond, and from the looks of his expensive car and suit, Pratt was going to have a hefty legal bill. He drove and wore the finest Harry had ever seen, except maybe Shelton from D.C.

Pratt held up his hand to silence his attorney. "I want to answer the question. I gave the documents to him." He pointed at Harry.

Flin tossed Harry a scowl. "That true?"

"Sort of," Harry said.

"What do you mean, sort of?" Flin seemed miffed.

"He told me where I could find them."

"I'll need the documents, Harry."

"I don't yet have them, I just know where they are. And I made him a promise that I'll present them during the trial."

"You what? You don't have no right to make such promises, Harry. That's about the worst thing you could've done."

"Sorry, but I did it." Harry had found out a long time ago that in some situations it was best to make decisions and apologize later than to get permission first. He suppressed a smile when he considered the philosophy of Theodore Roosevelt regarding making a decision. The most important thing was to make the right decision, the second best thing was to make the wrong decision and the worst thing was to make no decision at all. He had made a decision, whether right or wrong, so that was at least not the worst thing he could have done.

"So the man in the prison cell with Harry's father, who escaped from prison sometime after Harry's father had died in prison, is the old man who's been living up in the mountains?"

"Yes, Elmer Hall," Pratt said, emotionless. "He didn't exactly escape, but he wasn't officially released."

"Then how did he get out of prison?" Flin asked.

"Some favors were cashed in."

"By whom?" Flin dug deeper.

"A lawyer." Pratt's face seemed to reflect a sense of pleasure.

"Let me guess. Someone by the name of Jenkins?" Flin paced.

"No, but that's another story. Cost the man's family a large sum of money, and he has hidden out in the mountains ever since. He came up with the idea to impersonate Mr. Weatherholtz's father because he had run up a debt at Cutshaw's store. He schemed with Cutshaw to pull it off, with Cutshaw hoping to blackmail Judge Jenkins. The letter from Mr. Weatherholtz's father—the one Cutshaw gave Mr. Weatherholtz—was authentic … the man stole it from Elmer Weatherholtz's things after he died in prison."

"And what about the poem Harry talked to me about? Did he steal that, too?" Flin asked.

"I don't know how he obtained the poem. Evidently, Mr. Weatherholtz's father talked to him … maybe recited it to him … you know how prisons are, all kinds of time for inmates to do nothing but talk."

"You sound like a man with prison experience." Flin sat back down.

"Don't answer that," Stahl advised.

"So let me get this straight for the records." Flin wiped his brow with his fingertips and dried them on his pant leg. "Sorry about the heat in here, with no windows and all."

"It is awfully hot for my client, sir," Stahl said.

Flin seemed to ignore the statement and continued. "You originally told Mr. Weatherholtz the old man, Elmer, was his … Harry's daddy."

"Yes, I—"

The door opened and a deputy entered with a pitcher of water and four cups.

"Thanks, March," Flin said.

"Welcome, sir." He placed the water and cups on the table and left.

"Back to the question," Flin said. "You first told Harry the old man was his father?"

"Yes, I did, but that was not true."

"Why did you lie about that, or are you lying now?"

"At first I assumed that if Mr. Weatherholtz thought the man wasn't his father, he would not cooperate with me. The old carrot in front of the horse trick, I suppose." He paused. "When I lost my edge, I came clean with Mr. Weatherholtz and used the documents to make a deal. I assume we still have a deal, Mr. Weatherholtz." He looked at Harry.

"Harry may have made you a deal, but I haven't." Flin slammed his fist onto the table. He had turned into the role of bad cop. "I'll decide, after we've finished with this little conversation, if we have any kind of deal or not, 'course you'll have to take that up with the judge and prosecutor."

"I understand." Pratt showed no emotion.

"How did you meet Judge Jenkins?" Flin continued.

"Long story, sir."

"I have all day, unless you decide not to talk." Flin stared at Harry. "When did you start chewing?"

"It's bubble gum," Harry said. "I suppose Miss Rosie over at Grandma's Kitchen has rubbed off on me."

"Sorry. What was my—?"

"How did my client meet Judge Jenkins?" Pratt's lawyer reminded Flin. "That seems an irrelevant question, though." He conferred quietly with Pratt and finally said, "He'll go ahead and answer the question."

"It was during the war … England … I was a con man … a crook … running from the law … met him in a bar … he offered me money for some favors."

"What kind of—"

"Don't answer that, Mr. Pratt," his lawyer said adamantly.

Pratt agreed.

"Okay, how did you get to the States?" Flin continued.

"I blackmailed him … Jenkins. I said I would go to the police if he didn't take care of me, get me to the States and give me a job. Evidently, he realized I was a good man to have around, you know, birds of a feather. Of course, through the years I snooped into his personal life … his files. I found things. For starters, years ago, Jenkins' father had bought out Joshua Mullen's law practice, an attorney Mr. Weatherholtz's father had dealt with."

"The one who represented Harry's father in selling some property?" Flin asked.

"Correct. So the Jenkins Law Firm had the trust fund from the sale of Mr. Weatherholtz's … Harry's father's land. When Mr. Weatherholtz died in prison, the firm simply decided to wait it out, to see if anyone claimed the inheritance. No one did, as you can see, so Judge Jenkins eventually used the trust fund for personal gain. He never anticipated an inmate would end up with the letter from Mr. Weatherholtz's father, revealing the truth about the fund. The old man—"

"Elmer Hall?" Flin interrupted.

"Yes. He kept the letter for years without doing anything with it, but with Cutshaw breathing down his neck for back payment of groceries, he struck up a deal. Together they came up with the idea to pull him into their plot." He pointed at Harry.

"I still don't understand how the old man and Cutshaw, especially Cutshaw, expected to gain any of the money, and the old man won't live long enough to enjoy it if he did."

"He died last night," Harry injected.

"That's a shame … 'course he'd be headed back to prison if he'd lived," Flin said, in a matter of fact tone.

"I think he planned the scheme for his wife. She's destitute now," Harry added.

"She's also a crook, participating in the scheme," Flin said.

"She doesn't know," Harry said. "She believes the story about her husband being my father. I didn't bother to correct her. And as bad as you may think the old man was, he loved her dearly. He's a prison escapee and a criminal, but he's an old man who had love in his heart for a person that had been kind to him all these years. Love's a deep mystery." Harry stood, stretched his arms toward the ceiling and yawned. "A really deep mystery."

Flin stared at Harry. "It sounds far-fetched, Harry. And how did Cutshaw and the old man expect to get that money, money that belongs to you, if it belongs to anybody? That still doesn't make sense to me."

"It makes sense, alright," Pratt said. "The two of them, the old man and Cutshaw, had been trying to get money out of Jenkins for some time, threatening to tell the law about the embezzled trust, but Jenkins always called their bluff, since he knew that Harry … Mr. Weatherholtz … didn't know about the trust. When Cutshaw's threats fell on deaf ears, he and the old man concocted a plan to make Harry realize there was a trust that had been set up for him and his brother. Once Harry thought his father was alive and the letter was authentic, then Cutshaw was going to blackmail Jenkins with a deal he would negotiate." He spoke directly to Harry. "The only reason they pulled you in was to increase their chances of getting money out of the judge. Cutshaw banked on the idea that he'd be the mediator between you and Jenkins, and that you'd never accept money from your father. He and the old man would get the most of it."

"And how did you come about all this information?" Flin asked Pratt.

"I played both parties, Jenkins and Cutshaw. I knew of the blackmail attempt, so I approached Cutshaw from the concept that

I could convince the judge to give them part of the money to shut them up. Cutshaw agreed to cut me in on the deal, so he told me the entire plan … the letter … the old man. It was working pretty good until the judge sent me to destroy incriminating records he'd left in the mansion, and I had to shoot Jack Brady. Of course, I didn't destroy all of the records. I held some back. You know, insurance. That's what I have entrusted Mr. Weatherholtz to safeguard." He smiled at Harry.

"I'm going to ask you one more time. Where are these records?" Flin asked.

Pratt hesitated. His lawyer shook his head.

"I'm sorry, but I can't reveal that information," Pratt said.

"And I assume you won't either, Harry," Flin said.

"I'm sorry, Sheriff. I made a promise that I need to keep," Harry answered.

"Then there's no reason for this interview to continue. We'll have to take this matter up in court. Let a judge sort it out. Thank you, gentlemen, for nothing." Flin started for the door.

"I have one more question, for you, Mr. Weatherholtz?" Pratt turned toward Harry.

"What's that?" Harry asked.

"Would you have really shot me if I had not cooperated?"

"You said you were not coerced in any way, Mr. Pratt," Flin said. "Now you are asking if Harry—"

His attorney slammed his briefcase shut. "This meeting is definitely over."

Pratt stared at Harry. "Would you?"

"You'll never know for sure, will you?" Harry answered with a question and a smile.

Chapter Fifty-nine

Harry didn't bother to knock on the door to Jenkins' room. He charged into the room to find a startled Cutshaw who threw up his hands as if in surrender. The judge sat by the window, the curtains open, his bandages removed.

"How dare you barge into my room uninvited, Harry Weatherholtz!" It was obvious his vision had returned.

"If you were a normal human being, I would give you the courtesy of a knock, but you are not normal. In fact, you are inhuman … the most despicable man I have ever encountered, except maybe him." Harry pointed at Cutshaw.

Cutshaw started to respond but remained silent.

"Leave this room this instant or I will call the law and have you thrown out," Jenkins demanded.

"I welcome the law, but since they are not yet here, I have something to say to you … and Hurley … about the criminal activities you have been participating in."

"What are you talking about?" Jenkins asked.

"Ask Hurley. He may have a good explanation for his latest scheme. By the way, Hurley, it has backfired on you. And your accomplice is dead."

Jenkins stared at Hurley. "What's going on, Hurley?"

"I don't know what he's a'talkin' 'bout, your honor." Hurley's arms flayed like a crooked defense attorney called into the judge's chambers after he'd been caught in a lie.

"Sit down and shut up," Jenkins demanded. "What are you talking about, Weatherholtz? Has this toadstool been conniving behind my back?"

"He has, but that isn't what I'm here for. You'll have to take that up with him, unless the law arrests him before you get a chance."

"He's a'lyin' to you, judge. You're a liar, Harry Weatherholtz." Cutshaw leaped from his chair like the bell had sounded for the first round.

Harry crowded Hurley, and he fell back into the chair. He started to rise, but Harry kept a firm hand on his shoulder. "I have no issue with you, Hurley. Though you tried to hoodwink me, you have actually assisted me. I'll call that even."

"What's he talking about, Hurley?" Jenkins demanded.

Hurley didn't answer. The momentary silence gave way to a distant siren. Cutshaw tried to bolt, but Harry held him fast to the chair with a hand pressed hard against his shoulder.

"Here's the deal, judge." Harry slapped Cutshaw on the head. "Sit there till I say you can get up." He stepped toward Jenkins. "I know about what your father did."

"I don't know what you're talking about, Weatherholtz." Jenkins played the innocent role very well. "As far as I'm concerned, my father was a good man. Still, I can't answer for him regarding anything he may have done that was improper." Jenkins slipped into damage control mode.

"No, you don't need to answer for his wrongs for which you had no knowledge, but you must pay reparation for anything his law firm—which you inherited—may have done, especially if it was illegal activity."

"You've gone crazy, Harry Weatherholtz. I know nothing—"

"Then you can make this problem go away by simply doing the right thing now. And don't give me that surprised look, for you know good and well what I'm talking about."

Jenkins didn't respond. His head dropped, and he stared at his hands. They dripped with blood, the blood of perhaps hundreds of victims of his cruel rulings from the bench. All were selfish acts, none giving consideration to anyone, or anything, other than his personal gain, or venting the hate that raged in his heart. Only God knew the number of black children who had received cruel treatment because of his signature on a court ruling. Little Eddie was an indirect victim of his decisions. Those hands were responsible for pressing life from his lungs. At his decision, Miss Ann had languished for years under the control of Cutshaw, enduring his strap and surviving his threats, all because Jenkins sent her into that home. And these were but the tip of the iceberg. But none of these could be recompensed for, at least in this life. The avenger of the just would have to deal with these in time. Harry was not one to retaliate, but he held within his hand an opportunity to make a difference in the lives of the abused children of the community.

Harry shook his head in disgust. "I've allowed you to walk before, untainted, though your name should be tarnished in every town in this valley, the byword for all that is wicked, the embodiment of all that is immoral. I let you walk before because I did not want to bring additional harm to Miss Ann. But this is no longer about her. She's no longer a part of the equation. This is about you and me, about my inheritance that ended up in your trust. But you did not fulfill your legal role, and you withheld or perhaps even spent that which belonged to my brother and me. You allowed my brother to go to his grave without notifying him of an inheritance. I can only assume you were planning the same for me as well. But I've lived long enough to find out."

"Nonsense, Weatherholtz. Hogwash. You can't prove any of this." Jenkins managed a renewed rebuttal.

"I have the proof, sir. You prided yourself in keeping good records." Harry tossed a book onto Jenkins lap.

Jenkins scanned the cover but refused to touch it. "You stole my personal documents?"

"Then you admit your guilt?"

"Absolutely not, and anything stolen will not stand up in court as evidence against me."

"I stole nothing from you, but some incriminating evidence did come into my possession, and I'll let the legal system make the decision as to whether or not it's permissible in court. Anything I have may be disallowed in court, which is why I am offering you a deal instead of allowing the deplorable contents of the documents to be rumors shared by word of mouth in every household in this valley. And that's where I'm headed with this information, straight to a newspaper reporter. You know good and well that at the very least I can spread the gossip far and wide. And at the worst, I can have Sheriff Flin arrest you and haul you into jail. Won't that make a juicy news report? I'm holding Flin off right now, because he's feistier than a coon dog that's just picked up the scent, wanting to arrest you. He's so angry he'll arrest you just to prove he can. Do you want that to happen ... arrest ... booked into the county jail ... your face front page news all over the state?"

"I don't care what you do, Weatherholtz. Trash my name all you want, but it won't change the fact that I'm Judge Jeremiah Jenkins, elected by the citizens of this county for years. They'll remember me for the good that I've done, not for an error in judgment. I'll beat you at every confrontation. I'll apologize for all that my daddy did and deny I knew he was living above the law. I'll gladly let him take the blame to defeat you. And I'll dig up enough trash on you that will drive you from this valley and back to Ohio where you belong."

"I don't believe you will do any of that, and I know you don't want to be arrested. Oh, by the way, your butler ... Pratt ... he's in jail ... squealing like a stuck hog."

"So that's how you got this book?" He tossed the book onto the bed. "Just how much information did he give you? It's all stolen and inadmissible."

"It doesn't matter how I got it. I have it, enough evidence for Flin to arrest you without even running it by a prosecutor. You're too proud to spend one day in a jail cell, especially with all the Negroes that are in there. And some of them might just have had their sons or daughters taken away from them, by you, Judge Jenkins. You don't want that, but Flin is waiting outside in his cruiser just in case you don't accept my deal."

Jenkins turned toward the window, seemingly pondering Harry's case against him. Harry knew Jenkins had been in this situation before, when Brady confronted him, but he had Pratt back then to protect his back. With Pratt in jail and a turncoat, the cards were stacked against him. But he was a proud man. Still, that's what Harry banked on, the man's pride.

"So how much money do you want, Weatherholtz? Not that I'll give you one red cent. That is what it's about, isn't it?" He spoke with disdain, his face still turned away from Harry. "What kind of deal do you have for me?"

"Let me get one thing clear, it's not for myself. There is money involved, but it's blood money as far as I'm concerned, just like Judas' silver. There'll be no jangle of coins to torment my conscience, no guilt to drive me to a self-inflicted noose."

"I don't need a sermon, Harry Weatherholtz."

"To the contrary, sir, that's exactly what you need, but I'm no preacher, so I'll spare you. Here's my deal. You will put money in a trust called the Edward Tibbs Shaver Trust Fund. You remember the name?"

"Can't say that I do."

"He's the lad that drowned in my farm pond ... his death an indirect result of a childcare system you oversaw."

"And just what will this money be used for. It can't bring a kid back from the dead." His words were heartless, without any sense of regret.

"It will be used to fund a home for Negro children in need of care. It will never pay your debt, but it might grant you a speck of God's mercy."

Jenkins hesitated. He glanced at Cutshaw, who looked away. "How much money?"

"I've calculated the original amount left by my father, with interest for approximately fifty years, and I've included some extra to somewhat compensate for the crime against the children of this valley. I believe a beginning penance would be a hundred thousand."

"In your dreams, Weatherholtz. That's way too much—"

"Non-negotiable, sir. Either that or Flin makes the arrest."

"And how do I get a hundred thousand dollars?"

"Oh, you've got that and more. I spoke with Jack Brady. He didn't mind telling me what he paid you for the house."

"This is blackmail."

"Call it what you may, but I call it insufficient to pay for all the pain you've caused the black community in this valley. Do we have a deal, or do I call in the sheriff?"

"No adverse publicity whatsoever regarding the circum-stances of the trust ... only that I made a substantial donation?"

Harry hesitated. A dozen voices argued within his head. Some accused. Some questioned. But one won out. The voice of a little black child crying as he was pulled away from his mother and handed over to the scoundrel cowering in the chair beside Jenkins' bedside. "All I want ... all I'm demanding ... is your contribution into the trust fund. The legal system can do what they desire ... I can't control them ... I will not push that issue ... though someone else may. In that case, a donation to the black community might look good on your record." Harry withheld any information he had ac-quired from Pratt, especially that Pratt would be using Jenkins as a bargaining tool for a reduced sentence. But that was between them. It was not a part of this deal.

The room grew quiet. Cutshaw sunk lower into his chair, his facial expression one of despair, as he knew the plug had been pulled from any future shenanigans with the judge.

Harry had talked this over with Flin, and he had gotten Flin's nod, but he had also shared with Evelyn and Ann. His question: Am I breaking the law? Is this blackmail? But more so, is this morally okay? Ann, with another thought provoking analogy of the blood-root plant, had responded, "You're dilutin' the poison and lettin' the flower bloom. Seems there ain't no harm in that." Evelyn hadn't been as kind: "You're spraying the skunk with his own stink, a stink he meant for others."

Harry and Flin had both agreed, the system wasn't quite ready to deal fairly with the black community, so bypass the system and play hardball with the criminal, so long as no laws are broken. But would Jenkins risk his good reputation among the white folks by refusing any kind of reparation toward the black community? Harry knew it was a gamble … but it seemed his only logical option. Jenkins and his kind had controlled the system for decades. With his influence among peers, he could stall the legal community indefinitely. Harry could be dead and buried before the case ever came to trial. But perhaps he'd overplayed his hand.

"I'd think about this, your honor," Cutshaw said. "He's bluffin' and he knows it." Greed had resurrected his lifeless soul. "And don't worry none 'bout Pratt. Ain't nobody that'll take his word over yours."

"Be quiet, Hurley," Jenkins said. "You're beginning to annoy me."

The room grew silent. Harry could feel his heart racing, and he tried to calm himself by breathing slowly and deeply.

Jenkins stared at Harry. His expression was as stoic as a Grecian statue, and he was just as heartless. In all his years, Harry had never seen the like, cold and calculating. He'd lived as self-centered as a cat with a trapped mouse. Why would he be any different now?

"When do you want the money?"

Jenkins' response caught Harry off-guard, and he hesitated. Could Jenkins be toying with him? Surely not, for this was too serious for such. Harry glanced at Hurley, perhaps the one person who, next to Pratt, knew Jenkins' corrupt and devious actions more than anyone in the valley. His ashen face showed both disbelief and contempt.

"I'll do it," Jenkins said, his voice with a touch of agitation. "When and how do you want the money?"

"Immediately. Transfer the funds right now into the trust." Harry picked up the phone and dialed the local bank where he had set up the trust, and he handed the phone to Jenkins.

Chapter Sixty

The creaky, cane-bottom rockers kept rhythm as Harry and Sheriff Flin unconsciously pushed backward with the boot toe and slightly raised the same to rock forward. Push and relax, push and relax. They intermittently reflected upon the recent events, but they mostly seemed enchanted by the spectacular twilight hues of sunlight painting the rippled clouds that rode the peaks of the Alleghenies. Young Shep lay at Harry's feet.

"Ain't that sunset gorgeous, Harry?" Flin twisted open a peanut shell, popped a peanut into his mouth and tossed the shell onto the lawn, where a dozen bantams rushed to lay claim.

"Sure is." Harry retrieved an unshelled peanut from his shirt pocket and repeated Flin's actions. He chuckled as the chickens repeated their actions.

Shep stirred, walked to the edge of the porch and sniffed at the air. The chickens scrambled a safe distance and continued to tussle over the peanut shells. A rabbit hopped from the bushes to the edge of the yard, ears perked. Shep studied the situation a few moments before calling it a day. He lazily chased his tail in a circle and laid back down, his nose perched on his crossed paws, in the direction of the rabbit.

"Wonder what makes the clouds change into so many colors?" Flin tossed a shell at Shep, who swatted at it, sending it flying off the porch.

"I read somewhere that it has something to do with air molecules scattering the light. I don't exactly understand that, but you don't have to understand it to enjoy its beauty," Harry said, as he patted Shep, who had reclaimed his position beside Harry's rocker.

"I surely don't understand it." Flin stopped rocking and wiped his hands together to remove the dust of the peanut shells. "And there's something else I don't understand." Flin studied his knuckles. "It's about your ordeal with Pratt and. …" He paused.

Harry scratched Shep's neck, waiting for Flin to continue. He had assumed Flin would bring up the subject sooner or later, and they needed to clear the air between them.

"Though I've never seen it, I'm assuming you have the evidence Pratt talked about," Flin continued, staring at Harry, "the papers and stuff, whatever it was that Pratt had tucked away somewhere."

"Yes, I have the papers."

"Where'd Pratt have them hid?"

"A locker at the bus station."

"And you got it from the locker?"

"Yes."

"That takes a key, Harry. Who had the key?"

"It was held in the trust of the Topps Company."

"I'm not familiar—"

"The bubble gum company, Topps."

"Oh, that company." Flin paused, but Harry didn't offer any explanation. "Funny how addictive buying their gum can be, especially with the baseball cards that come with the gum … which ain't that good … the gum, I mean. But the cards, that's another story. I got me a hammerin' Hank rookie card, and that's better than the gum any day. The way that boy's playin', it might be worth some money someday. Are you into baseball, Harry?"

"No."

"Me neither … except sometimes I listen on the radio … you know, late nights patrollin' with nothin' to do … sorry, I got off base there." He paused and stared down the lane toward the sawmill. That was a crime he still hadn't solved, and it was a project Harry hadn't finished. "Off base, no pun intended." He chuckled.

Harry smiled.

"Do you know that company is Jewish owned, Harry?"

"No."

"Sure is. Started making bubble gum 'cause their tobacco industry was struggling."

"I didn't know that either. Interesting, failing at selling chewing tobacco and succeed selling chewing gum." Harry chuckled.

"Probably the cards that made it successful. Personally, I don't chew tobacco or bubble gum, but I enjoy the suspense of opening the Topps pack to see what card I get. I guess there's a kid in all of us. You don't chew neither, do you, Harry."

"No."

"But you was chewing the day I interviewed Pratt. Topps bubble gum?"

"I'm afraid I'm guilty as charged, Sheriff."

"That surprised me, the chewing gum, 'course I ain't figured any connection with you chewing and what was taking place in the interviewing room."

"The key was stuck underneath the table in the interrogation room in the jail."

"Stuck with bubble gum?"

"No, just stuck in a crack under the table."

"Then what does bubble gum have to do with the story? And just how in the world did Pratt—?"

"When the state police brought Pratt over from Richmond, he somehow kept the key hidden from them, then he tucked it in a crack on the bottom of the table in the interrogation room before you put him in a cell. Remember him changing seats with me the day we all met with his attorney?"

"Yes."

"That was so I could be near the key."

"And you took the key? Harry, that's called stealing evidence. What in the world are you thinking? A judge will—"

"I didn't take the key."

"Then how'd you get into the locker? Break in? That's a crime, too." He tugged at his collar as if it was constricting blood flow.

"I had a key, and I had permission to get into the locker and take anything I wanted. Pratt gave me permission before I turned him back over to you."

"Now I'm more confused. You didn't take the key, but you somehow had a key. How?"

"That's the reason for my Topps story. Back to you asking me about my new chewing habit, and I said Rosie had rubbed off on me?"

"Yeah, but what of it?"

"Well, I used that bubble gum to make an impression of the key that was hidden under the table. I did it while you were busy talking to Pratt. Later, I had a key made from the impression. But I put the real key right back where I found it—"

"Attached to the bottom of the table in the interrogation room," Flin interrupted.

"Right where Pratt hid it. That's where you can find it when you get back to the jail."

"And that's why he wanted you in the room during the interrogation?" Flin chuckled. "If that don't beat all! The whole interrogation was a ruse." He studied his fat knuckles for a long while. "One more question."

"What's that?"

"The same question Pratt asked you at the interrogation. Once you got the drop on Pratt, would you have really shot 'em if he hadn't cooperated?"

"No."

"That was awfully upsettin' the way he took you hostage. You sure you wouldn't have shot 'em, Harry? Not that I'd blame you."

"Yep, I'm sure."

"Come on, Harry. How can you be so sure about somethin' as uncertain and upsettin' as that was? You had to be mighty mad at him for the kidnapping."

"Oh, I was mad alright, but I still wouldn't have shot him."

"Why not? I would've." Flin gestured with an outstretched hand that mimicked firing a pistol.

"I couldn't shoot him, Sheriff, because my gun wasn't loaded."

Flin's head jerked like a pig shot between the eyes with a .22. He stared at Harry for a long while, then shook his head in disbelief. "Harry Weatherholtz, you're gonna get yourself killed someday."

Flin's frown slowly turned into a smile, and then he laughed. They both laughed. It was a wholehearted, belly laugh, the kind only true friends can share.

www.ingramcontent.com/pod-product-compliance
Lightning Source LLC
Chambersburg PA
CBHW071231250626

47163CB00001B/129